The Queerling

Austin Gary

AUSTIN GARY

Early praise for The Queerling

'Brilliant esoteric fiction! A standout! The epilogue will blow reader's minds and beg a second reading!'

'Gary is at the height of his literary powers, producing a character and a story that feels viscerally authentic long after the reality-bending conclusion.'

~Foreword Clarion Reviews

The Queerling

Austin Gary

Copyright 2013 by Austin Gary

All rights reserved. No part of this book may be used or reproduced in any manner—without permission from the publisher—except in the case of brief quotations embodied in critical articles and reviews.

This novel is a work of fiction. Any references to real people, events, organizations or locale are intended only to give the fiction a sense of reality and authenticity, and are used fictitiously. All other names, characters and places, and all dialogue and incidents portrayed in this book are the product of the author's imagination.

The Eighth Day quotation used by permission of Harper Perennial Modern Classics

Printed in the United States of America

Published by Deckle Press, Calgary, AB Canada

ISBN:

978-1-4923-2627-4

FOR BRAD

*...who discovered his voice and set his
feet on the path to greater things.*

DECKLE
PRESS

With Gratitude

Thanks to all those who gave of their precious time to read *The Queerling* in its various incarnations, especially early readers who patiently persisted out of friendship and kindness—offering invaluable feedback and encouragement. Foremost among them: Diane Gillespie, who also served as editor emeritus; Susan Maeder, an extraordinary poet and mensch; and Brenna Gray, whom I discovered through her blog on Book Riot.

My appreciation also goes to Deb Sacksteder, Drew Larson, Tenilla Sheehan, Libby Heindel, Lori Freeman, Dan Dundon, Molly Hueffed, Kathryn Brencick, Terry Lay, Leslie Shew and Lindell Bruce for reading and responding…and the many others who intended to but just couldn't quite.

I'm also indebted to several literary agents who showed early interest, but could not commit for any number of reasons. Those reasons, which were not stock rejection-speak but honest assessments, helped guide me in the revision process.

As always, I flourish with the love of my children and grandson. I remain ever grateful for my beloved husband, without whose support and creative and technical abilities this process would suffer.

And, last but not least, to my many former students, whose lives and struggles inspired me to speak out on the perils of adolescence and, especially, against The Drug War On Children. Preston's rants, some of which you may remember as my own, are dedicated to you…with Love.

Also by Austin Gary

Novels:

Miss Madeira
(Available on Amazon.com)

Plays:

Genius
Miss Madeira

The Queerling

AUSTIN GARY

Prologue

Should I fear looking back on my brief life, fear the Orphic gaze—risking the loss of innocence, the loss of myself by defying the gods, by observing my own existence, or should I embrace this transgression and discover the truth of my own godliness?

Is a bear Catholic? Does the Pope poo in the woods?

Forgive the conceit of this "journal," this introspective regurgitation ordered up by you, Dr. Thomas van Ittersum, psychologist and self-appointed savior. If I hope to be released back into the wild, you maintain that keeping a written account of my daily experience, a log of my innermost thoughts and a reflective ledger of my colorful past is my *only choice*. I'm *clearly confused* by this oxymoron, but in my *unbiased opinion*, it's *almost exactly* what one would expect in this era of *virtual reality*.

Okay, Shrinkmeister, you asked for it.

My given name is Preston Wilder Nesbitt. My *nom de plume* is Oskar Caulfield. However, I prefer my nickname, Achilles—not for Homer's great warrior but for its derivation from the Greek *achos*, meaning "pain," both for what I have endured and what I am to others. Besides, no one can prove Homer really existed, and the *Iliad* is an epic mix-tape from a long succession of storytellers—adding their own two drachmae worth.

Imagine…a mythologized view of history!

Though you refuse to admit it, this assignment is the result of a viral YouTube video that appeared April 29th—featuring yours truly—eclipsing a hundred million views faster than the soprano washerwoman with the scary uni-brow several years ago. Didn't think I knew, did you?

"No access to the Internet, Preston."

Fortunately, I can always count on one of the aides to violate ward policy.

Doc, you know me. I'm not just another precocious savant with a smart-ass mouth and a "Comedy Central" sensibility. I am all that to be sure. But, if I'm in any way unique, it's due to my ability to remember. It's positively Proustian.

I'm referring to my exceptional M.Q.: Memory Quotient. Unlike the dubious I.Q., my brilliance relies on the Emotions I've attached to said Memories. $M=E_2$, See? Call me the dyslexic Einstein. On second thought, Pres will suffice.

I've agreed to commit my thoughts to the page for one reason only: to convince you I know nothing about the YouTube video's origin and that my presence here is no longer required—one reason serving two purposes. May I suggest you read my modest musings aloud? Think of them as Performance Art: rhythm and meter my métier. If I could, I'd record this as an audio book…from my mouth to your ears.

As with my personality, you may tire of my bombastic, often digressive rambling and my passionate, hyperactive prose; however, you needn't take everything I say to heart. Like Sir Noël Coward, known for his wit and flamboyance, I have a talent to amuse. Nothing more.

I'm a throwback, pure and...not so simple.

NOTE TO POTENTIAL READERS

Doc says others may eventually read this nonsequential chronicle. (Inconsequential might be more accurate, although I hope it proves to be more enlightening than the average incarceration *cri de coeur*, like Wilde's *The Ballad of Reading Gaol*, written *after* his release.)

If you choose to venture into my sordid tale, unless you're a Sufi mystic, be prepared to suspend belief or open your mind to the possibility that *everything* is illusion, except for the reason I'm here...which is pure delusion.

Let me make it clear from the start, this isn't magical realism, unless you're willing to admit all life is magical.

~Achilles (ne' Preston W. Nesbitt)

AUSTIN GARY

~~THE THOUGHTS & LAMENTATIONS OF PRESTON W. NESBITT~~

QUIPS & QUOTES FROM THE QUEERLING

*There's something in the basic nature of human beings
that revels in the Theory of the Ideal
but finds its realization repugnant.*

~Oskar Caulfield

May 1st

First off, it doesn't require a PhD in English Lit to determine my pen name is a fusion of both Oskar Matzerath and Holden Caulfield. If this requires you to read *The Tin Drum* and *The Catcher In The Rye*, so be it.

I chose the former because, like Peter Pan, Oskar refused to grow up. Having technically celebrated only my 4th Birthday on February 29th (a Leap Day, the fourth since '96), that's rather appropriate, *n'est-ce pas?* I chose the latter, because Holden… On second thought, don't even bother to read *Catcher* if you haven't. It's about a self-indulgent little jerk-off with glaring self-esteem issues, who's a reflection of the very ideals he rejects. Fuck that!

Mihi ignoscas. I promised not to curse, but irreverence in language is nothing compared to the irreverence of war, religion, consumerism, parenthood and life in general.

Remember Doc, you wanted the Truth.

The Truth is: I don't trust anyone who doesn't drop the occasional "F-bomb." Keep that in mind if you're trying to earn my trust. And, of course, you are.

* * *

Preston, I mentioned that others may read this journal, but please avoid playing to the crowd. This is not theater. You get no points for performance. Though literary allusion may reveal aspects of your personality, don't incorporate them if your intention is simply to impress. No one is questioning your intelligence, and your ability to remember is not something you have to demonstrate to me. I need you to concentrate on <u>why you think you're here</u>. It's important you take this assignment seriously.

Gee, Doc. Thanks for trying to bust my groove. If I were a great basketball player, would you ask me to stop dribbling between my legs or blowing by the opposition with my first, lightning quick step? Would you tell a violin virtuoso to forego a breathtaking performance, with unmatched technical precision and colorful phrasing, and just fiddle for the folks? Were I a fine artist, would you have me shelve my masterpiece for inferior work? Not likely. The thought would never occur to you. But, when it comes to one's intelligence, it's considered "showing off" to put it on display...? I've suffered this kind of obtuseness my whole life. I expect more of you. Besides, we've known each other for almost eight years; couldn't you cut me a little slack?

You've taken away my freedom; now you're asking me to forfeit my intelligence. Other than my boyish good looks, it's all I have to offer.

May 2nd

No contact with Mom 'til the weekend? House rules...?

Why treat me like I'm in Drug Rehab? I've never even smoked marijuana, which puts me in the minority among my peers. When it comes to pot, Portland is to the U.S. what Amsterdam is to the Netherlands: Head Shop Heaven or Hell—depending on your proclivities.

I know kids who've been toking since fifth grade. Plus, half the student body at my high school takes *Adderall*, like your generation took No-Doz, to study for tests. Here's some advice you can pass along to parents: If your teen's mouth appears tense, his shoulder's stiff or her gaze unwavering...lock the medicine cabinet; it's today's candy store. Forgetting one's name and blacking out can also prove to be troubling signs.

Some parents prefer denial to believing their darlings are druggies. Last fall, there was a girl at my school who had so much trouble breathing she passed out in the hallway. They found *Oxycontin* in her purse. Though the girl's father took the painkiller for a back injury, the mother insisted her daughter's depressed breathing was a result of having to take Phys Ed. I kid you not. Some parents are just grown up children, incapable of accepting the responsibility that goes along with the job (like my Dad).

No drugs for Preston (hint hint). No siree, Tom. Personally, I prefer to be in control of my mind and other bodily functions. If I lack restraint, it's that I sometimes get a little carried away, linguistically.

Not certain I ever told you, but when I was in preschool, my teacher wrote a note to Mom:

'Preston's a sweet little boy, but he's a bit of a *motor mouth*. I'm afraid his classmates find him a bit *off-putting*.' A little harsh, wouldn't you say? I'd just turned four.

I know a little about a lot of things, a lot about a few things and I like to share. That hardly warrants being labeled "compulsive" by my kindergarten teacher:

'Please help Preston understand that it's rude to always be constantly interrupting and correcting his teacher.' (Note: split infinitive and unnecessary adverb).

Due to my interest in, not obsession with, all things Indian: arrowheads, burial mounds, chanting, drumming, shape-shifting, smudging, etc., a child psychologist at Familycare Medical Clinic told Mom I showed signs of an Autism Spectral Disorder—specifically, Asperger's Syndrome. He also said I had ADHD and would benefit from *Ritalin*.

Fortunately, Suzanne's not one of those drug first/ask questions later parents. She had me tested. My I.Q. was "off the charts," he said modestly. (That's how I skipped first grade.) She also did a lot of research and concluded I had "special abilities," not a disability.

Mom's always been my greatest supporter…'til now.

May 3rd

Being here Sux the Big One!

Are you and Mom trying to teach me some kind of lesson…like how Machiavellian you both can be? I know she called you in a panic about my "delusional fantasy," and that's why I've gone from occasional outpatient to *this*. But, what is *this*, exactly? What did I do to deserve *this*? And, what's most important, how long will *this* last? I can't be here. I get bored easily and *this* is already torturous!

I have to be out of here by tomorrow at the latest. State Forensics Competition takes place at the University of Oregon (Eugene), Saturday, May 5th. I'm competing in Solo and Duet Acting and Team Debate. Alix Fischer, my acting partner, the debate team and my coach, Mr. Wolff, are all depending on me. In addition, there are a slew of activities for seniors right up to Graduation Day. You'll be happy to know I'm slated to receive special recognition from the Honor's Society. Sure don't wanna miss that.

You want me to admit I staged the great video hoax, right? If that's what it takes to spring me from the Funny Farm, okay, fine…I did it. I wrote, directed, starred in, recorded, edited and put it on YouTube in my spare time. Simon says, "May I go now…?"

But seriously, if I'd hoped to create a viral sensation or wanted to send it to *America's Weirdest Videos*, I could see how you might think I was the mastermind. However, I was completely unaware of it, until Dad called and told Mom to check out the YouTube video, "Kid vs. Buick—and the winner is…?" and '…see what *your* son's been up to now.'

We watched it together. I was dumbfounded. Mom became hysterical.

"*Why*, Pres? Why would you do something so outrageous? It's not funny. It's sickening. What if you encourage other kids to try something similar and someone really gets hurt…or worse? *This* is the last straw."

(Aha! The answer to the "this" conundrum.)

I applaud the use of metaphor, but not when it's absurd. When Suzanne gets rattled, she abandons logic faster than a scorned lover. Camels routinely carry up to 500 lbs. Not to get too technical, but the addition of a single straw would never break a camel's back. Just sayin'.

She was in "no mood" for my explanation, nor would she believe I had nothing do with the video, which takes place in front of Mr. Wolff's. (Probably the real reason she was upset, as you shall see). Though I've driven by his house countless times, I've only stopped once—last year, when Alix Fischer and I went there to work on our duet-acting piece.

Doc, you of all people know I can remember, in minute detail, even the most insignificant incident throughout my lifetime, all the way back to the beginning. I honestly don't remember being there but one time, and especially not on April 28th when the video was recorded.

Hook me up to a polygraph. I'll prove I'm telling the truth. ~~Remember, I'm the victim here!~~ (There's a downside to preferring ink to graphite.) Don't get any ideas. I'm not suffering from a Persecution Complex, though in this case, I'd certainly be justified. This whole thing is some kind of bizarre SNAFU: S(situation) N(ormal) A (all) F (fucked) U (up)!

I've plenty more to say on the subject, but I must pause for now. A very flamboyant little Latino Aide just informed me that my presence is required in the Activities Room. For *CRAFTS!*

* * *

Preston, your mother and father are both concerned you're disavowing any knowledge of the video. That it exists is proof positive of your participation in its creation. Awaiting your explanation, I remain your trusted therapist.

I've told you I don't know anything about the video…and really I don't. Trusted therapist? Still waiting for you to drop the "F" bomb, buster.

May 4th

WTF! I'm missing the State Forensics Tournament because you 'haven't had sufficient time to process your current mental state?' Well, let me assist you. I'm fucking steamed to my very core and on the verge of a mental meltdown!

Don't you understand, I've competed all year to qualify for State in Solo and Duet Acting? Imagine how upset my acting partner is; we worked so hard, and the only time we didn't place first was at Nationals last summer as juniors. First place was a virtual lock this year. My contribution to the Debate Team's success is critical. On the affirmative, my rebuttals usually devastate any case made by the negative team. Mr. Wolff says my closing arguments are the best he's ever heard, *nonpareil*, and he's taken teams to State twelve out of the last fifteen years, although only once to Nationals.

In short, you cost me a chance to rack up at least two major Forensics awards, both of which would have looked great on my college admissions resume. Without me, our team won't even make the semi-finals. Devastating!

Need to breathe... Deep breaths.

Yesterday during free time on the ward, I was telling Ciera about my "writing assignment," and that the Oskar part of my pen name was a reference to Günter Grass's little anarchistic dwarf. Get this...she suggested I pretend to be dying of Hodgkin's disease and title my journal *Bang The Tin Drum Slowly*.

Love that girl, but she can be a bit of a downer. If you don't believe me, check out her Facebook profile: all those depressing quotations from Sylvia Plath, whose reputation puffed up like a cheese soufflé the minute she stuck her head in an oven. Another of Ciera's favorites is Virginia Woolf's suicide note:

> *I have the feeling I shall go mad. I hear voices and cannot concentrate on my work. I have fought against it, but cannot fight any longer.*

Not trying to tell you your biz, but you might want to deny access to the river and an oven to Miss Self. Among those you permit to read this unburdening, promise she will not be among them. Ciera Self lacks the creativity to commit suicide in some original way, but her determination can't be faulted. I'll share more about her later, none of which she needs to read. So, please exclude her from those permitted to peruse my innermost thoughts.

(Doing my best not to obsess about the tournament.)

For distraction, I decided to mingle with the prison population in *The Garden of Earthly Delights*, my epithet for the meditation garden. Jesus Hieronymus Christ! Richie Caytes pissed in the serenity pond. More outside supervision *please*.

Though only sixteen, I've already tired of the puerile and moronic. I know that's a bit unkind, but honesty above all things. The older I get the less I can tolerate stupidity, which eliminates 99% of reality T.V. and all of Faux News.

After dinner, having quenched my desire to hang out with the lunatics in the lounge, I figured I might as well record some more observations, re:

Ciera Self: Long-Suffering "Artiste"

In order to out-dysfunction me, Ciera recalled, in excessive detail, how "Daddy" tried to get in her pants when she was ten. Troubling, but also not very convincing. Between us, I suspect it's a figment of her fantasy life, an attempt to usurp her mother's place. She despises her overly-controlling mother, a woman who, to make certain she isn't obese like her aunts and cousins, has systematically starved her for years.

As a result, Ciera hears voices telling her to run away, eat Jalapeño Cheetos and steal her mother's diet pills. She binges on Ben & Jerry's, French fries and Skittles, gags herself and then carves Celtic symbols in her thighs. I admit that's some serious *sheiss*e—scoring major points on the DS (Dysfunction Scale). So, if she wants to paint her fingernails black and dress like an Emo Anne Rice, I hope you'll not judge her too harshly, though you might want to encourage her to find some new voices. Hers are intent on extinguishing her light!

Not sure what she's told you, trust being one of her big issues. Therefore, she's more likely to confide in me. Sorry, but it's true. Here's a little unsolicited advice: it's important she view you as an ally, not an adversary. Less interrogation, more support. Just trying to keep you clued in—hoping to be helpful. Let me know if I'm covering old territory, or if I can assist in unearthing other psychological motivations: be they biological, social or emotional.

P.S. Happy to cooperate with the journal-keeping. It helps chip away at the time, which passes very s-l-o-w-l-y. However, writing in longhand's putting a huge crimp in my style, which, like my taste in literature, leans more towards literary than popular, as fiction goes. Of course, this is autobiography, non-fiction...*vérité*. The only fiction is the trumped up reason I'm here in the first place. Don't go to too much trouble. Any old word processor will suffice.

* * *

I appreciate that you're trying to "help," but that is the very least of what you should be doing. You know what that is.

Hoping it involves consulting Dr. Jerkoff. That's what I'll be doing in the meantime.

May 5th

"*Cinco de Mayo, ése*," Caesar reminded me *mucho* times today. "The weekend shift…she can be a drag, *Señor* Preston. But, tonight…tonight at Dardanelle's, ees the kind of drag I live for!" He flashed his million-peso smile, winked and did a quick shine. Don't ask.

Not sure where you find these aides, but Caesar, in particular, is a hoot and a half (a hoot ho). He thinks we're *amigos* because I gave him the ashtray I made in crafts. This afternoon he was salsa dancing around Reza in the Nurse's Station—lip-syncing to Ricky Martin's "Livin' la Vida Loca." As soon as five o'clock rolled around, he was out of here pronto. *Cinco de Mayo*…here comes Carmen Miranda's love child.

Speaking of Reza: she appears to be a modern Muslim woman, but she was horrified by Caesar's antics. She thinks he's flirting. I suspect he covets her colorful tunics. Please don't discipline him. He's harmless and funny and, other than Ciera, the only light in this otherwise dismal abyss.

QUESTION: Do you intend to tell me what sort of observations/confessions you want in these entries? You know how random I can be. Or, is that the point? Do I get a Gold Star for pretending to be an adult about all this, or can I admit I'm little homesick without ridicule?

Last night while lying in bed, staring at the hideous popcorn ceiling, I realized I haven't been away from home for any significant time since I won that magazine selling contest in Jr. High (by virtue of Mom and Nana Nesbitt subscribing to a dozen periodicals to insure my victory).

Thirty boys and ten girls made the agonizing bus ride from Portland to Seattle, where we met up with other winners from the Northwest Region. I enjoyed visiting the Pacific Science Center; however, had I known then what a nightmare I'd have spending the night at Lewis-McChord Air Force base on our way back to Portland from a Mariners double-header (Boredom—thy name is Baseball), I'd have relinquished that honor to Bobby Vernon, who finished in second-place by a measly *Reader's Digest*.

Though I pretended to be worldly, kids from places like Tacoma, Yakima and Bum-fuck, Idaho quickly revealed me to be a pathetic naïf. I don't know what I expected, but it wasn't to be ridiculed for my "faggy" speech or "pantsed" by a bunch of homophobic teenaged troglodytes. Please explain to me how pulling down someone's pants isn't an indication of some "Mo" tendencies. I know, right?

I called home. The minute I heard Mom's voice, I choked back tears.

"Hi, hon. Are you having a good time?"

"Not really."

"How was the game?"

"*Boring*. Mom…I…I—"

"Oh, baby…what's wrong?"

"I ju-st…wan-na come home."

"Are you okay? Did something happen? "

My chest was heaving and words came in tortured spurts.

"Re-mem-ber when we read *Candide* to-gether? You know how he's so op-timis-tic…about ev-ery-thing? Like say-ing every-thing is well…ev-en when he's in hell?"

"Yes, honey."

"Well, I'm not an op-ti-mist an-y-more…"

Mom drove two hours, each way, to rescue me and bring me home.

Why am I sharing this pitiful vignette? I think you know. Though I shouldn't compare myself to other patients, I fail to understand how you can equate being in a video, even one that defies logic, with kids who have serious mental issues. Your inability to comprehend how desperately I need to get out of here has destroyed my last vestige of optimism. Was Candide just being rhetorical when he asked, 'If this is the best of all possible worlds, what are the others?'

P.S. Disappointed you couldn't come up with a word processor. I'm so used to typing on a keyboard, my cursive's suffered. FYI, many kids my age can no longer write or read it. (Imagine how incomprehensible SAT essays must be.) In some ways, this is as monumental as hieroglyphics being replaced by the Coptic form of the Greek alphabet in the 4th century. If the Power Grid fails or is shutdown by hackers (and I think you can count on it), we're ~~fucked~~ up Willamette River without a paddle.

P.P.S. Knowing my teammates were in Eugene today without me makes me deeply sad…*de profundis*. Note: Sadness is a feeling. So there!

* * *

Noted.

Guess it's just a coincidence Dr. Boullac showed up with an anti-depressant, right on cue. Why is it that your profession is so intent on medicating any feeling other than those associated with happiness? The medical profession's history in this regard dates back to the ancient Greek belief that melancholia was a result of excessive "black bile." They believed failure to eradicate this dread disease indicated "demonic possession." I won't even get into psychology's contribution to the nightmare of "conversion therapy," and its soul-killing attempts to "cure" homosexuality.

The passage from childhood to adulthood is an emotional firewalk, Doc. The way you and Mom are handling this YouTube thing, by imprisoning and drugging me, only adds to my feeling of alienation. (I'm sure GlaxoSmithKline has something for that, too.) Just so you know, I flushed the *Paxil.* What's next…blood-letting? Wanna see my spirits lift…? Let me outta here!

May 6th

From the looks of him, our little Caesar celebrated *demasiado*, a wee "too much," last night. He approached the patient lounge this morning rather sloth-like—cowering behind sunglasses. Burberry Aviators! (On an aide's salary)? When he removed them, I detected a few flecks of glitter still clinging to his droopy lids. As my Nana would say, 'He's suffering from Divine Punishment!'

"How was the big celebration? Looks like *you* had fun."

"Oh, *Señor* Preston, sometime Caesar have trouble saying no to Señorita (air quotes) Margarita." He gave me a knowing wink, then winced and grabbed his head like he was trying to stop dried beans from rattling around in his cranial gourd.

Funny when the aides are the ones requiring aid. Though I'll miss him, he desperately needs recovery time; fortunately, he's scheduled off tomorrow and Tuesday.

Any chance we could double up on the private sessions? I'm hoping to speed up the process so I can get back to my life. There's a special Parent Breakfast for graduating seniors on the 25th. Attendance is, once again, required. Mom will be sending you an invitation to my Graduation, Sunday, May 27th. No gifts, please. Your presence will be gift aplenty.

* * *

Two private sessions a week are more than enough, especially if you focus on the reason you're here and stop being distracted by the private lives of the staff. "Avoidance," as you know, is often used when someone is hoping to elude a hurtful or dangerous situation he's been in. What part of the video experience are you fearful of coming to grips with?

I'm not avoiding anything, but I would respect you more if you would *avoid* ending sentences in a preposition.

May 9th

You asked me to elaborate on why I think Ciera hears voices. First off, thanks for realizing I have something to offer. Secondly, here's something you should know about my generation. We *all* hear voices. Why? Because those voices are preferable to parents' meaningless yammering and the constant fear-mongering of the MainStreamMedia.

Therefore, most of us have created an Alternative Reality: a place where we can go mentally when the unreality of this reality grips one like a dentist-phobic patient white-knuckles armrests, as the drill reaches its high-pitched whir at 400,000 rpm and bloody spittle pools behind plaque-encrusted mandible incisors, before being suctioned, like potato chip crumbs and loose change from beneath sofa cushions and hope from the disillusioned, who, hoping to survive life's perpetual disappointments, have no choice but to create yet another alternative reality. (Confusing? Yes, indeed!).

Here's another thing. We don't "care" about anything because it hurts to care and be perpetually disappointed. Add to that the Gawker-like snark permeating our culture, and you can see why caring is facing obsolescence on a universal scale. That brings us to *Weltschmerz*. Though not proficient in German, allow me to translate: 'the world doesn't measure up to our idealized version of it.'

Consider us the GPD: the Generation of Profound Disappointment. Hope that doesn't pull focus from the almighty GDP, which is infinitely more important to your generation. Forgive me for sounding too philosophical.

Need Examples?

'This weekend, we're going to do something together…*promise*.' (Frequent message left on voicemail).

'Hey, kid…d'ja hear about the dyslexic man who walks into a bra? A bra, get it? Anyway, something's come up I can't get out of.' (Like your girlfriend's twat)?

'Hey, buddy…it's me. I'm reading a book about anti-gravity and can't put it down. Sorry, pal…*next* weekend. Promise.' (I'd be less annoyed if he'd skip the lame jokes and "promises" and show up once in awhile).

'Your dad loves you. He just doesn't know how to express it. He's emotionally impotent like his father before him.'

'Your mom's hot-to-trot for some English teacher at school. Keep an eye on her for me will ya?'

'Your dad has a GPS in his penis.'

On and on. TMI to the 10th power!

* * *

Thanks for sharing. Do you see any correlation between the examples you cite and why you're here?

No. But, let me ask you something. Do you see any correlation between the steady diet of drugs you shrinks feed us and our zombie-like countenance? I've never told you this, but when I was a kid, I actually looked forward to our monthly get-togethers. That was then, this is now. The shine is off the apple (another Nana expression). Too pithy? Try this…I'm seriously over this shit!

May 10th

ASSIGNMENT: Describe Your Parents (briefly)

Daddy's name is Steve: Steven Isaac Nesbitt.

He's a senior account executive at McNabb & Associates, Portland's largest ad agency. Steve specializes in selling worthless (insert animal excrement word) to people who don't really want it and usually can't afford it.

As you probably ascertained from the aforementioned clichéd broken promises, Steve-O's a workaholic and a complete failure as a father. He thinks he's funny, but he's really just "punny" and not very original. He believes the reason I don't laugh at his stupid jokes is because I have Asperger's. Strange, but I often find The Colbert Report a laugh-riot.

In our last private session, you asked if I'm still angry with him for baling on Mom and me. Hmmm, let's see? Yes, I'd say a tiny residue of perturbation remains. Are you kidding? Why wouldn't I be angry…*still?* Nothing's changed. He's a fucking jerk. He hurt my Mom. Please don't tell me forgiveness is a requisite for my release?

Deep breath…

Mom's name is Suzanne: Suzanne (Preston) Nesbitt.

It's true she got boinked by Mr. Wolff, my English teacher. Can't say I blame her. If Steve had paid a little more attention, said boinking would never have occurred. He says it's the reason they got divorced. She says it was due to his insatiable penis and his inability to connect. Me? I wish they'd never married in the first place. Not a death wish Doc, just stating the obvious.

Suzanne is head librarian at my high school, Willamette Preparatory Institute (WPI). She isn't one of those, 'Shhh! Quiet!' old-school types. No, she's the kind who slips you a copy of *The Tropic of Capricorn, The Story of O* or *The Swimming Pool Library* and asks you to do some comparative research on literary eroticism verses the crap version found in romance novels.

Obviously, she gave me her family name: Preston. But, what of my middle name, Wilder? It's an homage to the author of one of her most beloved novels, *The Eighth Day*, and one her most revered authors, Thornton Wilder, whose success as a playwright often overshadowed his fiction.

This is Mom's favorite quote from what she calls, "one of the great forgotten works of the 20th century."

> *Nature never sleeps. The process of life never stands still. The creation has not come to an end. The Bible says that God created man on the sixth day and rested, but each of those days was many millions of years long. That day of rest must have been a short one. Man is not an end but a beginning. We are at the beginning of the second week. We are the children of the eighth day.*

"You're my eighth day child," she told me many times, "the beginning of something new...something better." Pretty hard not to feel special when you have someone anointing you with that on a regular basis.

Mom annually appears before the school board—refusing to ban *Huck Finn*, *Slaughterhouse Five* and *To Kill A Mockingbird*. Don't people have more important matters to address, like protesting the overmedication of today's youth?

Most thirteen-year-olds aren't ready for Henry Miller, nor was I. But, in order to let her believe my precociousness extended into my teens, I read it.

> *Once you have given up the ghost, everything follows*
> *with dead certainty, even in the midst of chaos.*
> *From the beginning it was never anything but chaos...*

I could relate to the *Tropic's* opening lines, but I wasn't into the "outrageous sexual exploits" of Miller's protagonist. Call me old-fashioned, but I prefer to have sex with someone I'm making love *with*, to performing sex *on* someone I've managed to seduce. Don't tell my friends. Most of them regard sex as less important than texting or playing video games.

To my generation, with the exception of brain-washed TAGs (Teen Abstinence Groups), sex has the kind of import necking once did for my grandparents, except now it involves fellatio and cunnilingus (especially for TAGs). Actually, BJ's aren't even considered sex. Girls who like to believe they can fellate someone and still retain their virginity cling to this absurdity. Boys, of course, encourage this "fellacy." (Daddy would be proud.)

Snack time in the lounge. Later...

That's the skinny on my folks. However, were I able to assemble a Fantasy Family, I'd choose Thoreau for an unmarried uncle; Emma Goldman for an unmarried (and intimidating) aunt; Noam Chomsky and Howard Zinn for grandfathers; and Hannah Arendt and Ursula K. Le Guin for grandmothers. (Once, I literally bumped into Ms. Le Guin at Powell's Books, but I was too embarrassed and shy to tell her I think she's amazing.)

I would hope those anarchistic familial influences might have a profound effect on Steven—transforming him from a money-grubbing capitalist into a real father, more concerned with the decline of civilization and his family's welfare than his own pecker and his persistent longing for an American Express Centurion Card—requiring he rack up expenditure$ of at lea$t a quarter million a year. (What a lofty goal, Dad). Susan, though less emotionally incestuous, could still be Mommy.

Seems to me children are here to recreate our parent's issues and try to resolve them. That's certainly a description of my life so far. Unlike Suzanne, I'm looking for someone who shares common interests and a genuine concern for others. In case you couldn't tell, Daddy doesn't give a fiddle-dee-fuck about anyone but himself. As for his obsession with money and his inability to connect emotionally, I'd say I'm his antithesis.

What about you Doc? How's your attempt at being less anal-retentive than your mother going? Any idea how often you realign and restack the papers on your desk? Yikes…and you think I'm compulsive.

I'll forgive your foibles if you forgive mine.

May 11th

I've yet to report on the lovely digs here at The Healing Place. In order to survive the mind-numbing boredom, permit me to have a little fun.

Fun (and humor), unlike the plethora of meds, is in short supply around here.

Consider this my humble attempt at *definite jest*...

ROOM 2-C

(Boy's Wing)

My micro-condo is a 10' x 12' rectangle. It's actually a 12' x 12' cubicle, with a 2' x 6' quadrilateral closet space. The walls are institutional, baby poo brown concrete blocks; smart not to use drywall—knowing how fast this place would resemble the Siege of Sarajevo. It's rare an hour elapses when one of the anger addicts isn't using his or her fists to express what a limited vocabulary can't. The doors are solid hardwood, a cinch to turn adolescent knuckles into something resembling rheumatoid arthritis.

Is there a WalMart in Vladivostok? Pretty sure the small chest of drawers and twin bed are standard issue in orphanages throughout the former Soviet Union.

The simple writing desk is also a homey touch. How thoughtful of you to keep Mennonites employed.

I'm guessing we can't have a desk lamp because you're afraid someone would 'unscrew bulb and insert tongue in socket.' I've only had the displeasure of talking to Richie Caytes a few times, but he would be my first choice for lingual electrocution.

If you were going for a Cold War, interrogation-room atmosphere, the overhead ultra-violet lighting's an inspired choice. It took a restless night or two, but now I'm rather fond of the low *humming sound. When I'm feeling lonely, I pretend it's coming from a "roomie," whom I imagine to be a geriatric patient with advanced dementia.

Mentioned it to Miss Vines, but she ignored me—treating me like I'm just another one of the whackos! (Footnotes: my sort of homage to David Foster Wallace. RIP, dude…really).

I suppose it would be cheeky to request sheets be changed more often. Aware that I shed approximately one million dead skin cells a day and spend up to a third of that 24-hour period in bed (though not always asleep), I'd like to know I'm not over-feeding the dust mites.

Note: I believe positive affirmations and proper hygiene to be the Castor and Pollux of mental health.

Speaking of sanitation…several of your recent admittances are either itchy-twitchy due to crystal meth withdrawal, or they have cooties. You might want to institute disinfectant showers for those who've managed to avoid bathing this decade. Having to feature a bedbug infestation would seem incongruous in your otherwise *impressive institutional brochure, a copy of which I purloined during my intake. I was bedazzled by the photo of Koi fish swimming in the meditation garden pond, though I soon discovered there are none and never have been. Staging is everything, even when it comes to selling psychotherapy.

**I find it ironic and somewhat disconcerting that the 4-color booklet was designed by Steve's Ad Agency.*

My assessment of the décor may sound like carping, but I find it difficult to be comfortable, psychologically, in an ambience more befitting *The Shawshank Redemption.*

Though I AM hoping for some redemption!

* * *

Very amusing. Your father had nothing to do with the brochure. I will have someone check on the humming noise.

Thanks, Doc. You and Miss Vines are a peach of a pair.

May 12th

Suzanne visited today. She was all smiles and positivity. I made sure that didn't last long.

"How're you doing, honey?"

"How could you let Doc keep me here—knowing I'd miss Forensics competition at State? Was Mr. Wolff upset?"

"He was disappointed, but he understood."

"Understood what? That I'm being held here on spurious charges?"

"That you're here to…work on some things."

"You told him that? What did he say?"

"He hopes you get better soon."

Mom's skilled at changing the subject to avoid confrontation. Thinks I don't notice.

"Oh, before I forget…I saw your room. It's nice, but a little stark. Maybe they'd let me bring you some things from home. Pictures and books. You'd like that, wouldn't you? Assuming they let you have books."

"In case you haven't heard, this isn't a library. It's a fucking mental institution."

"I just thought you might be more comfortable if—"

"Are you two conspiring to make this my permanent residence?"

"What? Who? *No*…I only—"

"You've talked to him haven't you? What did he say? Planning to keep me here until I confess I had something to do with the video, isn't he?"

"Dr. van Ittersum's concerned, as am I…that your insistence you had nothing to do with the video…is—"

"What? Proof I'm crazy…delusional?"

"Sweetie, please don't get upset."

"I'm in a fucking psych ward, Mom. If I weren't upset, then you'd know I was nuts."

"Your dad and I agree you need to be here working with Dr. van Ittersum on a more intensive basis until—"

"Until I admit the video's fake…that I somehow perpetrated an amazing CGI prank in hopes of becoming a YouTube superstar? Come on! The fact that you and Dad agree on anything is what's fucked up."

"He cares about you, Pres. We both just want you to be okay. We both love you."

"I hate it when you use first person plural. The only *we* is you and me. He opted out a long time ago."

Big Brother's watching! Next thing I know, Antoine's in the visitor's room telling Mom it's time to go. She looked relieved.

"I'll be back next weekend. Things will be better by then."

"Why so certain I won't already be released? Help me, Mom, *please*. I can't take this much longer."

"I have to go now." She glanced at Antoine, her eyes imploring him to help her escape. "Try to cooperate, sweetie. I love you."

"Wait. Have you talked to Chris? Seen him at school?"

"No. I called him, but he never returned my call. Does he know anything about…?"

"The *video?* No! Why would he?"

"I just thought maybe he—"

"Believe me, I'd tell you if I had any idea who made the damn thing. In case you can't tell, I hate it here."

"Sorry, M'am. Time's up," said Antoine.

She gave me a quick hug.

"Get better, Pres. I miss you."

"Please get me out of here. High school graduation comes but once in a lifetime. Nana's coming. I can't believe you agreed to this torture because that's what it is…torture!" I was desperate to make her realize how badly I needed to be released. "Being here's killing me…seriously. You've got to help me Mom…you're my only hope."

She made every effort to appear unfazed. Turning to leave, her high heel skidded on the concrete floor, but Antoine steadied her, and she continued on. Just as the door was closing behind her I gave it my best shot, "I'm sorry I'm such a *disappointment!*"

For a second I thought I detected a shudder. Her shoulders stiffened, but she kept walking. Nothing. No response. I'm beginning to think Suzanne's finally had enough of being the perfect Asperger's Mom?

I'd appreciate your thoughts on the subject Doc. Also, I could use a little assurance you're not keeping me here because you find me more fascinating than my peers.

* * *

Nothing would make all of us happier than for you to attend your graduation. Please understand I'm not taking sides when I say your mother is one of the most supportive parents I have ever encountered in my 25+ year career.

A ringing endorsement.

May 13th

BONUS ENTRY (today being another soul-numbing Sunday).

Weekends are the worst. As much as I loathe the idea of Group, I prefer sitting around listening to damaged and deranged cuckoos, rather than vegging out until your return: Monday @ promptly 7:45. (Not stalking, just needing someone with a triple digit I.Q., other than Ciera, with whom to converse).

In response to your request…a story from "The Bizarro Childhood of P.W.N."

One Little Indian Boy

I've long had a fascination with fire: the repercussion of numerous past lives as an Indian—and other aboriginal incarnations—on present reality.

By the time I was five years old, I *knew* I was an Indian. I repeat, an Indian (not Native American, you greedy *Wasi'chu*). I didn't pretend to *be* an Indian. I *was* an Indian. Not a five-year-old Indian, a wise old Indian in a five-year-old's body.

I dreamed Indian dreams. I remembered what it was to have an arrow impale a lung, or the white-hot shock when it pierced the heart. The gaminess of dried venison and the seductive redolence of soft deerskin would summon my native past.

On sultry summer days, I peeled white birch bark from a tree— fashioning it into a miniature canoe. When I ran, I drew power from the Earth and the Wind and sailed like my spirit animal, the red-tailed hawk.

Ancient drums resounded in my head and reverberated in my soul. Watching *Drums Across The River*, I cheered on Jay Silverheels and the Indians. Of course, it didn't hurt that the baby-faced war hero, Audie Murphy, was on the side of the Utes. Like Johnny Sheffield (Boy in *Tarzan Finds A Son*) before him, there was something about the cherubic Audie that got my young blood going. No homo. (Okay, maybe a skosh). I also

THE QUEERLING

developed a crush on Margaret Sullavan and Alice Faye. (Thoughts…?)

*Testament to my fascination for old movies. Most of my peers think the motion picture industry began with "Toy Story" or "Lord of the Rings." God bless The Movie Channel and Turner Movie Classics.

The many fires I built as a kid awakened familiarity in my cell-memory. At first, I feared I might be a pyromaniac, but then I realized it was a longing for the countless native campfires that once swirled up into my nostrils. The smell of burning leaves would somehow recall the *olfactory splendor of smudging with sweetgrass, cedar and sage—jolting my memory and searing my lungs, while I stared into the flames as if mesmerized by lifetimes of repetition.

*Somewhere deep within us, smoke is the perfume, the spice and savory condiment of dozens of lives. No one who tastes the earthy piquancy of smoked meats or catches a whiff of an oak-born draft from a fireplace is immune to the momentary recognition of fire's favorite offspring. (Okay, I concede heat is fire's favorite offspring. But, for the sake of a mini-extended metaphor, allow me that conceit, s'il vous plaît?)

I thought like an Indian. I moved silently over broken twigs and brittle leaves like an Indian. I reclined on spongy mounds of moss in shady glens and breathed in Nature. And, when we played Hide 'n Seek, no one could find me, the Indian. I'd shinny up a maple tree, wrap myself around the branches and *become* the tree. *No one had a clue.

* I might add that most of the neighborhood kids were clueless mofos!

Once, at dusk, I lay down in a small hollow, covered with barely foot-high grass. Only forty feet away, Danny and Donnie Jenson, who always had to be 'it' together, pretended to cover their eyes as they counted to fifty. As the droning of numbers faded in my ears, I *became* the Earth…the Grass. The pungent smell transported me back through the millennia.

"…forty-e-i-i-i-ght, forty-n-i-i-i-ne…FIFTY. Here we come, ready or not!" they bellowed in tandem.

"Phssst," Danny hissed. "He's over here. I saw him go over here."

"Where…?" Donnie grumbled—squinting through the dusky half-light.

"Right over he… What the heck? He was right here a few seconds ago."

"Yeah, right, dumbass. He ain't here."

"But he *was*."

They were practically standing on top of me, the Earth, the Grass. Their cotton T-shirts radiated an incandescent blue-white in the evening twilight. In ancient times, I could have risen up and slit their useless throats—ridding the world of two more pale-faced clods.

"Where the hell did he freakin' go…?" demanded Donnie.

"Telling Mom you cuss."

"Shut up, shit for brains, and help me find the little queer."

"I swear I just saw him," said Danny—shaking his head. "That's really weird."

"*You're* really weird," concluded his brother. "Come on, moron, let's go find the others." Donnie ran on ahead.

Danny stood motionless—cocking his head from side to side like a baffled beagle. Finally, he whispered, "I *know* you're here. You ain't foolin' me you little *queer*." One more futile compassing of the area and off he ran—muttering.

I could see them, but they couldn't see me: the Indian. No one ever found me, unless I got bored and let him.

Doc, I can only imagine how excited you get when you think you've discovered a patient with this level of delusion. However, that assessment would indicate a mental inflexibility and lack of receptivity necessary to understand me *in toto*. You do want to understand me, right? Or, have you already determined I'm hopeless?

I assure you my Indian exploits are no less real than the spiritually uplifting hallucinations you experienced during your LySergic acid Days at the Stanford Research Institute.

You might want to reconsider which photos you display on your credenza.

* * *

Interesting story. Let's discuss this further in Tuesday's session.

When it comes to shape-shifting, I can offer no plausible explanation other than a sense of knowing, an unwavering belief. And, frankly, I'm not interested in hearing you debase an incredible experience with psycho-babble. So, I'll pass on further discussion, kemosabe.

May 14th

Today, you referred to our initial meeting and the circumstances that occasioned my first visit to The Healing Place. Wow! Almost eight years ago. Can't believe you asked me if I remembered. Never forget…the first word in memory is ME.

So, here's a little back story, per your request. Nostalgia time, Tommy Boy…

En Génesis

Where did Suzanne get the idea she'd birthed a genius?

It all happened quite by accident. As a fourth-grader at the end of W's first term, I was given a national two-day exam: reading comprehension—including vocabulary and inference, my specialty, since everything my parents ever said to each other was inferred: a dialectical puzzle meant (puzzlement) to hide the real meaning from their innocent offspring.

Call it Fate, Dumb Luck or a thesaurus-like grasp of the language (thanks, Mom), but I managed a perfect score—resulting in two representatives from AETC, the Acme Educational Testing Company, flying from Palo Alto to Portland to validate my dubious achievement. Following a lengthy powwow with my teacher, Miss Eleanor Dawson, in an attempt to determine if I might have cheated, or if she'd helped me cheat by failing to properly monitor the test, the twosome questioned me.

"Nice to meet you, Preston. I'm Ms. Dilbeck and this is Mr. Simms. We'd like to ask you some questions."

Ms. Dilbeck, in her early 30's, had obviously spent a great deal of time polishing, nourishing and replenishing her skin. It was as shiny and tight as the fake plastic buttocks I wore to school for our class Halloween party 3rd grade year—culminating in a one-day suspension.

"Is this about that stupid test?"

"Why do you refer to it as stupid?" she asked—glancing at Mr. Simms, as if I were about divulge the answer they'd flown 600 air miles to hear.

I stared at her just long enough for him to intervene.

"No fourth grader's ever made a perfect score on the Acme 2000 Multiphasic Reading Comprehension and Dynamic Vocabulary Inventory Test...not even close. Plus, our records indicate you're a year younger than the rest of your class."

I shifted my gaze to him. Though he dressed the part, Mr. Simms, in his early-to-mid 40's, was obviously uncomfortable in this pseudo-academic role—possessing a demeanor more akin to that of used-car salesman.

"You think I cheated?" I appealed to Ms. Dilbeck with my deeply-wounded look.

"*No*...not at all," she said. It's just sometimes students receive unfair help through no fault of their own. We're not saying that happened, but we want to make sure—"

"Ever hear of Charles Van Doren?" blurted Simms—cutting her off. Thinking the reference impossibly old for my generation, he seemed self-satisfied.

Embarrassed by her colleague's ineptitude, Ms. Dilbeck lowered her head.

"I believe he was a contestant on one of those rigged quiz shows back in the golden age of television." (Score! Fortunately, Mom and I watched *Quiz Show* several times on TMC. She has a crush on Ralph Fiennes; we've watched *The English Patient* three times.)

"That's *right!*" exclaimed Ms. Dilbeck, who perked up again.

Without missing a beat, I fired one back at Simms. "Ever hear of Tomás de Torquemada?"

"Thomas who...?"

"Torquemada. The first Inquisitor General during the Spanish Inquisition." (Booyah! Nailed him).

His face contorted as he struggled to make the connection. A humiliated and angry Miss Dawson had returned to the classroom; however, our Principal, Dr. Harriet Werner, was in attendance.

"Stop showing off, Preston. I mean it. This is *serious*." She shook her head in disgust. "Sorry, he does this."

Ms. Dilbeck decided to take charge. "What we want to know...and you're not in any trouble...is whether or not Miss Dawson assisted you? Do you understand?"

I wanted to say, 'I made a perfect score on your friggin' test. Of course I know what assisted means. Aided. Abetted. She provided the answers.' Instead, I looked perplexed.

"Answer the question," growled Dr. Werner, using her authoritarian voice, tempered, so as not to appear the Nazi we all knew her to be.

Adopting my patented self-serving tone, I inquired, "Dr. Werner, wouldn't you say my previous I.Q. scores might be an indication of my abilities when it comes to test-taking?"

"Personally, I don't put much faith in I.Q. tests," said the woman most students referred to as BORE, the Bitch of Reimer Elementary. "Scores can fluctuate wildly. Never once did my I.Q. score indicate I would someday hold a doctorate degree."

She served it up, and I smashed a torpedo-of-an-overhead just inside the baseline. "Mom says, 'When it comes to online degrees, all that's required these days is a computer and a credit card.'"

Blood rushed to her face. I feared laser beams would come shooting from her reptilian eyes. She dropped all pretense. "That's enough. Answer the question *now!*"

Instead of answering, I concentrated on what my dog, Scottie, looked like after Steven backed his classic 280ZX over him on that infamous weekend he walked out on us, or as I like to call it: Abandonment Saturday/Depression Sunday. Within seconds, I managed to squeeze out a big ol' fat tear that trailed down my cheek, like thick sugar-syrup right before it reaches the soft-ball stage.

"Great. Now what do we do?" sighed Simms.

"Please don't be upset," said Ms. Dilbeck. "We're not accusing you of anything, just trying to determine the legitimacy of your score."

"Here, blow your nose," said Werner—forcing a perfumed tissue that contained a faint lipstick blot into my hand. *Ewww.*

I scanned their faces, took a deep breath and lowered my eyes. "She didn't help me, but she did whisper the meaning of *charity* to Amanda Sue."

"Are you sure?" quizzed Werner.

"Uh huh. But, she was just being charitable," I added, straight-faced. "That's the type of teacher Miss Dawson is. Accommodating. Altruistic. You know the meaning of altruism don't you...? It means Amanda Sue's her niece."

I'm not certain in what manner Dawson was reprimanded, but she retaliated by giving me a "D" in Conduct and dedicating herself to making my life miserable.

Suzanne was irate, but I managed to dissuade her from confronting my dear teacher—fearing it would only make things worse. Besides, I had other means of retribution in mind.

Not unlike the head lice epidemic that plagued our elementary school the previous September, word quickly spread that Preston Nesbitt aced a National Reading Test. One would think this might be a lauded accomplishment; however, much like the sores caused from scratching and the toxic chemicals used to kill the little buggers, it only further alienated my fellow classmates and the faculty, most of whom feared any student with a brain and a modicum of independence. (A bit forced, but I feel compelled to use an occasional figure of speech, in hopes of enlivening this pedestrian assignment.)

The ridiculous interrogation, Dawson's disciplinary action and my subsequent counteraction set the stage for my first psych evaluation and an opportunity to meet you, my dear *Dottore*.

How's that for memory? Unlike Borges, who described memory as a "stack of coins," the possibility of one memory distorting the next, I'd say my recollection is spot-on.

Today, in our private session, you said something rather intriguing.

When I asked why you have me write about things we've just covered "to the best of your memory," I scoffed at the irony.

"Why do you act like memory's my *hamartia*, my tragic flaw? You of all people know it's my greatest gift."

You smiled with that patented 'How naïve you are,' patronizing look you've perfected over the years.

"Hopefully, someday you'll learn that having memory of something is very different from having perspective."

I'll have to get back to you on that one…someday.

P.S. Ciera said you asked her if I ever talked about the video. I've told you everything I know. But, let me ask…is pumping a patient for another's personal info even ethical? She also mentioned that most of her entries are a scant paragraph or two. Since some of mine are *whoppers, I may not journal every day.

As in 'exceptionally big or remarkable'…not as in 'a gross untruth!'

(Surpassed 40-pages of journaling. There goes my plan of turning this into a chapbook).

* * *

Re: Your story. Are you still feeling misunderstood? Re: Perspective. Like aesthetic distance, perspective requires a slight remove. To be clear, I do not think you are naïve, but you do not currently have access to the perspective time will afford you. For instance, with a little perspective, you would understand that identifying the cause of someone's condition doesn't automatically lead to a cure, far from it. Re: Criticism of the staff. Though you may disagree, my colleagues and I are in this profession because we, too, want to help others. Re: Journaling. Your journal assignment and Ciera's are alike only in that you are both recording your thoughts. You may write as little or as much as you choose. The length isn't as important as the content. Several patients and staff members have said you questioned them about whether they'd seen, and what they thought about, your video. My question to Ciera was simply a follow-up to her mentioning it.

Wow! You answered every question but the most important one. When am I getting out of here?

May 16th

No doubt you'll be convinced my Indian story was concocted as justification for setting fire to Miss Dawson's garage, revenge for the "D" in Conduct. Think I'm that petty? Never mind. In case you've forgotten, it was an accident…of sorts.

To show my outrage at having my intelligence questioned by two boorish emissaries from AETC, and at Dawson for failing to validate my intelligence and making the rest of the school year pure Hell, I created her effigy—affixing a mock-up of that hideous pomegranate seed-of-a-wart alongside her nose. (No detail is insignificant when one is trying to drive home a point). Admittedly, I waited until the last day of school before committing the incendiary act. After all, I was vindictive not stupid. Well…

This was no scapegoating effigy, like the ones created of Judas, to be flogged, hanged, burned and exploded with fireworks by Christian fanatics every Easter. No, no. This was a political effigy—protesting the lack of moral, emotional and intellectual support by an old crone posing as a teacher.

Not only did I feel justified, I was certain others, former students who may have been psychically damaged by Dawson, would feel the same. That's why I made an anonymous phone call from my trusty pre-paid

Nokia to KATU-TV, affectionately known as K2—alerting them to a newsworthy "happening."

Hanging the crude replica from the clothesline in her backyard, I waited until I was alerted—via walkie-talkie, by my buddy Chris Roberts, who was stationed in the Reimer Elementary parking lot—that she was only ten minutes away before igniting it. What I neglected to calculate, and this is where my judgment, not my motive, should be called into question, were the forceful wind gusts that spring day. Plus, the lame way I attached the object of ridicule to the clothesline—using only a twist tie.

I watched in horror as the flaming manikin took flight—scoring a perfect "10" landing on the roof of her garage (really no more than an old shed) and setting it ablaze. In a panic, I attempted to extinguish the fire—only to discover that her pitifully short garden hose was attached to a rotating sprinkler and the water pressure was insufficient to do more than christen the side of the building.

I contemplated whether or not to dial 911, but not certain whether a disposable phone could be traced, I opted for not. Instead, I hid further down the alley—hoping for a miracle afternoon cloudburst. No such luck! By the time Dawson appeared in her vomit green, 1983 *Yugo*, the fire was raging.

Believe me, the conflagration was an accident, not to mention her own culpability for failing to notice the flames until *after* she'd parked the barf-wagon in the belly of the inferno.

I should've received an award from the Neighborhood Improvement Association; however, that was not to be, as the Wicked Witch of the Northwest decided to press charges. It didn't help that the K2 news crew arrived in time to capture both the shack collapsing into a fiery heap and me hightailing it down the alley.

The combination of obtaining a perfect test score and igniting a garage, plus irreparable damage to the worst car in automotive history, resulted in a whopping fine and a Psych Eval for me here at The Healing Place: "For children who have difficulty functioning in mainstream community settings." (Biting my tongue).

As for the hearing: Accompanied by both Suzanne and Steve, I found it to be a most memorable day…"The Family Together Again." And, to think, all I had to do was accurately answer two hundred and fifty questions and torch a hovel.

Anyway, you know the rest. That's how I ended up here in this fabulous state-funded facility, with the meditation gardens and the ubiquitous Feng Shui. Balance and Harmony abound at The Healing Place, though it's apparently lacking among its residents.

Any chance I racked up some points for protecting Chris from possible prosecution? Do you hold it against me when I resort to a bit of theatricality in the retelling? Is there a timetable for when you plan to release me? So many questions, so few answers.

Potty break…

Of course, your initial evaluation didn't result in my confinement (I mean residency). It merely culminated in our weekly get-togethers for almost a year. I could play it smart, avoid asking what I'm about to ask, but you know how impulsive we ASer's can be. Besides, as Oscar Wilde so famously aphorized, 'I can resist everything except temptation.'

So, here goes: Does it ever bother you that after almost *eight years* of intermittent outpatient therapy, I ended up here as a full-time inmate? According to the quantum entanglement theory, where the future can impact the past, do you think our current situation is affecting our previous interactions?

Think of them as a koans: nonsensical or paradoxical questions which demand an answer. I'll let you ponder both awhile. May I recommend the lovely meditation garden for your rumination?

May 17th

What was your impression of today's Group Therapy? Hilarious, yet mind-boggling, right? Masturbation's rather ho-hum. But, *bestiality?* Awkward.

I have to admit, I was taken with Joey's honesty. Though he's not someone I would choose to befriend under normal circumstances, I have to admit there was something sincere, almost poetic about his description of the act itself. Let me attempt to record the outrageous and revelatory:

Confession Session

"Does anyone else have anything to share?" you asked. "Remember, you're safe to talk about anything. No one will judge you. No one will criticize you." (Now which of us is living in a fantasy world)?

Misty Johnson volunteered first. Wish I could simulate her weak, languid speaking voice, the result of years of *Lexipro* and *Luvox*.

"I wanna say thanks to everyone for letting me talk about my…masturbation trauma. Haven't told that story to anybody, except like a few people I chat with online."

"You've discussed this with people on the internet?"

"Uh, yeah. But, most of them think I'm like a 35-year-old Japanese guy talking about my niece. I call her Yuki. I'm really into anime. Do any of you guys watch AnimeFreak TV online? It's so cool. Book One…"Water" is really rad. Watched it like at least fifty times. You know those pictures in my journal, Doc? That's her…Yuki. Don't you think she's beautiful? *I* do. I love her. I've even learned a bunch of Japanese words. *Kakkoii*. It means cool. Anime's like way cooler than manga!"

"I see." (Very doubtful). You made a quick notation. "You mentioned this wasn't the first time your mother…walked in on you while—"

"Yeah, but this was kinda worse. She was supposed to be cooking supper in the kitchen. But, she like came charging into my room without even knocking. Right when I was…doing it. And I was like, 'Mom!' And she was like, 'Misty! For God's sake! Give me that! First a cucumber and now this!' She made me feel really ashamed…catching me with the…dildo."

"Thought it was a zucchini?" said Joey Gentry. Like many of the homeless who find their way to Portland, there's something feral about him.

"Another veggie dildo," said Richie Caytes, forever the little rich-kid asshole. "That makes her a *vagitarian*." He led the group in laughter. I abstained.

"Steely Dan," I said—raising my voice in an attempt to cut through the hilarity.

Richie looked at me with disdain. "Huh?"

"She used a Steely Dan."

"Yeah, right, mister brainiac. She's not talking about some 70's rock star." He quickly scanned faces for agreement.

"First of all, Steely Dan's not a *guy*, it's a group. And, furthermore, it's another name for dildo, Dildo."

"You know the rules Preston. No name calling."

"Sorry Doc, it was just a st-st-st-stutter."

"Yeah, right," said Richie—glaring at me with pure enmity.

Like him, you also seemed uninformed. "Where did you come by this information?"

"*Cum* by…LOL!" blared Misty, who's harmless but rather Hannah Montana, as our generation likes to refer to the perpetually stupid. Everything provides a sexual connotation for her, particularly any food resembling sexual organs. If you don't believe me, join us in the cafeteria sometime. Dare ya.

"Steely Dan…? So glad you asked Doc. It's what William S. Burroughs called a strap-on dildo in *Naked Lunch*. Suzanne suggested I read it my freshman year, when I was contemplating becoming a Nouveau Beat, an heir apparent to Jack Kerouac."

"You're so full of crap!" said Richie. Under his breath he added, "…and that mother of yours is a whack-job."

Before I could get my hands on the little bastard, Antoine grabbed my shoulders and held me back. For those who haven't seen him, Antoine's 6' 4" and weighs at least 300 lbs. He says he was drafted by the Seahawks but blew out a knee in training camp. I know what you're thinking, Doc, but Antoine isn't the aide who told me about the viral video. He's more into the Trailblazers than YouTube.

You attempted to restore order. "Let's all settle down, shall we? Joey, you look like you have something to say. What's on your mind?"

"Since Misty was like, you know, so honest and all…I wanna get something off my chest, too. Not really a confession, you know, but more like just wantin' to see if any of you guys have ever…have ever…"

"Come on Street, spit it out," said Richie.

"Beat off a dog."

"Wut da fuck!" blurted Antoine, involuntarily. "Sorry…" If any question remains about whether Black people blush, it was answered by the rubescence in Antoine's visage.

"I'm outta here!" said Richie—springing to his feet.

"Sit down, please…and listen."

Antoine moved to assist Richie in resuming his seat.

Ciera's hands, fingers spread, shot to her cheeks and her eyelids fluttered like Aunt Pittypatt in *GWTW*.

"Forgive the interruption Joey. Continue please."

"Well, it's just somethin' I did one time, you know, because this neighbor's dog was all tied up. It's chain was wound round and around the pole 'til he couldn't move. They never let the poor dog off that chain."

"So you got him off?" said Richie.

"HA! Got him off. LMFAO!" squealed Misty, whose wheezy laugh is as contagious as a fever blister.

Richie shifted in his chair. "Do we have to listen to this shit?"

Antoine placed his catcher's-mitt-of-a-hand on Richie's shoulder.

"Go ahead."

"Well…sometimes I'd come home from school, and the chain would be twisted around the clothesline pole, and this poor dog was, ya know, like about chokin' to death. I felt really bad for it. It looked real sad."

"So, you thought givin' it a hand job would make it feel better?"

"I ain't tellin' this story if he keeps buttin' in with his nasty comments," said Joey, who'd lived on the streets of Portland for more than a year when he was arrested for breaking into Pets on Broadway and court-ordered into treatment.

"You flogged a dog's log, tickled a canine's lipstick dipstick and *I'm* nasty? How high were you?"

"I may've been sniffin' a little glue, but that ain't why I did it."

I'm unfamiliar with all the background details, but I know Richie Caytes (Caytes Reality, anyone?) has been in several behavior modification programs and wilderness camps. Apparently, none were effective. I heard him brag he's only here 'til his mother can get his latest legal problem fixed.

Not only is he a classic sociopath…he's a bully.

"Speaking of *buttin' in*… Sounds like you may have been sniffin' more than glue," said Richie.

"Huh…?"

"Probably let him sniff yours, too."

I'd had enough. "You're a douche, you know that?"

"Asslicker!"

"No more of that now." (What a forceful moderator you are.)

Ciera, who usually sits quietly by with both legs pumping up and down like hydraulic pistons, covered her ears.

"Actually, it probably would…make it feel better," said Misty. "J/K. Not really!"

"Doc, ancient civilizations believed all animals represented a moral lesson…that they were, in essence, a living allegory. This is probably a case of Joey subconsciously trying to save the world."

"How do you mean?"

"The Ukrainians believed there was a dog chained beside Ursa Minor—"

"Not more of that astrology crap," interjected Richie, who rolled his eyes, crossed his arms and slumped down in his chair.

"Let him finish!" said Ciera—raising her voice, which was a rarity.

"…and this dog tries to gnaw through his iron chain. If he were to succeed, Ukrainians believed the world would perish. So, Joey, in his own way, was just trying to prevent world annihilation."

"By poundin' a dog's pud? This little perv's one whacked-out dude and so are you. When I tell my mother what kind of incredible bullshit goes on in these sessions, I'll be out of here in a flash."

"Not unless there's a moratorium on setting cats on fire."

"Fuck you, faggot!"

Before I could even respond, Ciera sprang to her feet.

"If this is how it's going to be, you'll have to excuse me." She headed for her room. Miss Vines, a hefty female aide, attempted to stop her.

"It's all right. Let her go. The rest of you…settle down, please. And no more name-calling… Continue Joey."

"That's about it. One of the reasons it kept gettin' tangled up was 'cause it kept tryin' to get to this female dog across the alley. I felt sorry for him…"

"Very touching…"

In your most modulated, non-judgmental voice you inquired, "Why so critical Richie? You seem angry."

"I'm *angry* because we have to listen to Mr. Urban Camper here talk about beatin' a mongrel's meat because it can't get laid, when he's really talking about himself."

I had to agree Joey was projecting his own sense of inadequacy onto the situation, but I hated the way Richie was verbally abusing the poor kid.

"I can get laid. I've *been* laid."

"Yeah…but not within your own species."

You closed the cover on your leather-bound notebook.

"That's enough for today. Misty and Joey, thanks for sharing. Back to your rooms. I want you to journal about what went on today. We'll discuss it in your private sessions. Richie, I need to see you in my office."

So, that's how it went…from memory. What grade would you give me for accuracy, detail and nuance? A great big ol' hairy "A," right? They don't call me a memory prodigy for nuttin'.

All in all, it was a little livelier than some of our sessions, I'll admit. But, just how any of this is going to heal us, I fail to understand. It doesn't seem to be helping Ciera. When I found her later, she confessed to shoving a paperclip through the webbing between her big toe and distal phalanx the minute she got back to her room.

"It helps, Pres. You should try it. If it doesn't work...these will," she said—handing me two tabs of *Zoloft*.

I don't know how you think she's doing, but personally I'm worried. You might want to rethink the potpourri of pills you're giving her, or make sure she's taking them.

So ends the Nesbitt Report for Friday, May 17th. This is your humble reporter, Achilles, signing off. Bless the Beasts...and the Children.

* * *

Very amusing. Your reinvention of the details shows a great deal of creativity. However, let me remind you that it's not necessary to make this entertaining. Other than myself, only a few colleagues will likely read any of it. You should, perhaps, think about becoming a comedy writer.

I checked. Comedy Writing for Film and Television is actually an advanced course offered at NYU's Tisch School of the Arts. Though I can recite the Gettysburg Address, the Preamble to the Constitution and *Hiawatha's Childhood* (Gangnam Style), for some reason I have difficulty remembering jokes. Weird, I know. However, here's the first joke Steve-O ever told me...one of the very few I've retained. Keep in mind I was only nine:

Two deaf mutes are on a date with these two "hawt" girls. They are all making out at a drive-in movie (this joke is obviously from another era). The deaf mute in the front seat pauses and (imagine I'm wiggling my fingers like a mad man, "signing") says to the one in the backseat...

"Got the condoms?"

(More finger wiggling). "No," says the other. "Thought you had 'em."

Frustrated, the driver pulls out of the drive-in and races to the local drugstore. He rushes in, but doesn't return for ten minutes. He heads back to the drive-in. When things get hot and heavy again, the guy in the back peers over the front seat and signs...

"Need a condom now."

"Sorry. Don't have 'em," signs the other.

"What happened...you were in the drugstore a long time?"

"It's complicated. I searched every aisle. When I couldn't find 'em, I went up to the pharmacist and tried to make him understand what I wanted. He couldn't read sign language. Having no other way to make him understand, I unzipped my pants, took out my penis, flopped it down on the counter and put a five dollar bill beside it."

"Yeah, what happened then?"

"At first he seemed confused, but then he unzipped his pants, took out his penis and flopped it down on the counter. His was bigger than mine...so he took my five bucks!"

This story has two points: First, my sense of humor has nothing to do with genetics. And second, being misunderstood is a bitch.

May 18th

Just reread yesterday's recap of that amazing Group Session. My, my...how I do go on. May I remind you that excessive talking is not a disorder. Admittedly, it might be a symptom of ADHD. But, in my case, I think it's a result of extreme *ennui*.

May 19th

ASSIGNMENT: A little Family History, culled from the Annals of P.

W. Nesbitt's Memory Bank. Thus, a Family Historectomy. Had I extracted it from the Anals instead, it would be a Family Histroscopy. (Putting on Serious Face).

The Steven Nesbitt Family

Steve's father, Raymond, was a Vietnam vet. Upon graduation from high school, he actually volunteered for the conflict. When he completed his tour of duty in 1967, he used the G. I. Bill to enroll at Occidental College. Once he received the $130-a-month service man's benefit, he was, as we like to say, stylin'.

In a local bar (this is unconfirmed family lore), Ray allegedly met Terry Gilliam, a former graduate of Occidental, who later joined Monty Python's Flying Circus. At the time, Gilliam was working for a local ad agency as an illustrator and growing supremely unhappy with U.S. Imperialism. After a few beers, the two took off in Gilliam's Hillman Minx—tooling around Glendale—when a cop pulled them over for no apparent reason. According to the future Python, this was not the first time the local Gestapo had harassed him, and he was beginning to take it personally.

Asked why they were being detained, the cop said, "You two look like a couple of trouble makers."

That incident finally induced Gilliam to leave the country and join the "Circus." He told Grandpa Ray that if he stayed any longer, he'd end up being a "bomb-making terrorist." If you've seen *The Man Who Killed Don Quixote* or *The Imaginarium of Doctor Parnassus*, you'd know he became one anyway. (Tee hee!)

That's the fun part of the Nesbitt family history. It gets darker.

Raymond moved into Occidental's first Co-Ed dormitory in 1970, where he met Nana, the lovely Nancy Siddons, a scholarship student from a relatively poor family near Bakersfield. It was "love at first sight" for Ray. Nana says it was really "lust at first sight," and though he was ruggedly handsome, she wasn't smitten, initially. After all, he was a Vietnam vet and she detested war.

She helped stage a student protest of the Kent State shootings and the invasion of Cambodia, and somehow persuaded him to join her in the cause. That backfired, because some of the students taunted him for his involvement in the conflict—calling him "murderer" and "baby killer." (Oh, how some of them ever-lovin' Hippies could promote Brotherhood.)

Nancy then began a letter-writing campaign to protest U.S. involvement, one of the first in the country. Because she was adamantly opposed to our polices in Southeast Asia and dedicated to protesting everything involving "the war-mongering government," it eventually created a fissure in their relationship.

In addition, Ray developed a hard-core drinking problem, a coping mechanism for his undiagnosed Post Traumatic Stress Disorder. His bouts of erratic behavior and inebriation led to more conflict between the two. Nana's father was an alcoholic and she was determined not to get involved with "a dipsomaniac." This is a beautiful example of how the *"best-laid schemes o' mice an' men gang aft agley' (go often askew).

*I prefer Robbie Burn's original to the bastardized translation. Call me a purist.

During one of their frequent verbal skirmishes, in a effort to stop her from sermonizing about the atrocity that was the My Lai Massacre, a shit-faced Raymond pushed Nancy—causing her to fall down the dorm steps. Though not seriously injured, she refused to forgive him, so he transferred to Caltech and finished a degree in civil engineering. He immediately got a job working for The Aerospace Corporation in El Segundo, near the U.S. Air Force Ballistic Missile Division, where he assisted in the creation of the new Global Positioning System (GPS) for the Air Force.

According to Nana, Gramps dated a few other women, but he couldn't shake the thought of "the lovely Nancy," his pet name for her. So, he devised a campaign to win her back, and by doggies it worked. What was it? Oh, 'twas devious to be sure. (Obviously, Raymond's genes skipped Steven, except for those craving alcohol, and were passed along to yours truly.)

Upon discovering a First Edition copy of Steinbeck's *Of Mice and Men* in a local used bookstore, he tracked down the great man at his home in Pacific Grove, where the Nobel Prize-winning author consented to write the following *dedication:

> To the lovely Nancy,
>
> I believe a strong woman may be stronger than a man, particularly if she happens to have love in her heart.
>
> Forever,
>
> John Steinbeck.
>
> P.S. Forgiveness is a great virtue.

*Apparently, cliché and sentimentality are prerequisites for snagging the Nobel.

Upon receiving the surprise gift, Nana accepted Ray's accompanying proposal. That's where the next line of Burn's poem is most apropos: 'An' lea'e us nought but grief an' pain, For promis'd joy!'

They married during Christmas break in '71. Stevie was born in '72. Nana says the marriage was a disaster from the get-go, but she tried to cope until she realized Ray was working on a GPS system that would aid police in tracking people, not just criminal suspects but POI…"people of interest."

Over the next few years, his drinking escalated, as did the flashbacks. He became increasingly paranoid, and in 1979, when Stevie was seven, Ray came home early from work, went to the basement of their Glendale ranch-style home, grabbed a 12-gauge shotgun from his handmade, walnut gun case, shoved it into his mouth and blasted his brains all over their hideous green, indoor-outdoor carpeting.

Seven-year-old Steven, a latchkey kid until Nana arrived home (usually) around 4:15 p.m., wandered into the basement, where he stumbled upon his father's body. Ms. Nancy, who'd acquired a Master's degree in English Lit from Stanford, was teaching at nearby Glendale Community College. Waylaid by a student needing to discuss an "unfair grade," she finally appeared thirty minutes later than usual.

Hearing the TV blaring, and figuring Stephen was absorbed in the program, she yelled down the steps, "Hi, honey. Hope you had a good day."

She then started supper before venturing into the basement, where she was greeted by the body of her dead husband. Several feet away sat little Stevie—watching "The Dukes of Hazzard."

Lovely stuff, eh? Should I, perhaps, be more forgiving of Daddy's Attachment Disorder? Forgiveness still pending.

On the morrow, the equally tragic story of the Michael Preston Family.

May 20th

The Suzanne Preston Family Saga

Suzanne's parents, Michael and Julia (Illingworth) Preston, immigrated to Seattle from Brighton, England in 1973. Michael, an endocrinologist, was hired to teach in the Med School at the University of Washington. Julia aspired to be a poetess. She stayed home and raised Suzie Q, who was born in '74, and her older brother, *Ian McEwan Preston, named after Julia's first beau.

*According to Suzanne, her mother was so disgusted McEwan named one of the incestuous characters in The Cement Garden "Julia," she never read another word he wrote.

The Preston's lived a comfortable life in a large Victorian home on Queen Anne—overlooking Puget Sound. Mother remembers life as idyllic. She had a horse, stabled near their summer cottage on Bainbridge Island, and took ballet—aspiring to become a professional ballerina, until her 'ever-burgeoning breasts refused to stop burgeoning.'

She also kept journals and, during her junior year at *Ballard High School, she wrote a novella about a torrid love affair between a young Snohomish Indian girl and an early white settler. *Rain Falling on Wooden Huts* she entitled it, though later she would say the pedestrian title was superior to the actual novella.

*Mom jokes that the writing would have been better had her brain not been negatively impacted by the asbestos contamination in the old school building. She says if, in the future, she contracts COPD, mesothelioma, or T.B., to make sure I'm part of any Class Action Suit. She also made mention of how the novella was praised by one of her former English teachers, who later became a novelist.

When Suzie (as she was then known by friends) discovered a new next-door neighbor to be a famous British travel writer, her desire to become an author deepened. However, that dream faded soon after she was accepted into Stanford's Creative Writing program, where her work was assailed by what she termed, 'a gaggle of preening Stegner fellows.'

During her freshman year in '91, she met Steven at a Chi Omega Sorority Rush. She thought he was sexy and funny. Hormones, like the cannabis they both smoked ('just a few times'), obviously impaired one's perception of reality. She did, however, opt out of the Chi O pledge class, so apparently her ability to reason wasn't permanently destroyed. Anyway, they married over Christmas Break in '93. Ms. Suzie believes she married him mainly because she loved Nana Nesbitt and their shared passion for literature.

Looking at their old college photos, I have to admit Steve, a typical beer-ponging Frat Boy, was a dashing Lothario. I'm certain that also played a part. As previously noted, Mr. Wolff's a hunk-a-doodle. So, I'd say Suzie Q. isn't immune to "fucking faces," as Leonard Cohen so graphically termed it in *Beautiful Losers*, another work my well-intentioned Mother exposed me to at a too tender age.

Young Ms. Nesbitt graduated with a B.A. in English in the summer of '94—completing her Master's in Library Science in May '95.

The following December, six people—including her parents, a UDub colleague and his wife and their mutual friends (a Weyerhaeuser executive and his wife) were all flying to the Exec's summer home in Cabo San Lucas, when the private Cessna Citation crashed near Bakersfield—killing everyone aboard. I made my appearance ten weeks later: a leap day to remember, following a year to forget.

This is where the Steve & Suzanne Saga takes a steep nosedive (like the Cessna did into the Greenhorn Mountains). Up to that point, Nana and Steve had managed to conceal Raymond's suicide, saying he'd been killed in an accident. It wasn't until shortly after I was born, Mom discovered the real story, when her brother, Ian, an investigative reporter for the "Seattle Post-Intelligencer," sent a copy of an article from the "Glendale News-Press"—detailing the suicide. That revelation created a schism between Suzanne and Nana that never completely healed, although Mother still encourages me to visit her in Glendale every Spring Break.

Do schisms heal? How 'bout fissures, ruptures and rifts?

I'm all for nostalgia, but I find it rather bizarre that the green indoor-outdoor carpeting remains. On Spring Break visits, I avoid Nana's basement, because its FUBAR energy repels me like Steve's emotional distance.

Da-Duh! And that's what I like about the West. (Jazz hands)

* * *

Would you say "avoidance" of painful scenarios would be the theme of these two family histories, as regards both of your parents?

Feel free to employ a little subtlety in your questioning. You say you admire my intelligence, yet you insist on insulting it.

May 21st

Not up to writing today. Exhuming Family Skeletons was a downer. Is it possible I was adopted? Did I, perchance, escape from a hole in the wallpaper, or emerge from an alien starseed? Any of those origins would be more comforting.

REMINDER: Senior/Parent Breakfast <u>this Friday</u>. The juniors cater the Senior Brunch. It's a WPI tradition. There's a special video tribute—consisting mainly of seniors' baby pictures. For the record, I was a tow-head with "an adorable smile."

Let's aim for a Thursday release, shall we? Let me know if there's anything you need from me between now and then.

May 22nd

You re-read my in-depth journal report on the bestiality debacle, and take issue with what exactly: my 'recreation of the dialogue?' 'Forced' I believe you called it. 'Doesn't quite ring true' the way you remember it?

Listen, if I can't take a little poetic license in recreating these vapid and dreary sessions, my brain will start melting and run out of my ears. I'm bored. *Really bored!* Remember how the actor George Sanders reacted to boredom? Unlike him, I have no intention of offing myself, but I do understand the urge.

You can't imagine what it's like being confined. Well, maybe you can. The only difference between the jailer and the jailed is one gets to go home at the end of the day. That…and you have a nifty set of keys dangling from your belt loop.

As for enlivening the dialogue, etc., I am inclined to add a little patina to the mundane. Why wouldn't I? It's what artists do. Picasso had his grandchildren piss on his bronzes—believing the oxidization created by urine increased their ornamental value. It's the same thing, really. I'm just adding a little gloss without piddling (too much).

Misty, bless her, is a monumental mess. The "asides" I've added, while juvenile, are meant to provide comic relief. Think Greek Chorus. As you may know, The Greek Chorus often represented the audience's hidden thoughts and fears. But, in Misty's case, her text-speak is symbolic of 99% of the scintillating exchanges you'll find on Facebook badinage. In another millennium, this journal can serve as a valuable snapshot of how far we'd fallen, linguistically, as a species.

I admit Richie's put-downs were not nearly as clever as the ones I provided, but I was just trying to lighten the mood. Name a memoirist, worth reading, who doesn't "juice up" the dialogue.

Life here is Dullsville. Admit it, you get bored, too. I can tell you're often amused by my witty banter and bombastic style. Bet our sessions are uplifting, compared to the mounds of dispiriting excreta you trudge through on a daily basis. Great image, eh? I can see you now—slipping on your psychological hip waders. Besides, I'll be gone soon…and you'll miss me.

ATTENTION: All Seniors must be at Rose Garden Arena <u>by 9:30 a.m. Saturday morning</u>. Graduation practice begins 'promptly' at 10. Attendance is mandatory. There are no exceptions! If for some reason I haven't convinced you I'm sane by Friday, the 27th, I <u>promise</u> to report back on Monday, the 30th. Nana's coming from California. This is a pretty Big Deal!

May 23rd

Before I bid farewell to The Healing Place, I'd like to be of further assistance. It's my way of showing my concern for the well-being of others.

CIERA SELF

(A psychological evaluation by Dr. P.W. Nesbitt)

Who *is* Ciera Self?

Ciera's atypical of most girls, the ones interested in being popular, getting ahead and "livin' the life." She's really bright and *really* sensitive. Unfortunately, all that sensitivity makes her a walking raw nerve. It's like she has all these invisible tentacles surrounding her, and people are unintentionally stepping on them or bumping into them—"hurting her feelings."

She's a natural blonde but dyes her hair jet black. I joke she's raven-haired but bleaches the roots (as lame as Steve, I admit). Her skin is like translucent porcelain, so the contrast is rather stark. She has the most amazing eyes, just bulbous enough to be prominent without being bug-eyed. And, a blue that shames the Caribbean.

You might guess Ciera's into vampyres and zombies, but you'd be wrong. Her whole deal is she wants to be a "serious" writer. Between you and me, she doesn't have the chops. Oh, it's all dark and emotional, but also rather clichéd and camp.

She's been influenced by a bunch of Emo bands: The Used (their signature song, "Buried Alive," contains the scintillating line: 'I puked the day you went away,' and their 'brilliant' video shows each band member trapped or dying; Escape the Fate (their debut album, "Dying Is Your Latest Fashion"), enough said; and the classic Emo group, Christie Front Drive. She thinks we were fated to be together because CFD's first label was "Caulfield" Records. (Remember my *nom de plume?*)

Her favorite movies are *Sid & Nancy; Girl, Interrupted; The Hours* and *Sylvia*.

She's collected her short stories under the title, "The Vacuum Chamber," a thinly disguised reference to Plath's *The Bell Jar*.

I hope you've read some of them Doc. Morbid, wouldn't you agree? Being raised Catholic, she's already set sail on the Purgatory Express.

Last week she slipped me a copy of her latest poem. Here 'tis:

"Reunion at Egg Rock"

Digits aflame,
Violating sacred flesh,

> Searing emotion,
> Simmering shame.
> Smugness sickens,
> Childhood despoiled.
> Festering boils of sorrow
> Ravage chalk white skin.
> Fragmented reflections leap
> From Soul's shattered mirror.
> Temptation beckons.
> Blood-soaked memories
> Part my hair like a razorblade.
> There must be a reckoning!

The title, of course, is an allusion to one of Plath's suicide poems. Doesn't require much analytical ability to determine it's about Daddy-As-Violator.

When it comes to creativity, it's not necessary for something to have actually occurred if an artist can construct a plausible reality. However, in my opinion, this angst-ridden "Ode to Incest" fails to convince, and its overwrought imagery lacks artistry. Might I add that capitalizing "soul" perished with Dickinson.

God, I'm a critical bastard. But, admit it, I'm cute and cuddly.

I loathe terms like "co-dependent," but Ciera Self is a leading candidate for poster child; her suffering knows no bounds and her enmeshment is instantaneous. I find her attractive, but her neediness—terrifying and exhausting. If I'm a little down, within milliseconds, she's also depressed. If I'm having an up moment, she's automatically manicky, like a spastic Chihuahua.

I sense you getting a boner over this description of Bi-Polar Disorder. No need to confirm.

Oh, the power of suggestion. Need a short break to "Portnoy." I believe I've failed to mention May is considered "Masturbation Month" by many sex-positive organizations. What a month it's been!

Back!

In spite of the above, I really do care about Ciera.

Never tell her Antoine's from Haiti; the death and destruction there several years ago plunged her into the depths of despair. And, by all means, shield her from the knowledge that Juma, the male night nurse, is from the Sudan. Trust me, she couldn't handle it. Her justification for cutting: a self-inflicted homage to Female Genital Cutting in sub-Saharan Africa. Co-dependent enough...?

"Pres, the world is so full of pain. If everyone was more sensitive to it, life would be bearable. As it is, no one cares. So, I must. Don't you see...I must?"

Au contraire, I say, "The world has enough pain. It doesn't require any contribution from you. And, since you're going to be a writer, you should know that *if* indicates the Subjunctive Mood and requires a plural verb. If everyone *were* more sensitive."

Wowsers! That pissed her off. But, it's true. How can anyone believe being in pain over someone's tragedy improves the situation? I think Jackie DeShannon had it right, 'What the world needs now is Love.' Let's hear it for PureGold Rock N Roll Radio. (Didn't know I was such a softy, did ya?)

As for why I care, a brief explication. But first, an elucidation:

Pain is a common addiction, one most difficult to break. People like Ciera are mired in the misery of the past, where all the pain resides. When it comes to rehashing her painful past, she's the "Princess of the Pity Party," he said—angling away from the microphone to avoid popping the plosives. Perhaps one day she'll figure out that every time she hosts said party, she's the only one in attendance.

I suppose I care, because Miss Self has a good heart and I hate to see her suffer. Still, suffering IS a choice, and until she stops reliving every slight—replaying old painful scenarios—she'll remain a victim of her own choices.

How's that for analysis? Any room for me on staff? Wish I *were*. Thought I'd throw in another example of Subjunctive Mood. Mom says I'm a born teacher.

As for being on staff, you have to admit I have more insight than Dr. Boullac…or, as I prefer to call him, Doctor Bollixed. I know he's your colleague, but ya gotta admit he's as clueless as a Tea Partier at a wine tasting. Psychiatrists, with their prescription pads at the ready, frighten me. Boullac fires off prescriptions with the ferocity of a quota-driven Meter Maid on a steady diet of amphetamines.

That demands a speedy change of subject.

Caught a glimpse of my chart from our last session. You should take it with you when you have to whiz. While you're at it, you may want to have a blood test and a prostate exam. Your frequent urinations could be a result of on-set diabetes, but I wager it's an enlarged prostate. You sit all day. Prolonged sitting raises your risk of dying from cardiac and metabolic diseases. May I suggest you get up and move around occasionally—providing some relief for your inflamed rectal grape?

Always happy to be of assistance.

Hugs,

Me.

Back to exposed chart:

I find "Delusional" to be very dismissive. Just because many of my commentaries border on the oracular, and just because I survived that freak accident, don't assume I think I'm omnipotent. Far from it (though our shared "divinity" is what connects us to everyone and everything).

"Delusions of Grandeur...?"

Come on Thomas...you're better than that.

(Oh. This was slipped under my door tonight. Thought you'd find it amusing.)

Dear Preston,

I'm glad your (sic) here. Why? Because I was lonely before you came. I like your quirky sense of humor. You're also really cute.
Don't get a big head, I said cute not drop-dead gorgeous.

There's another reason. It's because you have some bigtime problems and you don't even know it, since you were one of those super precocious kids with a grownup vocabulary so that when you were little people always told you how smart you are and how clever and how everything you say is so witty and hip and you use literary illusions (sic) and pop references that nobody but a 60 year old nerd would know or care about.

While I'm at it I hope for you're own sake you stop quoting Noel Coward, that French guy Marcel I can't remember his name right now and what's her name oh yeah Gertrude Stein and Oscar Wilde and all those other homosexuals and lesbians you keep talking about since it just gives Richie the chance to diss you and besides no one really understands half of what your saying which I guess makes you feel superior but really just makes you come off as sort of snobbish. *(Jesus...and you think I run on).*

You remind me of Seymour Glass or Ender Wiggin or that girl in

The Golden Compass who's kind of a genius. I know her name but I can't think of it now because of all the meds I'm taking. Just remember those are characters in books not real people!!! I know you can be real sometimes because I've seen you try to help people who I can tell you think are hopeless and messed up. I admit that you know a lot of stuff most adults don't even know, but please stop preaching and teaching all the time. It's really irritating!!!

Just try being a kid, or is that like your psychological condition? The preaching and teaching part, not the part about knowing how to be a kid, though you sometimes seem kind of old fashioned compared to kids I know. I'm sure there's a name for whatever it is that makes you have to constantly being showing off, or at least a drug that might help you stop doing it. If there is please take it. I'm not saying your not one of the smartest people I ever met, and your funny like I already said, but the point I'm making here is <u>who cares</u>? Stop trying to analyze things wrong with me and everybody and use that big brain of yours to figure out what's wrong with you!!!!!

I'm not even talking about that weird video, because that's a whole other subject. I'm talking about how believing everything I already mentioned is true has made you kind of an A-hole. Are you even aware practically everyone here thinks so??? No!!! And don't say you are and your just being an A-hole on purpose to get back at people who you think are A-holes like Richie!

Pres, they don't know you like I do. You're definitely not as bad as everyone says. Sorry. I really like you, but you should know your not perfect. No one is!!!

Your friend who's telling you the truth,

Ciera

* * *

Why do I feel compelled to point out that Ciera is exclamatorily overly-emphatic, comma-cly under-punctuated and practically clueless when it comes to "your" and "you're?"

May 24th

Just got off the phone with Mom. Today's her B'day. Hoped to be home in time to help her celebrate, but even a belated arrival tomorrow will still be a welcomed gift (for both of us).

I believe the occasion is worthy of a heartrending story. Here's one…from sorta near the aorta.

The Little Baker Boy
By Oskar Caulfield

Eight years ago today, I decided to bake Mom a "surprise" birthday cake. She knew I was up to something culinary because she'd been banned from the kitchen. With my allowance, I'd secretly purchased a cake mix (Strawberry Supreme), which I kept hidden in my room for several weeks in anticipation of my baking debut.

To make it even more special, I borrowed a heart-shaped pan from my best friend's (Chris Roberts') mother and planned to whip up the strawberry cream cheese frosting from scratch. The pièce de résistance would have been using local strawberries to decorate the cake, but after calling several area U-Pick farms—discovering none had ripe berries for another six weeks—I opted for frozen.

Following the simple directions, I combined the mix, eggs, oil and water into a carnation pink batter, and poured it into the greased and floured pan. I'm omitting the description of the counter and floor from that procedure. I believe "lightly dusted" would be a gross understatement. Proudly, I carried the batter-filled cordiform pan to the oven—placing it on the middle rack of the new Antique Reproduction Cook stove Mother cajoled Steven into purchasing when the kitchen was remodeled. Years before, she'd spotted the turn-of-the-century classic in a copy of the *Old House Journal*. She saved the picture for nearly a decade in a folder marked, "Suzanne's Wish List." Now, it provided me with my first baking opportunity.

Though beating the batter with an electric mixer was pretty heady stuff, the part of the process I most anticipated was lighting the gas oven. I pressed in and turned the porcelain knob, as I'd often seen Mother do. Then, remembering a lighter was required, I hurried to the newly refinished oak pie safe and yanked open a drawer. Somewhere amid wooden kebab skewers, various corkscrews, measuring spoons and more obscure kitchen gadgets, I spotted a large plastic baggy filled with matches.

So many choices: various colored paper matchbooks from every dive Steven ever haunted; a large box of safety matches; and long fireplace matches. Then, buried under a half-dozen hand-forged feasting tools (never used), I spotted a Coleman (Child Safe) lighter wand. Always one to promote safety over negligence, I selected the wand.

Returning to the oven, I held the tip near the pilot light opening, unfastened the safety latch on the wand, clicked the trigger and *Kablooey!*—an explosion, like Mount Mazama's volcanic blast, hurled me backwards into the massive antique butcher block island, where I cracked my skull on a large spindle leg. Sliding to the floor like an addle-pated Barney Fife, I remained there on the black and white checkered tile, spraddle-legged, wide-eyed and stunned.

Within seconds, Suzanne burst in—screaming, *"Preston!* Preston…?" She rushed to the stove and switched off the gas, audibly gasping when she saw the oven door hanging from only one hinge. Turning, she spotted me.

"Oh, honey, are you all right? Pres…*say* something."

"The oven blew up," I mumbled in a vacant monotone. I was suddenly aware of a hideous, acrid smell, and it wasn't strawberry batter.

She knelt down in front of me. For a few seconds she just stared, as if she were studying an enigmatic abstract painting. Then, in spite of trying hard to stifle it, a smile snaked across her face. I couldn't believe she found hilarity in my near-death experience.

"It's not funny," I said, my voice breaking. Tears, surpassed only by the torrent of Multnomah Falls, streaked down my face.

"Come here, babe," she said—helping me to my feet. She dried my tears with a dishtowel that smelled like garlic and bleach. Leading me into the bathroom, she hoisted me to the mirror above the sink.

At first, I noticed nothing. But, then…! Where Mount Mazama's eruption had merely destroyed its enormous summit (creating Crater Lake), this thermal fulmination had eradicated my eyebrows, melted the tips of my lashes and deforested, like the proposed clear cutting in Clatsop State Forest, the fine filaments of my arm hair.

Curious, I raised a singed appendage to my nostrils and inhaled. I will never forget the stench of scorched hair and skin cells…*ever*. It was then I vowed to become a vegetarian, and, in spite of that minor setback, a pastry chef.

No need to recall the entire verbal skirmish that ensued when Steven got home, but I will share this, verbatim: "You think because he's smart, he's an adult. Well, he's not! Treating him like one's fucking him up big time! Keep it up and we'll all be sorry."

Man, who would have guessed Dad and Ciera were kindred souls, I mean Souls?

REMINDER: Senior/Parent Breakfast tomorrow.

* * *

Interesting story. I think it would be helpful if you'd explain what effect your stories have had on you psychologically. You indicated you want to be on staff. Here's your chance.

Point well taken.

I think the story is about the importance of carefully reading the directions on the box, especially the fine print regarding additives and preservatives…and, of course, understanding why some cooks prefer electricity to gas. As for the psychological effect of having my loving gesture greeted with an explosion that eradicated my eyebrows and rattled my cranium, I'd say I learned that no good deed goes unpunished. (Just so you know, I think that cliché is as ridiculous as you asking me to analyze my stories.)

You make the big bucks. Isn't it about time you ventured into Interp Land?

May 25th

WTF! I missed the Senior/Parent Breakfast.

Called Mom to ask what time she's planning to pick me up for graduation practice in the morning. Momentary silence.

"*Mom…?*"

"You'll have to talk to Dr. van Ittersum about that."

I don't know this woman anymore, the Stepford Suzanne. I can't tell if you've brainwashed her, or if she's brainwashed you. You both need to spend more time locating the source of the video…and less time questioning my sanity!

Bottom Line: If you fail to release me in time for graduation, you can forget about me cooperating ever again!

May 27th

You knew all along you weren't going to permit me to attend graduation. Mom knew it, too. Nana didn't even bother to come, and she's had an airline ticket for months. Graduation's a once-in-a-lifetime experience, and you deprived me of it!

Are you all trying to break me down so I'll admit I engineered the video "scam?" I've tried to cooperate. Under truly deplorable conditions, I've done my best to stay positive and upbeat. <u>NO MORE!</u>

I'm over writing in this dumbass journal. And, you can forget about me taking part in those idiotic Group Sessions. I thought I knew you. I hoped I could count on you (and Mom) to do the right thing. But, just like everyone else, you've let me down. I wish that stupid car had… Oh, fuck it! I'm done!

May 30th

Notes from today's session:

"I know you're upset about missing graduation."
"What insight! That's why you're Chief Cook and Bottle Washer."

"Preston, I've given you a month to address the issue of the video. You've yet to acknowledge your participation or take responsibility for putting it on the internet."

"I've already told you I don't—"

"I'd hoped your desire to attend various school activities would prompt you to admit your involvement."

"I can't admit to something I honestly know nothing about."

"So you've said…but, let's be clear. You appear in the video do you not?"

"I've verified it's me."

"Then, please explain how a video of you, Preston Nesbitt, standing in the middle of a residential street, being struck by a fast-moving car that appears to pass through you, came to be?"

"Am I on trial now?"

"Just answer the question, please."

"Sir, yes sir!"

"Are you the young man being struck by the car?"

"I've never denied it's me."

"After the car magically passes through you, do you not get in your vehicle and drive away."

"Why are you asking me this again? Yes!"

"Then given your understanding of reality and your prodigious memory, can you explain why it is you don't remember participating in the video's creation?"

"I—"

"And given the fact that cars do not routinely pass through solid objects, especially people, how do you expect anyone to believe you had nothing to do with the creation, the editing, the visual trickery behind this video?"

"I've already told you that I don't know. And, really, I don't. Have I spent countless hours trying to figure out how this happened? Who's behind it? Why it is I don't remember even being in front of Mr. Wolff's house…standing in the street…being struck by a car that, as you say, 'magically passes through me'…? By the way, that's done by superimposing two images. There's nothing *magical* about it. Still, I would remember something. But, I *don't*…believe me, I don't. Have I thought I may actually be delusional? I've contemplated it, of course. Hundreds of times since I first saw the video on YouTube. In fact, thinking about is…is…"

"Breathe. Take a breath. I've been seeing you, off and on, for nearly eight years. Not once, in all that time, have I known you to forget anything. Exaggerate a little, perhaps…embellish for effect, but never ever fail to remember even the minutest detail. Can you understand why this video, and your inability to either admit willfully participating in its creation or recall being present when it was created, completely defies credibility or logic? Though I'm concerned you *may be* delusional in this regard, I'm simply perplexed."

"So, you're planning to keep me here until I either admit I staged the whole thing, *or* until I remember participating, *or* until you're no longer perplexed?"

"What I'm saying is…let's work on removing whatever it is that's blocking your ability to recall what happened. It's critical, wouldn't you say?"

There was more, but it was more of the same.

Okay. I'll cooperate, but only if I don't have to take any more anti-depressants; they cloud my thinking. More importantly, they suppress my libido. I happen to be very fond of my libido. You've taken away everything else. Hands off my libido!

That being said, I have a few questions of my own:

For the sake of absurdity, let's pretend I planned the whole thing and am faking amnesia. First off, there's the little matter of the car. Whose is it...? The thing's a rust bucket. The only person I know who owns a car older than a year or two is my buddy Chris Roberts, and it's not his.

Secondly, who's the Mystery Woman behind the wheel...? It's unlikely I could persuade a stranger with two small children to play major supporting roles in a video flimflam, wouldn't you agree? Could someone at least attempt to trace the vehicle (with magnification, I believe the license plate is readable) and locate the poor woman, who gives a remarkable performance of a person either freaking out or laughing maniacally? Imagine what she must have thought when she saw it.

And finally, has anyone bothered to determine the location of the camera? From that angle, it appears to have been shot from the second or third story of the apartment building across the street from Mr. Wolff's bungalow. If it were like most apartment buildings in the area, you'd need a code to get inside. Whoever did it has gone to a lot of trouble to pull off this prank.

Not I, Sherlock.

P.S. There's a fourth thing, but it should be pretty obvious. Don't you think if I knew the origin of the video, I'd tell you so I wouldn't have to stay here another fucking second? I hate this fucking place! And, though it pains me to say it, right now I don't like you very much either.

May 31st

I had a weird "what if" thought today. What if Ciera's right and I do have some big problems I'm blind to (I know...but to which I'm blind sounds stilted)? What if the video isn't the reason I'm here after all? What then is the etiological explanation? What if I'm suffering from some legitimate mental illness, one that prevents me from even realizing I have it? What if Dad knew it all along and left because he couldn't deal with it? What if his leaving contributed to my need to create the video to get his attention?

* * *

This is good Preston. These questions are a starting point for further exploration.

Gotcha!

June 1st

True Story…As Allegory

Several years ago, while waiting for Mom to finish up in the school library, I read an account—in *Ms. Magazine*—of an Indiana woman who had a stroke at age 37. She ended up in a nursing home. While recovering, her brother's family sought and were granted power-of-attorney. They sold her house, her car, cashed in her savings bonds and stock portfolio, and—after treating themselves to extravagant vacations and other luxuries—spent every last penny on bribing a judge, who declared her "incompetent."

Several times she escaped, but each time she was caught and returned to the nursing home. The authorities concluded her "wandering off" was proof of her incompetence.

Completely rehabilitated from her stroke within a year, she spent her days helping other patients suffering from dementia, or bedridden from various ailments. In short, she became *free labor*, an unpaid nurse, whom the staff adored.

After nearly a decade of forced confinement, a local female attorney heard of the unusual situation and took on her case, *gratis*. She arranged for a new hearing and this time, an unbiased judge ruled in her favor. Following her release, she sued her brother's family and was awarded $2.5 million. Court testimony implicated the original judge, who was removed from the bench.

I mention this because I'm quickly assuming a similar role here at The Healing Place. And, whether or not Ciera, you or anyone else gets it, it's intended to be helpful. Hopefully, it will be rewarded…not with a financial settlement but <u>with my release!</u> Not sure who will come to my (legal) aid. As far as Mom being reprimanded for abusing her "power-of-attorney," and for you being "removed from the bench," we shall see what we shall see. You can both choose to be offended by my story, or you can see it as allegory, learn from it and adjust your behavior accordingly.

In my quest to prove my usefulness, let's have a little chat about Cody McCrary, a fine example of what psychotropics and stimulants can do: Diagnosed *at age four* with Bi-polar Disorder, the kid's been on a deadly mix of medication for the past dozen years. Any idea how those chemicals affect a brain that's in a critical stage of development? No, and neither did the so-called "doctor" who prescribed them.

When you consider what his brain's endured, he's a medical miracle. Not surprisingly, Cody's also become an incorrigible sociopath, but it has a lot to do with the narcotics and misdiagnosis, not to mention being treated like a defective most of his life.

I dare *you* to consume all those killer pharmaceuticals at once. Think breaking into houses is bad? You might be more understanding of his plight once you found yourself wielding a machete in Group, or blazing a new trail through the Meditation Maze out back.

Perhaps it's time for a re-evaluation of his meds. Helpful, right?

* * *

Need I point out that it isn't your job to analyze your peers? I'm not questioning your motive, I'm simply saying it's not helpful as regards your own healing.

Healing? Is that what you really believe happens here? Holy Mother of God…I'm doomed!

June 2nd

On temporary hiatus.

June 3rd

If I'm forced to be here awhile longer, I'd appreciate having a few things from home, nothing big, just some familiar objects of affection. I realize that the austerity and deprivation of this institution might be necessary for those who need no reminder of a place where abuse—either mental or physical or both—may have occurred. But, that's certainly not true in my case. It's just that I'm a little fragile at the moment. Having to cope with the sardonic me is definitely preferable to having to deal with me "adrift." Ask Mom. She'll confirm I've been there once or twice.

Granted, I'm an expert at camouflaging my feelings, but if you haven't figured it out yet, those feelings often come veiled in sarcasm. At the moment, caustic words and outright cynicism are the only underpinning I have to keep me from being flung into the void.

Therefore, I'm sure my whole attitude would improve if I could have just a couple of little meaningful tokens: any of the books from my collection of "best-loved" tomes, especially my first edition, signed copy of *The Tin Drum*; a small decorative plate with a picture of Crater Lake that Chris Roberts gave me as a reminder of our trip there the summer after sixth grade; and a red-tailed hawk feather—hanging from a leather binding on the edge of my computer monitor. Mom will be happy to bring them once you give her the "OK."

If I'm only permitted to have one, I'd prefer the hawk feather. In case you're wondering how I came by it, it's a perfect example of how deep meditation can reveal not only "past" lives but also "future events" (déjà vu).

The summer before high school, while floating in a sensory deprivation tank (if you ever need to free yourself from the bonds of the physical world, you should try it), I had a vision of a red-tailed hawk. All I knew for sure is that I would find the hawk at a roadside location and that it would somehow bring me comfort.

A week later, while Mom and I were driving to Medford, where she was to attend an Oregon Library Association meeting, we came up over a hill on I-5 and I yelled, "Stop, Mom. Pull over!" It was rather foggy that morning, so she wasn't driving her normal breakneck speed.

She didn't ask why, just hit the brakes, pulled onto the shoulder and flipped on her emergency lights. I jumped out and ran back about a hundred yards. That's when I spotted the hawk's body lying in a small ravine. It wasn't even visible from the interstate, but somehow I "knew" it would be there.

I could still feel its warmth. Apparently, it had flown into the side of a vehicle, most likely a semi, only minutes before. The feathers were barely ruffled, but its neck was broken. Reverently, I carried the hawk back to the car. Though Mom protested, I insisted on keeping it. As always, she was running late, so, reluctantly, she gave in. I wanted to hold onto the magnificent bird, but she made me put in the trunk.

When we returned to Portland later that night, I had a burial ceremony in our backyard. I'm sure it may have looked bizarre to the neighbors, what with me drumming and smudging, but I didn't care. Before I placed the magnificent hawk in the shallow grave, I removed a tail feather.

Call it a coincidence, but I *know* I drew that hawk to me. I desired it, was grateful for it…and it manifested. It's my Spirit Animal. It speaks to my Indian heart. That's the back story. I just know I'd sleep better if I could have the feather in my room.

I think you'd have a better understanding of what it means to me if you read *Return of the Bird Tribes*. I can ask Mom to bring you my copy.

June 4th

Thanks for putting me on blast!

Yes, I questioned your "therapeutic style" in front of the others, but it was justified. Encouraging the Group to 'Please call Preston on his use of vocabulary to deflect *real* feelings,' struck me as unprofessional.

I admit when I'm challenged, or when I need a little validation, my default is a formidable stockpile of words. But, unlike others here, who prefer drugs, petty larceny, felonious assault, and threats of suicide or failed attempts, I think my use of vocabulary is a pretty harmless way of acting out. Besides, I have feelings…and they're *real*. So, calling me out in front of the Group felt like a personal attack.

Between Joey and Misty, I'll now be lucky if I can use any word with more than five letters. Forget idiomatic language. Having to explain to her that "caught with your pants down" has nothing to do with exposing one's self was a complete waste of time, and, frankly, irritating—especially when she was "ROTFLMAO!"

You're hardly the first person to point out I sometimes employ my intelligence as a defense mechanism…nor am I the only guilty party. Everyone in Group has his/her own method of deflection.

Richie uses anger, and you reinforce it—daily. Just like kids who hate school and would rather be idling away in Detention, he loves being removed from Group. You fall for it *every time*. BTW, Antoine, who has to hustle him off to the Quiet Room or your office, figured it out weeks ago.

Ciera relies on "shyness." Oh, poor Ciera. She's "so sensitive." Being shy is just another form of Ego. 'Can't you see the "me" hiding in here is *special?* If you work really hard, maybe I'll let you get to know me.' Never thought of it that way, had you?

All Misty and Joey have to do is look confused (which is most of the time), and you let them off the hook. Actually, thanks for that.

Just so you know: singling me out isn't very *equitable*. My bad, I meant "fair."

* * *

You're quite right. I'm sorry, Preston. Please accept my apology.
Done.

June 5th

Another brain-numbing Tuesday, so let's discuss the Jefferson twins, new to our cohort. You have to admit they're pretty amazing. Virtually incomprehensible…but amazing.

Celia and Ophelia Jefferson are here, primarily, because no one can decipher their enigmatic speech. That makes them what…linguistically challenged? I know Developmental Expressive Language Disorder is considered a "learning disability," but that's hardly justification for ending up in The Healing Place.

They're the perfect example of "idioglossia."

Look it up. It's pretty rare, but there are other documented cases. Check out *Pittman's Journal of Commercial Education, Volume 51*. Another example of my snapshot memory. No biggy. I thumbed through a copy once while waiting on Suzanne to close up the school library. Who's to say what info is useless?

Covertly, I've observed them, and it's obvious they're not backward, quite the opposite; they've invented their own language! Instead of being here, they should be on "Entertainment Tonight," or maybe Oprah could give them their OWN show.

Spend a few minutes with their insane harpie of a mother, and you'll see why they figured out how to communicate in a way designed to cut her out of the equation. No one would argue that it's easy being a single, African American parent, but trying to remake her daughters—into the perfect young black women she herself failed to be—has turned into a tragically failed enterprise, unless you're a linguist looking for new vernacular.

I urge you to try this. Record what they're saying. Then, slow it down and separate the words. You'll see it's just English slurred together, with emPHASIS on the wrong syLABbles. Damn clever, if you ask me. I just went onto the ward and asked Ophelia why she thinks they're here. "SelNmeLahkmahTHERINTHclaZET."

Translation: "Celia and me locked mother in the closet."

Can't say I blame 'em.

* * *

Preston…need I say it? "Heal thyself."

Are you aware Jesus prophesied that those who opposed him would still use this phrase as he hung on the cross? I'm just noting the irony…not drawing a parallel.

June 6th

Called Mom early this morning. Asked if she'd made any progress finding the source of the video. She acted like she'd never heard of it. Once I'd refreshed her memory, this was her unsettling response, "Honey, please don't talk about it anymore. The thought of it makes me sick to my stomach."

What!?!? Is this the next phase of your treatment plan: Mind Fuck 101? The video's why she called you in the first place. What other possible reason could you have for keeping me here? First, you refuse to consider my release until I admit I'm its creator. Now, I'm not supposed to mention it to my own Mother because it makes her queasy?

The call resurrected some "Mommy Issues" I haven't discussed with you previously. I love Suzanne, but she's violated my boundaries with a frequency rivaling the border disputes between Canada and the U.S. As you shall see, some even involved territorial "waters."

Boundary Wars—An On-going Struggle

I'm *not* Suzanne's surrogate husband, nor am I the confidante she needs. However, those are two of the many roles thrust upon me when the marriage went kaput.

"Do you think Mommy's pretty?"

Wearing only a sexy black lace bra and panties, she asked this question while applying make-up in front of her dressing table mirror. She is, in fact, a knockout. However, what she really wanted to know was, 'Do you think I'm desirable?' Yes, without a doubt, she's *très souhaitable*...but *ewww*.

"Dad's out-of-town on business this week. Would you like to sleep in here with Mom? We can watch *Oedipus* on *PBS*."

If I were a five or six-year-old...sure. But, at nine...not so much. (As a nine-year-old in the Congo, I might've been a child soldier/murderer.) Though hers was a King-size bed and we could be comfortably apart, it still felt a little creepy. On top of it, it felt even worse because I even had that thought. Maybe it wouldn't have if she and Steven had actually gotten along, but all that emotionally incestuous B.S. only added to the "you and me against him" thing.

"Oopsie...sorry, hon, I'll be out of here in a minute. Need to get some fingernail polish remover out of the medicine cabinet. Go ahead, finish your...bath. You can tell me all about your day while I remove this chipped polish."

Sure thing, Mom, but please ignore my boner! Hopefully, a tenting washcloth requires no further explanation.

"I know Dad told you about Kirk...Mr. Wolff and me. We only...you know...a few times. Both of us realized it was a mistake. It won't ever happen again. It's just that he's so unlike your father. He reads. He's a foodie, too. We can talk about anything. I consider him one of my best friends, and he's extremely good looking. Still, it was wrong...the heat of the moment. We both regret it. You understand, don't you?"

I was *ten* for Christ's sake! I totally got it. Steve's a jerk and Kirk's a hottie. *But,* I didn't need the mental image of her blowing my future English teacher or him humping my Mother terrorizing my thoughts, okay? I admit I was very mature intellectually, but she shouldn't have assumed just because we were pals, able to discuss post-modern literature and moral and political philosophy, that my Emotional Self was on par with my ability to parse syntactic relationships. (I've since directed her to some Katie Roiphe essays in hopes she'll discover a way to parent with less enmeshment.)

I'm rambling, I know. But, it's not like I'm readying this for publication.

Oh, FYI, my YouTube video's approaching 475,000,000 views. <u>Lots of people think it's real.</u> Better add on a wing or two. The Healing Place can't begin to accommodate all the whacko's.

You asked me not to mention the video in Group, but until you tell me why you continue to keep me as an inpatient, I'm ignoring your request.

* * *

How would you feel about us doing a session with you and your mother? I think it might be beneficial for you to discuss boundaries with her, don't you?

Just a moment while I consult my Magic 8 Ball. Sorry. 'My sources say NO FUCKING WAY!'

June 7th

I was totally unprepared for your final question in today's private session: "Now, what's this about you and a great blue heron?"

For a moment I was dumbstruck, mouth agape. I struggled to respond.

"Apparently, you and Suzie Q are conferring behind my back."

"Nothing so clandestine. It's standard procedure to talk to a patient's parents. Does that surprise you?"

"Nothing about this place surprises me as much as the total violation of my civil rights."

No response.

"Did you discuss my boundary issues with her? Were you digging for evidence of my 'delusional state,' or did she volunteer the information?"

"Why do you assume I only talk to your mother?"

"Because Steve's too busy mesmerizing some 23-year-old ex-Portland State co-ed with his trouser snake to care about what's going on in here."

"Actually, it was your father who first mentioned it. When I asked your mother to elaborate, she was a little reticent."

"That's because some of my more bizarre childhood tales frighten her. She hates that story, in particular."

"Do you think your stories are bizarre?"

"I think you and the majority of those disguised as humans would find them a little unbelievable, given very few people seem to have similar experiences. At least, no one I know."

"Why is it, do you think these unusual experiences are happening only to you?"

"Look, I get what you're trying to do."

"What would that be?"

"For one thing, you're hoping to get me to admit I make up "stories." Or, trying to determine how deeply delusional I am. Just so you know, it's coming off as pretty accusatory—considering how practically everything out of your mouth is in the form of a question."

"Asking questions is an important part of my job. Does that bother you…?"

"I rest my case!"

It went on this way for another three or four minutes, until there wasn't time to tell the story. So, I'm writing it.

My homage to G. G. Marquez and H. Marukami:

A Hundred Minutes of Solitude
or, The Wind-Up Heron Chronicle

It occurred one summer day when I'd escaped to the modest creek that trickled beside the neighborhood park, my favorite place in our suburban jungle…to *be* an Indian. This particular July day, I was sitting on a sandbar in the middle of the creek—having waded through the only semi-deep puddle to be found.

As I sifted through the sand, I uncovered rocks, whose colors were reborn in water. When I found an unusual one, I'd ask the rock's permission to be moved, like any respectful Indian would do, before adding it to my take-home pile. Or, if it were a reject—tossing it back into the puddle. The plunk of pebbles echoed in the silence as they sank to the bottom.

Under the pellucid sky, the sand grew hotter and more unbearable by the minute. Suddenly, the stillness was shattered by a *whoosh!* Out of the corner of my eye, I saw a flash. I turned to see an enormous bird swoop down and land on the far end of the sandbar. I recognized a great blue heron. The sunlight caught the indigo shimmer of its gray wings, like when raindrops illumined a driveway oil-slick from Steve's classic 280ZX—creating an iridescent mandala.

Without pause, the majestic bird stabbed its beak into the edge of the sandbar and extracted a snail. With surgical precision, it held the shell with the tip of its claw, and in one deadly peck, detached the bucolic escargot from it home. Then, it tilted its head back and I observed the slimy *hors d'oeuvre* inching its way down the bird's sinuous neck.

In my Indian World, everything made sense: the snail succumbed to the heron—becoming its morning snack; the heron dignified the death by spreading its great wings in tribute to the snail. And, had I a bow and arrow, I would have continued this reverent chain of honor by wearing the heron's feathers with solemn pride, using its claws to etch into soft stone and draping its magnificent wings from my hoop-stick.

But alas…

Enraptured, I watched for another few seconds before sending a mental message that I was "a brother."

There was an immediate energetic connection, nearly visible, between us. The giant bird cocked its head from side to side, its piercing eye dotting its black feathered eyebrow like a *fermata*. Suddenly, he fanned out his gray-black and indigo crown feathers, extended his tremendous wings and launched himself back into the air.

As if falling into an immediate trance-like state, I closed my eyes. I still remember the feeling, the sensation of rising up in great swoops from the sandbar. I could see me, the Indian, sitting down there, cross-legged and still—growing smaller by the second.

The creek bed spread out before me like *The Hinterlands of the Eastern Kingdoms, the verdant trees rushing past me. Up, up I climbed…nearly weightless like a helium balloon, yet powerful, buoyed by the flexing and contracting of muscles and tendons that ran the full-length of my wings. Up, up, above the trees. Oh, the breeze…the breeze rippling my feathers.

Hated to break the spell, but I had to throw in at least one World of Warcraft reference, for this was truly an Elite Mount!

Then, for an instant, I let a bad thought creep in: the "reality" that little boys do *not* have wings and can*not* fly. It was the fear voice, the one that so often spoiled moments of sheer exhilaration: the voice I hated. That voice made me think what would happen if I fell; that fearful instant ended my glorious flight.

I came crashing back into my body. It was jarring and unnerving. An oppressive foreboding settled over me like a dirty blanket—smothering my joy. I sat there stunned, while the realization of what it is to be a bird vibrated within me.

As if my nervous system had been shot-through with electrons, I began running up the creek bank, through the empty park, past SUVs and over-priced, cookie-cutter home—all the way to our over-priced, cookie cutter home—anxious to share this fantastical out-of-human-body into-bird-body experience with Suzanne. But, it was a Saturday, and she was at Costco stocking up on enough paper towels to get us through to the End Times.

Steven was "watching" the British Open, though actually napping on the sofa and only occasionally waking long enough to see Tiger Woods blazing his way to another double-digit drubbing.

"Dad…wake up. I have something amazing to tell you."

"*What…?*"

"You awake? Steve!"

"Huh…? Yeah. Move out of the way son, you're blocking the TV."

"While I was down at the creek— "

"Where's your mother?"

"Gone shopping. Listen, Dad, this great blue—"

"When did she say she'd be back?"

"How should I know? *Listen*…when this giant heron took off from the sandbar, I—"

"Did you see that? You can kiss Nichlaus' majors records goodbye. Tiger'll have 20 by the end of the decade."

I like Tiger, I do, but I was trying to share one of the most incredible experiences ever, and Tiger somehow took precedence. So, I thought,

'Fuck you, Tiger, and your perfect life. May it all come crashing down.' (Doc, do you think somehow my curse contributed to his unraveling? Hope not. I take some solace in knowing that unlike most schmucks who relished the *schadenfreunde* when it all went to hell for Eldrick, I didn't.)

By the time Suzanne made it home with 48-rolls of toilet paper; 6.8 kg of penne pasta; a 10-lb wheel of Parmigiano-Reggiano ($219!); a dozen avocados (certain to turn fibrous and inedible in two days); a 2-gallon container of chocolate-covered pretzels and a plastic vat of fresh salsa, large enough to garnish all the nachos in Portland, my need to share had waned.

Besides, I knew, like all the other times, it would elicit one of her empathetic smiles. If you have AS, you know the one that says, 'Oh, that's nice, dear,' but really means, 'For the love of God, never tell that to anyone...they'll think you're a *freak!*'

See the connection Doc? The YouTube video isn't the first time my sanity's been called into question. This is but one example. I'm not trying to give form to fable. This is my life we're talking about, not some metaphorical principle!

Now...my turn. *Why does everything that belies our understanding of reality come off as apocryphal?*

That's my question to you. And, boy howdy, I'd really love an answer.

June 8th

I know you take home some of our journals with you on weekends. I'm sure I'll hear all about my heron story on Monday...more probing questions. So today, I'm making every effort to be introspective, because I want you to take me seriously. I know sometimes I come off as an obnoxious child and a pontificating bore, but <u>I am serious.</u>

Do you think it's easy being a psychological sponge—soaking up other's emotional turmoil, and, worse yet, remembering it with such intensity? I'm not being grandiose in saying I'm different in many ways from your standard issue teen psycho. Dare to look beneath the surface of my palimpsest existence, and you'll discover layers of ancient memories.

My personal diagnosis is that I "suffer" from *Savantism*. Perhaps because I don't exhibit typical mnemonic skills, you'd disagree; however, I do possess a prodigious memory, my little island of genius.

Imagine what it's like having to live with someone like me, someone who remembers: *everything*. Mom's a Saint, (well, she used to be).

Let's assume this unique form of Asperger's Syndrome is responsible for my *je ne sais quoi*. Doesn't it make sense that a lot of us AS folk, people who wrote sonatas at age five or advanced mathematical or theoretical understanding in their teens, were/are more important to our species' evolution than the nitwits on "The Housewives of (insert location)" or the troglodytes on most of "reality" TV?

Admit it, the finest minds are almost always idiosyncratic and capricious, qualities that should be celebrated not punished.

Einstein's parents thought he was a mental defective because he couldn't string words together into a comprehensible sentence by the time he was nine. Before a truly crazy person put a bullet in his back, the seemingly undistinguished President James Garfield, was most distinguished because he could write Latin with one hand and Greek with another <u>at the same time.</u> (Savant skill, anyone?).

Mozart, Beethoven, Mahler, Strauss, Newton, Edison, Tesla, Dickinson, Austen, Kafka, Twain and Nietzsche. The list is packed with geniuses in the arts and sciences. I could go on and on...

Van Gogh's depression, legitimately based on the frustration that no one understood the artistry of, therefore bought very few of, his paintings, eventually led to suicide (or allowing some local juveniles to get away with murder because he didn't have the guts to pull the trigger).

Admit it, if Dr. Boullac had been Vinnie's attending psychiatrist, he'd have ended up a slobbering, drugged-out zombie, incapable of painting his toenails, let alone "The Starry Night."

I'm <u>not</u> suicidal. However, I *am* perpetually frustrated by the greedy, unenlightened assholes in charge of making decisions that affect the rest of us. Still, that doesn't mean I want to exit the planet. You probably know all this. And, if you do, you should be ashamed for playing it so close to the vest. Don't leave it to me to be your exegete; I'm fighting for my life here.

Admittedly, I get wound up, but why wouldn't I? Someone has to be the voice of a new generation. Why can't that be me? Unlike most of the anesthetized, who are "lost in space," I've got plenty to say! Danger, Will Robinson, danger…here it comes:

'All men are created equal.' HA! The way I see it, equality's an illusion, and only a hypocrite would say otherwise. The world is controlled by the moneyed elite, multinational corporations posing as "persons."

As Nana Nesbitt says, "The rich get the goldmine and the poor get the shaft." (Remember, she's originally from Bakersfield. That's Nashville West).

America *isn't* a Democracy, and unless you were a white, male landowner, it was never intended to be. Now, it's a Corporatacracy. Name one elected official without ties to Big Business…? They've all drunk the Korporate Cool-Aid.

Why would I trust any government that protects the wealthy and pays lip-service to helping the underprivileged…? If that makes me a Liberal or a Socialist, I'm happy to be in cahoots with J.C., Gandhi, King *et. al.* of that ilk.

The point is…it's time for parity when it comes to prosperity disparity, but this barbarity will continue because of our own temerity!

Somebody stop me, or accompany me with a beat box!

June 9th

Random musings for a spiritless Saturday.

Who said, 'If you talk to God you're praying, but if God talks to you, you're a schizo?' Someday, we'll discover people sleeping under the overpass are hearing actual voices: bleed-throughs from alternative realities, different frequencies, like when FM 94.9 interferes with 94.3. Not saying it isn't problematic, but there may be an explanation. This just in from the father of *The Little Prince*:

> *Only the unknown frightens men. But once a man has faced the unknown, that terror becomes the known.*

Not a word about my heron story in today's private session. A little too Carlos Castaneda for you to even mention it? I hope you don't think I'm being impertinent when I say your version of reality's on par with the medieval belief that the world was flat. With every passing day, I'm feeling more and more like Galileo: imprisoned, tortured and infinitely misunderstood. I feel an oration coming on…so I'll pause. Deep breathing… New mantra: "I am free of the need to rant."

Better now.

Sometimes, I watch from the Break Room window as you walk to your champagne beige Lexus SC430 (by the way, that coupe usually appeals to the wives of stock brokers and dentists), especially Friday evenings, because you always seem so burdened from the long week. You remind me of the disheartened pack mules at the Grand Canyon that carry people across the Red Rock Bridge and down those treacherous slopes—leading to the canyon floor.

Our trip there was the last we ever took together as a family. I loved the Painted Desert and the canyon itself, but Steve ruined it by insisting we all take the mule tour of the south rim.

"No way," I said.

"Yes, way! Suzanne, I would appreciate a little help here."

"Preston, let's all do this together as a family."

"Mom, I know you don't want to go either, so why force me?"

When I tried to explain how cruel and exploitive I thought it was, Steve got furious, threw up his hands and shouted, "Will you please stifle it for once!"

Dozens of people stopped what they were doing to see who dared disrupt the harmony and peacefulness of that spectacular vista.

"*What?*" he howled at them like a mad man. Then, like a childish brat who didn't get his way, he stomped off towards the car. But, not before admonishing Mom. "I've had it with his fucked up condition. And, as always, thanks a lot for the support!"

Hadn't thought about that in ages.

Doc, metaphorically, you're trying to guide me down some treacherous slopes. Any chance we'll safely reach the "canyon" floor in my lifetime?

When you talk to Mom this week, ask her to bring along Chris Roberts next time she visits. Or, better yet, ask her to encourage him to come on his own.

* * *

Will do.

Thanks! I'd be forever beholden.

June 10th

Sunday Morning comin' down... Whatever you gave me Friday, just about put me out of commission. Pretty sure it contributed to yesterday's disjointed post. Time to adjust my meds.

On my way to breakfast, Miss Vines, who sees herself as both Den Mother and Spiritual Advisor, asked if I'd be interested in attending a "church service" if one were available on the ward. I thought about letting it go, but passing a kidney stone the size of a grapefruit would have been easier.

"Seriously...?"

"Oh, honey lamb, Miss Vines is *very* serious. A little dose of Jesus would do you kids some good. For what ails ya."

"And what *is* that, exactly?"

"Why, *sin*, sugar! We all's sinners. Prayerful worship's what this here hospital sorely needs. Gotta let da Debbil know he ain't got hold of y'all. (Betcha couldn't tell she's originally from the Deep South.) "You okay, baby. But, some in here ain't doin' so good. If you catch my meanin'...?"

I couldn't resist. I asked what day of the week the service would be held.

"Why, Sunday, darlin'...the Lord's Day."

"But, Miss Vines, some of the patients are Jewish, not to mention several of the administrative staff. And, what about a Muslim like Reza, the in-take nurse? Pretty sure several of the psychologists are atheists. Would they be expected to attend?"

"Everybody be welcome, sugah."

"You're aware, of course, Muslims pray five times a day and Friday's their Day of Assembly. The Jewish Sabbath is Saturday. Actually, both days are less pagan than a day set aside to worship the sun."

No response.

"*Sun*-day…the day of the Sun, practiced by the Babylonians? Don't forget what happened to them, Miss Vines."

"Mister Preston, *everybody* know God created the world in six days and rested on the seventh."

"If true, that would've been Saturday, according to the *Bible*. The Book of Daniel to be exact."

"But—"

"Sunday Sabbath was chosen by Nimrod, the one who built the Tower of Babel. Interesting man, 'ol Nimrod…married his mother, Queen Semiramis. Not the kind of fellow you'd want to follow, considering how he defied God's Law."

She struggled for words. When they weren't forthcoming, she walked away—shaking her head and mumbling. Luckily, I was able to comprehend a phrase or two.

Miss Vines is a good worker, reliable. However, you should know she thinks 'Y'all goin' to hell.'

That would include you.

June 11th

Last week, as you approached your sedan, I spotted my journal sticking out of the pocket of your briefcase. Needing some light reading, a little homework, perhaps? Dying to revisit my heron story—hoping to discern if I have a skewed perception of time and space because of that Out Of Body Experience? Could have saved you the trouble…I don't.

Do I appear to be an automaton merely observing life? No, quite the opposite; I actively pursue it. Furthermore, I don't experience life as a movie, and I don't feel it's a dream (well, maybe a little). All of that would indicate Depersonalization Disorder—suggesting I experience non-reality subjectively. I would amend that by saying I see a lot of what passes for reality as mere illusion.

I started seeing the man behind the curtain a long time ago. And no, I don't believe it's G-O-D. It's M-E. That's ol' Pres pulling the strings in my puppet show, just as you're creating your own version of reality. If nothing else, it invalidates the idea of blame and takes the onus off God when bad things happen to good people. Omniscient and omnipotent involvement would indicate a sadistic Divinity, not a loving one.

We're made in the image of The Creator…and that's makes us (surprise!)…*creators*. This mess is our co-creation, our game, our rules and it's ridiculous to think a Loving Being would be responsible for the fucked up tragi-comedy *we* created. We wanted Free Will (like we did the Knowledge of Good & Evil) and, baby, we got it.

Didn't know you were dealing with such a little evangelistic prick, did you? We don't need another Messiah or Swami. We just need to do what's just…what serves others and ourselves, simultaneously.

In short, I remain a Disciple of Onan. It serves me and should have no negative effect on anyone who stands at least five feet away from Mr. Winky.

June 12th

Forgive me, but Monday Night Guest Speaker Sessions are a farce! If you're paying these people to come enlighten us, save the cash. Or, better yet, reduce the outrageous prices you charge.

Last night after dinner, when we were forced to listen to Visiting Child Psychologist, Dr. Sylvia Cranston's lecture on *"The Importance of Matching Your Insides to Your Outsides," Ciera pulled me aside.

*This is proof I'm a hypercritical bastard, but the incongruity of Dr. Cranston's topic cannot go uncommented-upon! If her outside is, in any way, a reflection of her inside, it's more than an outward manifestation of her inner turmoil. Alopecia, extreme obesity, a penchant for rainbow serapes, exotic moo-moos and enough beaded necklaces to simulate a horse-collar, cloaked her lecture in an aura of irony not experienced since that firehouse in Tillamook burnt to the ground. I was grateful Ciera needed my help. (Fortunately, Dr. C's tedious disquisition had quickly reduced the aides to a catatonic state, and their resultant stupor allowed us to sneak away, undetected.)

Ciera was beside herself. Believe me, that's one Ciera too many.

"Psst...Pres!," she whispered. "Misty's in my room. Come help."

"Help?"

"She's on the floor in hysterics."

"Again? Why not tell Miss Vines? She could try to pray her out of it."

"Please. She's hearing that voice."

"You mean *da Debbil*? Battling Beelzebub is Miss Vine's specialty."

"Show a little compassion. She's terrified. Oh...never mind."

"Wait...! I don't know what you want me to do, but—"

"Just talk to her. Do that thing you do with your hands."

"That *thing* I do with my hands? Oh, how she'll love that."

When we got to Ciera's room, Misty had tried to squeeze under the bed, but the bed was having none of it. She was scrunched up in a semi-fetal ball—repeating, "*He's* in me...he's *in* me!" I spent the next five minutes trying to convince her she was safe with her friends and that "he" had no power. I did do 'that thing' I do with my hands. I've never mentioned it 'til now (for fear of being labeled), but back when I was meditating on a steady basis, my hands would get blazing hot. Once, when Suzanne was complaining of a rare migraine, I placed my hands on her forehead, and they heated up faster than her new convection oven.

"That feels wonderful," she said. And, within a minute, her migraine was gone.

I've also used it a few times to help ameliorate Ciera's anxiety attacks. Ask her…it works. I'm not claiming healing powers, though we may all possess that ability. Just getting Misty to breathe deeply also appeared to work miracles. When she calmed down, I had her describe what happened.

"It starts whenever he's coming for me." She mentioned a 'fire burning in my chest and throat.'

"Are you lying down when it happens?"

"Uh huh. Pressure right here in my chest…like one of those suck-you-beasts or an Inca-beasts sitting on me."

I glanced at Ciera, who quickly turned away.

Wait for it, wait for it… Fooled ya. I let it slide. See, I'm Healing… must be this Place. ☺

For the record, Misty's the perfect example of polypharmacy. She's been on oodles of drugs since she was five—receiving her first antipsychotic for *insomnia*. *Really…?* Insomnia in children is an indication of psychosis? That's criminal! Giving her *Aripiprazole* so she can sleep is like using a surface to air missile to eliminate a gnat. Not to mention it has more side effects than there are stars in Old Glory. (There, but for the Grace of Suzanne, go I. As Nana would say, "Bless her little heart.")

Eighty pounds overweight, she suffers from Type II diabetes and cardiac problems. I've seen her drench her fries with half a bottle of ketchup. That crap's loaded with high fructose corn syrup. A normal amount's comparable to eating a candy bar. She pours the equivalent of a box of chocolates on her fat-soaked and sodium-drenched carbohydrates every lunch and dinner. There's no oversight in the cafeteria. None. How about a little consideration of her physical, as well as her mental, health? Even a half-assed holistic approach would be beneficial. Better food, fewer drugs. Try it, betcha it helps.

That 'fiery burning' in her chest and throat…? Has anyone bothered to see if she might have acid-reflux? The Devil may be in the details. Just talking calmly and rationally, with an emphasis on breathing, settled her down. Perhaps more talking, more breathing and less poisoning her brain? Radical, I know.

No doubt you'll alert Dr. Boullac about this episode, but please try to monitor the situation. You're her therapist; he's her drug dealer. Not every kid who loses his or her temper, argues with adults or is annoying has Oppositional Defiant Disorder and needs to be drugged.

* * *

I've known Dr. Sylvia Cranston for over twenty years. In spite of her appearance, she is an expert on healing the inner-child. In the future, I would advise you to put your particular prejudices aside and listen to what our guest lecturers have to offer. They are here to help you, not amuse you. As for Misty, I will review her medications. Had she had a full-blown seizure, she could have been seriously injured or worse. I repeat, focus on your issues and leave it to the staff to assist others.

You're right. Next time I'll wake them! (Clearly, Dr. Cranston's inner-child is alive and well. *Namaste.*)

June 13th

From today's Private Session:

"I'd like to hear why you seem to be preoccupied with your ability to remember."

"I wouldn't say I'm *preoccupied*. Is this another complaint from Mom?"

"Do you think your mother complains about your compulsions, as a result of your Asperger's?"

"Assuming I even have Asperger's... (Not even a blink. You're my hero). "I'm sure she's exhausted by my need to explain, but she handles it pretty well, considering. However, I wouldn't call it a compulsion."

"What would you call it?"

"A blessing and a curse...like *Amedei Procelana*, the world's most expensive chocolate."

We got waylaid for the next forty-five minutes—discussing why I feel the urge to "orate." (Your description). So, let me address your original question. You may think my preoccupation with memory is merely a "compulsion." So what...? Has anything of true merit ever been accomplished without it? Whether in scientific invention or literature, compulsivity is a requisite to be cherished not medicated. Imagine Michelangelo trying to paint the ceiling of the Sistine Chapel while on *Atomoxetine*—sixty-five feet above the cathedral floor?

"No, your Eminence, we have no idea why he got distracted and fell from the scaffold to his death." Think Pope Julius II's physicians would have had their asses in a sling?

But, in today's pharma-culture, medicating any behavior out of the norm is standard practice. It's terrifying how it's accepted as "normal" instead of reprehensible Every third commercial on television is hawking a drug, with many more side-effects than "cures." (My favorite is *may result in death*.)

As far as Asperger's is concerned, you must admit I'm not typical. I have no problem being touched, appropriately. I welcome hugs from most people, even the unwashed if they have love in their hearts. I'm a cuddly little fucker, truth be told. I don't have many OCD traits; I'm not a slave to routine. I'm remarkably flexible in my thinking and I embrace change.

I do, however, have a few proclivities when it's comes to food. I prefer my over-easy eggs on top of my country-fried potatoes, sectioned off in bite-sized rectangles. I'm aware that qualifies as a food ritual, but who gives a rodent's rear-end, a hyena's heinie, a kangaroo's keister, a possum's posterior, an aardvark's anus, or a baboon's badonkadonk? (Showing restraint. I could go on *ad infinitum*.) Playing Tic Tac Toe with my breakfast doesn't negatively impact anyone. So, what's the big deal? I'm not cutting it up—hoping to affect the calorie count. That would be ridiculous. I just like the way it looks, and it facilitates the whole eating process.

Judges: That'll be five points for plating and five points for creativity.

June 14th

No sign of Caesar today. I have to admit I prefer the days when he's on the ward. He's a sweet little man and always has an upbeat attitude. He refuses to let Richie get to him. Typical exchange:

"How's señor Richie today?"

"What's it to ya, Fruit Loops?"

"Caesar just wants to see a big happy smile on your face. You have such a nice smile."

"Faggot."

"*Mi amigo*...when you say that word you should *not* be saying...it look to everyone like you're smiling!"

That shut him up. (Paradoxed him! I once used that trick on Dad, who was yelling at me for no reason. "Why are you shouting?" I asked, calmly. He started to yell again but stopped—realizing he'd only prove my point.)

Anyway…when I asked Miss Vines why Caesar wasn't here, she sneered. "Ask Dr. van Ittersum." (Apparently you said something to her about my reaction to her church service idea. Wish you hadn't.)

Caesar showed up a little before noon with quite a shiner. Did you see it? The whole left side of his face was still kind of puffy, and his eye resembled a bloody gaping wound. This was one time he needed to wear sunglasses.

I asked how he got the black eye and he "shushed" me—pulling me aside. "Oh, señor Preston, there are bad people in the world."

"Someone hit you? Who?"

"Well, you know Dardanelle's…on 2nd Avenue?"

"The drag bar?"

"A showplace… Okay, *si*, a drag bar. A friend, Enrique, he move here from El Paso two month ago. Me and him, we go las night. About 11:30, we leave from the club to go walking down by Hawthorne Bridge. You know this place…?"

"A few blocks from the…showplace."

"*Correcto.* Jes walking, minding our beesness…when dees men come up behind us…and…" A large tear spilled over the rim of his eye and trailed down his cheek.

About then, Miss Vines noticed Caesar talking to me. She waved him over to the Nurse's Station.

Brushing away the tear, he said, "Don't say nothing, okay?" I nodded but didn't promise. I thought you should know. Please don't *do* anything. Caesar's harmless. Besides Antoine, he's the best aide you have. All the kids here like him, except maybe Richie, who doesn't like anyone. What's wrong with people?

* * *

Preston, I know your concern for Caesar is genuine. But, I feel I must discourage you from addressing him as a friend. He's a professional staff member, and as such, I will remind him as I'm reminding you.

Thanks for your predictable response.

June 15th

Haven't told you much about Mr. (Kirk) Wolff, except that he boffed my Mom. Lest that leaves you with a bad impression, you should know he's an amazing teacher and one of the best people I know. In addition to teaching AP English and Theater I-IV, he directs the plays and sponsors Forensics. Unlike entrenched teachers who expect you to parrot back the same ol' manure they've been shoveling for decades, he encourages creativity and individuality.

He not only instills hope in those without it, he challenges every student to find his or her true passion and pursue it, relentlessly—believing the only real failure is not learning from one's mistakes. Love that man with the lupine name, ironically the poster-boy for every Bear Cub's fantasy.

My freshman year at WPI, I took his acting class. It was mainly improvisation and sense-memory stuff. You can imagine how that appealed to me. He told me I showed real promise, so I asked if I could be in the fall play. He said auditions were only for juniors and seniors, but I could work on one of the backstage crews. I kept bugging him, until he gave in.

"Okay, work up a short comedy monologue. If it's good enough, you can perform during the intermission between the first and second acts."

I was really stoked. I chose to do an impersonation of Dame Edna Everage. In case you don't know, Dame Edna's a big ol' drag queen with purple hair. She was really popular in the UK in the 80's for her send-up of Thatcher's "caring and compassion." She has a cult following in the U.S. as well. Mostly gays. But, believe me, even straighter-than-an-arrow you would think she was hilarious.

I spent hours perfecting her over-the-top, high-falutin' Aussie accent and working up a routine. In the meantime, Mom found a Plus Size spangled evening gown in a vintage clothing store and ordered a "wisteria-hue" wig and huge cat-eye glasses, encrusted with dozens of rhinestones. I needed some padding, so I built a body stocking with sagging breasts, a paunch and padded posterior. I looked fabulous and couldn't wait to show off my Thespian skills. When I finally performed it for Mr. Wolff, he thought it was "hilarious."

The night of the performance, he introduced me. "And now, ladies and gentlemen, for your entertainment, we have something really unique and wonderful. Please welcome a freshman, the very talented Preston Nesbitt, as Willamette's own Dame Edna Everage."

There was a mild buzz with mixed applause. However, when I came out in front of the curtain, some guy in the front row said, "Jesus Christ!" loud enough for everyone to hear.

Undaunted, I launched into my routine, most of which was original material, but some I'd borrowed from one of Dame Edna's DVDs. I really went for it. At first, there was some laughter, then a few giggles; however, soon my jokes were all falling flatter than a flitter.

The spotlight blurred my vision, but I could see silhouettes of people leaving in droves for the restroom and the concession stand. By the time I'd finished, there was scant applause, led by Suzanne and Chris Robert's mother. It was horrific.

Steven Isaac Nesbitt has missed practically every program I've ever been part of, but for some unknown reason, he allowed himself to be dragged to this one. When the play was over, I waited until the auditorium cleared, then I met him and Mom in the lobby.

"How was it...?" I knew she would lie, and I was counting on it.

"Oh, honey, you were wonderful. So funny. Wasn't he, Steven?"

He produced a forced smile.

"People barely laughed or clapped."

"Those who sat around us said you were great, didn't they Steven?"

He mumbled something.

"I don't get it, Dad. I thought I was really good."

He reached out and put his hand on my shoulder. "You were, son. That was the problem. You were a little *too* good."

I don't think this requires any further psychological interpretation on my part. Do with it what you will.

June 16th

They just keep coming! And, Saturday is the most popular day of arrival. The Portland court system must be swamped on Fridays. In the spirit of consumerism, it seems determined to keep the streets and shopping malls clear of misfit teens for the weekends.

Crystal Strickland: fifteen, exotically attractive and hypnotically fascinating made her debut this morning. Unlike Ciera, who immediately labeled her "...trouble with a capital 'T' and that rhymes with 'C' and that stands for C*nt," I was smitten. (I was also surprised by Ciera's *Music Man* reference...another shared interest.)

"Hi, my name's Preston. What's yours?"

"Like that actor who played the traveling salesman in *The Music Man*...Robert Preston?" (You have to admit that was a random and weird co-inky dink.)

"Yes, except Preston's my first name."

"Crystal."

"Sorry?"

"Name's Crystal."

"A gem of a name!" I said, doing my best jocular Steve impunsonation.

"Guess you've heard that a hundred times?"

"You're the first."

"May I ask why you've graced us with your presence?"

"Graced? What are you, some kind of fucking retro nerd?"

"What I meant was—"

"Got nabbed taking 5-HTP from GNC. Can't sleep."

"5-Hydroxytryptophan...an amino acid. Tryptophan...the chemical in turkey."

"Yeah, the thing that makes everyone fall asleep after Thanksgiving dinner."

"Actually, I believe that's a combination of gluttony and football."

She smiled. Crystal's disarming and I was already in her thrall. She's like a beautiful but deadly butterfly, the amazing Blue Crow. In case you're unfamiliar with Lepidoptera, it's one of the *Danaines*. Gaudy and colorful. Attractive but inedible and highly poisonous. I knew hanging around her would not only incense Ciera, it might compromise my desire to be released.

"Listen, adorable," she said, leaning in close, her warm breath caressing my ear. "If they're giving you downers, I'll buy them from you for twice what you'd get on the street. If you don't need the cash, I have other, more pleasurable ways to make it worth your while."

* * *

Do you know if many of the patients here are exchanging medications? You've indicated as much before, but I'm just wondering if this is a widespread practice?

Sorry, Doc. Those are staff questions. I don't feel qualified to answer.

June 18th

Apparently, you read my "Dame Edna" story over the weekend. In answer to your unsubtle inquiry, I don't consider myself to be gay. Yes…I've had what's labeled "homosexual experiences," though Alfred Kinsey would say I only deviated from a "4," the mid-point on his sexuality scale. I think sexuality is fluid not fixed. Personally, I find certain people of both sexes attractive…always have. Guess that makes me *ambi*-sexual, another confining label.

Over the years, you've hinted at the question several times, but never this directly. I've always avoided answering to your satisfaction because I abhor confining labels weighted with tons of baggage. Truthfully, it often felt like your interest was a wee bit prurient. Sorry, that's how it felt. However, if it will shorten my stay, settle back and tend:

The Tale of Chris & Preston

I've mentioned Chris Roberts many times in the past. He's been my best friend from pre-school 'til… I'll get to that. Our families were never really close since his was strictly blue collar, and because Steven was a class-conscious snob. Suzanne liked his mother, Ginnie, but due to Mom's involvement in all kinds of local causes and her various positions with the Oregon Library Association, the two never had time to get to know each other.

In the 90's, Chris's father, Charlie, was head of maintenance operations for a large company that exported logs and lumber to Japan. It was a good paying job, and they could afford to live a couple of blocks away from our rather pricey neighborhood. However, by 2000, environmentalists' restrictions on the logging of public lands had crippled the company; Charlie lost his job, and they were forced to move. I was happy the lumber companies stopped clear cutting, but I was sorry he was out of work for nearly a year.

Mr. Roberts became head of maintenance at Willamette Preparatory Institute in 2002. I didn't find out 'til last year Mom helped get him the job.

In 2006, when I enrolled at WPI, Chris was forced to go to a public junior high, until Suzanne lobbied to allow the children of non-certified staff to attend without charge, which the trustees approved. He joined my 7th grade class mid-year.

Chris was built like an athlete, but he wasn't very athletic; he wasn't much of a scholar either. However, he had a winning personality and was way more popular than I. (Shocking, I know.) He was also really cute: a ginger bear cub, with the whitest teeth, greenest eyes and thickest auburn curls. He and Amity Jenkins hooked up only a few weeks after he enrolled, and they dated all through junior and senior high.

I loved him because I could just be myself around him, which meant he tolerated my crap. We stayed at each other's house, three or four nights a week for years. I preferred being at the Roberts's because Ginnie was a fabulous cook. Her sugar cookies were melt-in-your-mouth yummalicious, and she made a big deal about anything I did. I would say really outrageous things—prompting her laughter, which sounded like ceramic wind-chimes or a welcome case of *tinnitus*.

I could tell it bothered Chris when she fussed over me; I felt bad when she compared the two of us. I did stop showing her my grade card, because every quarter it was always the same. "Would you look at that? A in

English, A in math. *All* A's! Christopher Lee, why can't you ever bring home grades like Preston's?"

Like Mom, Ginnie worked outside the home, but her department store job was strictly 7:30 to 4, so she was always home by the time we arrived. Sometimes, Mom didn't get home until 6:30 or 7.

If Chris stayed with me, we'd heat up leftovers or a pizza and go play The Legend of Zelda, WoW or mess around in the basement playing foosball or watching TV. Steve was frequently out of town. Even when he wasn't, he rarely got home before 8:30. Unless he ventured into the basement, we'd only see him for a second on our way to bed. After the divorce…never.

The summer following seventh grade, we'd gone to see the new *Transformers* movie; Chris liked it, I thought it was mindless dreck. We were lying on my bed, talking about the special effects, and before I realized it, he had his hand down my jammie bottoms.

At first, I fought him off—pretending to be offended, though instantly aroused.

"Stop struggling…stop!" He was very persistent. "That's better. Feels good, doesn't it?"

My response was non-verbal. It took all of ten seconds to experience my first orgasm. For the record, there wasn't a lot of evidence, but I'll spare you the visual. Though somewhat inept, I managed to return the favor. Following a quick mop up, he was ready to go to sleep; however, I was primed for Rounds Two and Three.

I soon discovered the penis to be, in structure, flexibility and utility, more intriguing than Leggos. I'm not saying the mysterious va-jay-jay isn't fascinating in its own impenetrable—as in mysterious—way, but you learn to work with what's at hand. And, that would be Chris's joint. It was soon evident he'd unleashed a monster.

This routine became a regular occurrence anytime we were together, usually with me initiating it. Before you ask, we stuck with mutual masturbation. We did try fellating each other a few times, but we were particularly inept in that area and—lacking proper technique—hoped to avoid permanent teeth marks or worse. Likewise, I was convinced anal penetration was akin to a car careening into a Freeway Exit, hazardous and potentially fatal.

Our hand-job-orgies had slowed by senior year, partly because he and Amity were having frequent intercourse. I really liked Amity, so even though I was a little hurt things changed, I understood. Then, in January of our senior year, she informed Chris she was pregnant. Several weeks later, her parents removed her from school. The story was: she went to live with an aunt back in Maryland so she could more easily visit potential colleges (like anyone believed that). When she returned in March, she was no longer pregnant and completely avoided Chris.

Kids at school knew we were close, but no one thought anything about it, or if they did, no one cared. After all, dozens of students identified as "bi," even if they'd never had any same-sex experience. Bisexuality was the current fad, behind only Sudoku and Sexting in popularity.

Unfortunately, this one jerk, Jason Berkowitz, a typical bonehead jock, started a rumor about us a few days after Amity left. Part of the crock he concocted was about how Amity, whom he'd always liked and tried to date once when she and Chris broke up for a week, found out about us 'being "queer" for each other'...blah, blah...and 'that was the reason she left'...blah, blah. It was all over school. Mr. Wolff heard it, but thought it was ridiculous.

I told Chris I was going to call Jason on it, but he said, "Let it go." He was really insistent, and I couldn't understand why. I kept bugging him until he finally admitted that when we were freshman, he'd stayed all night at Jason's house. Said they drank beer and smoked a joint.

"Promise you won't be mad."

I said I wouldn't. He told me they were both high and Jason had more or less forced him into having anal sex. He said it really hurt, and when he said it, he got all teary—something he'd never done. He'd wanted to tell me before, but was too ashamed. I thanked him for being honest, and said how sorry I was that it happened. Though I felt bad for him, I couldn't help feeling a little betrayed.

Everything: getting Amity pregnant, having her leave and then dump him, enduring Jason's rumors, and having no post-graduation plans, drove Chris into a deep funk. I watched him morph into a stranger. He got a job after school, and anytime I suggested we get together, he manufactured a flimsy excuse. Mom kept asking why we'd stopped hanging out, and I said it was because he was too busy.

I miss Chris's furry, ginger bear chest and lying next to him—twining the hair between my thumb and index finger as we chatted late at night. I miss the way he would mold himself to me before falling asleep. And, though he never said the word, I know he loved me, too. But, he's made no effort to contact me since I've been here, and that's left me feeling not only disconsolate but also a little abandoned.

Was that the big same-sex story you hoped to hear? If you ask me, it's about love and friendship...feeling totally comfortable with someone. Sex was never a big deal, no more than playing WoW or eating his mother's lasagna. Honestly, it was more like a natural sleep aid. Whack each other off (a couple of times) and fall sleep. Now that I think about it...not very romantic.

Does that satisfy your curiosity? Here's my question: If my sexual experiences with Chris (such as the were) made me "gay," did the times I had sex with Alix Fischer (actual intercourse) make me "hetero?" Does either term begin to encompass the feelings attached to those experiences? Labels are meaningless, except to people who spend more time labeling than experiencing. As Nana would say, 'Put that in your pipe and smoke it.'

* * *

Would you be comfortable with me inviting Chris in for a session with the three of us? Would you be open to a session with Alix Fischer?

A *ménage* à *trois*? Hmmm. Intriguing idea. Once again, I must consult my Magic 8 Ball. ☹ 'Outlook not so good.'

Okay, I'll cut the smart-ass routine for a second. I know you mean well, but there's absolutely no way Chris would agree. And, if he thought I'd told you anything about our relationship, I'd never hear from him again. Like most ambivalent Heteros, he's pretty much in denial about everything.

And, Ali Fischer is off-limits. That relationship was over long before you wrecked our chances of winning Duet Acting at State. Besides, as a result of her experimentation with me, she discovered her True North in Nicole Tomlinson. Without regret, I acknowledge my contribution to helping her finding her sexual preference. So, as a reminder of the legal strictures regarding confidentiality, please keep it zipped. Mom doesn't know, and unlike her, I sincerely believe some things should remain private. Although Stevie Boy would wet himself, it's none of his fucking business. 'Nuff said!

June 19th

Apparently, you've enjoyed cogitating over the connotation of my little confession. Though you pride yourself on the subtlety of your interrogation methods, your questions today were pointedly obvious. Just what my sexual preferences have to do with why I'm here is beyond me…yet I cooperated.

"So, you're suggesting my sexuality is somehow related to the video."

"I'd rather hear what you think."

"I'm sorry…that's just weird. There's no connection."

"What about Mr. Wolff? Why were you at his house that Sunday?"

"I've already told you, I don't remember being there. If it weren't for the video, I wouldn't have known about it."

You paused a moment. I could tell you were carefully considering your words. "Your mother found some things…poems and other things."

"She's been going through my shit? Great. Was that your suggestion?"

"Of course not."

"Good to know."

"What I'm asking is…do you think the video was your way of trying to get Mr. Wolff's attention?"

"What are you insinuating?"

"Nothing. I'm just asking."

"Well, the answer is no."

And that ended the conversation. It did, however, get me thinking.

Could there be a physical or psychological reason I've blocked being there, why I no longer remember willingly participating in the video? Could the limbic system of my brain have been damaged in an accident? Or, could my amnesia be a result of some devastating psychological trauma? Wouldn't it be the ultimate irony if a Memory Prodigy forgot something so extraordinary…?

Sometimes I wonder what you're like, when you're not poking and prodding around in my psyche. Time for role-reversal.

"No personal questions Preston...remember?"

Now I ask you...is that fair?

I know it's important for you to retain a position of power and control. However, if I knew whether or not you had a successful marriage, or if you're twice or thrice divorced, it would lend credence to your authority or, dare I say, humanize it.

It would help if you acknowledged having any kids: if your son's a recovering drug addict or your daughter's a klepto with an eating disorder. Just a hint of how successful you've been as a parent might validate you as "Head Shrink to Troubled Teens." Then again, it could expose you as a fraud, who talks a good game but fails to deliver on a personal level.

So many questions. No answers.

Are you a Child Of Alcoholics or a victim of sexual abuse? Do you carry your 20-year AA chip in your pocket? Did you become a psychologist in an attempt to fix your own dysfunctional family? How about some clues to your Circle of Tears?

I'd feel more like sharing if you admitted to having a sex life, or to being impotent and praying an ED pill will resurrect your erection and magically morph your surroundings into an opera house, an orange grove or theme park—with you and the Missus ending up in separate bathtubs, staring into a lake and smiling like idiots. (*I'm* delusional? Puh-leeze! Wanna get it up? Get in one bathtub *together*. "*See Alice*...it worked!")

Come on, Old Pachyderm, loosen up. If you'd reveal a little something about yourself, maybe I'd be more open to exposing my innards. I'd like to know I was talking to a fellow human instead of a smug dispassionate tool. To be honest, you do come across that way sometimes, Dr. Thomas *van Itte*rsum.

Far be it from me to point out the character-revealing flaw ensconced in your surname. I like to think of it in its pre-15th Century meaning: less about ego, more about futility. Never let anyone catch you staring longingly into the reflecting pool; it's a dead give-away.

June 20th

Still carting my journal home with you, eh? In Group today, it was apparent you'd read my previous entry. Couldn't wait 'til Friday? You covered nicely, but I know you well enough to have perceived your pique. Frankly, I thought discovering the hidden anagram in your name was kinda brilliant. Apparently you don't agree.

If you've determined I'm just projecting my "Daddy Anger" on you, you'd be wrong. Don't tell anyone, but I think of you as being more of a father than Steven ever was. I know you're getting paid to listen to my B.S., but he never spent five minutes of his valuable time listening to anything I had to say. He thought my Asperger's gave him an automatic pass.

Suckin' up? Maybe a little.

June 21st

Mom's not coming tomorrow. As if the weekends aren't boring enough. I'm pissed, and I don't care who knows it. And, thanks for blowing off our session today. Were you really out of town on business, or did you just stay home and whack off?

June 22nd

A surprise visit from Chris! Mom asked him to come. Maybe you told her it was a good idea. Anyway, thanks. (Sorry about my little snit yesterday.)

Antoine didn't say who was waiting to see me, just "Sir, you have a visitor." So formal.

I figured it was probably Dad—making one of his rare, ten-minute duty-stops. But, when I saw Chris, I practically jumped into his arms. Antoine quickly excused himself.

There's something about Chris that's off. Physically, he even looks different. I know I haven't seen him for two months, but it's more than that. It was awkward; he seemed embarrassed. Maybe it was just being in this place, but more likely it was because he'd stopped coming around and abandoned me weeks before I was spirited off to this place.

I thanked him for coming, but then I asked why he hadn't come sooner.

"I wanted to, but I've been real busy working at Simpson's Garden Center. Saturday's are crazy. (Uncomfortable silence). Weekends are the worst. I had trouble asking off."

I can always tell when he's dancing around the truth.

"Other than school, I've seen you exactly twice since Christmas. I need to understand why…"

He lowered his head. When he looked up, his eyes were brimming with tears. "*Why* do you think? You're the smart one. You must have a theory. You're full of theories."

"No theory…other than you being hurt by Amity. I figured—"

"Amity had nothing to do with it. Sure, none of that helped. But…"

"What?"

His eyes seemed to be pleading, as if he hoped I'd figure it out so he wouldn't have to say it. Finally, with resignation, he said, "You're going away…"

"To college. Yeah, we've known about that forever. So…?"

"*So?* How do you think I feel…knowing you'll be gone four or five years? Am I just supposed to be happy for you…? Sit around and wait for you to come home on break? Pres, we've been together almost all our lives."

"Since kindergarten."

"I said almost… Didn't you ever *once* think that maybe…? I mean, doesn't it even bother you a little bit that after all this time, after…*everything*…you're going away and leaving me here…? Don't you understand…? I stayed away so it wouldn't hurt so much."

Let's just say I've never known Chris to be so emotional. That's always been my role. He couldn't say the words. He didn't have to. He loves me. When he got ready to leave, he hugged me for the longest time. And, then, he kissed me on the cheek. He didn't even care that Antoine was standing there.

I'm really happy, but now I'm also really sad. Is there a word for that…?

Found it! (Love the Internet).

I searched but couldn't find any English word that encapsulates both feelings, the ambivalence. But, the Portuguese have a word—*saudade*—that comes close. It means that when you think about the person you love, you're happy. But, melancholy accompanies the happiness when you realize the one you long for may never return. It's a deep yearning, a heartfelt nostalgia for what was.

Saudade…it's the love that remains.

Thanks for arranging Chris' visit. I know you orchestrated it.

June 23rd

Mom's last visitation was strained, especially when I asked about Mr. Wolff and whether she'd talked to him about the video. Today, she dropped off his letter. Here it is in its entirety.

> Dear Pres,
>
> Hoping this finds you in good spirits. I think of you often. You are at the very pinnacle of my list of favorite students.
>
> Not having you around the last month of school was a downer. Not having you at State was really depressing. (You were sorely missed.) But, not getting to see you graduate was the biggest bummer of all. Your mother and I did everything we could to convince your other instructors to go ahead and give you the marks you had going. It made no sense to have you repeat the last quarter, as your grades made you exempt from taking Final Exams.
>
> Even so, it was a struggle. The inflexibility of traditional schools diminishes my respect for them with each passing year. I'm more interested in non-cognitive variables than I am Bloom's Taxonomy. I'm seriously considering a move to Terra Nova, where some of my more progressive ideas will meet with less resistance and where students can have a "real world" learning experience. I've always approached education as "one student at a time," as you can attest. Willamette's rigidity, elitism and super-authoritative attitude are beginning to wear.
>
> Enough negative news. I realize I wasn't being very "power of now." I'm spending my summer vacation at the Naropa Summer Writing Program in Boulder, Colorado. You know how I am about

learning things. Outlier that I am, I needed to add to my 10,000 hours of scholarship.

Naropa University was founded by a Tibetan Buddhist teacher and named for the 11th-century Buddhist sage. The actual writing program was developed by the likes of Allen Ginsberg, Anne Waldman, John Cage and other avant-garde artists. They came up with the name for the "Jack Kerouac School of Disembodied Poetics." Rad, huh?

Everything about this place is rather esoteric, which really resonates with me, as I know it would with you. Before we begin writing, we meditate—something I'm copping for my acting classes as well as for Honors English. That should make for some interesting parent-teacher conferences. In addition, there are occasional Japanese tea ceremonies. Though I'd like to, I'm not adopting those, as I know students would sign up for class just to sip tea and nosh on Tansan Senbei, those thin sweet cookies I've come to love.

Due to another cutting-edge class, I've become fascinated with Neo-Shamanism, specifically practices concerning communication with the spirit world. So far I've managed to summon my favorite grandfather and a spirit, claiming to be Charles Bukowski, who told me he was "disgusted so many would-be poets adopted my lifestyle without learning the fucking craft." Sure sounded like something he'd say, but I may have been hallucinating.

Oddly enough, while in a meditative state recently, you appeared. You kept repeating, over and over, "Why? Why?" I recall the vision, but I have no idea what it means, do you? You were very upset and insistent. I strained to dislodge a memory that seemed to be bubbling just under the surface (cliché, I know), but nothing emerged. When I came out of the meditation, I felt ungrounded and grief-stricken. Who knows what lurks in those inner-recesses?

Anyway, I wanted to check in with you and let you know you're never far from my thoughts. Though I have a tendency to compartmentalize, you seem to have a way of breaking down my most reliable psychological barriers. That's a compliment, an acknowledgment of the mutuality of feeling.

Please try to co-operate with the staff so you can be released. You're not crazy, not even close. However, you are smart enough to tell them what they want to hear. Do it! NYU starts September 6th. Get with it, Achilles. Your life awaits.

I know your mother misses you terribly. And, I miss you, too.

Fondly,

Mr. W. (Kirk)

It really bothers me that he made no reference to what occurred on my visit that led to the infamous YouTube video. I'm certain Mom told him to avoid the topic. Since my memory of the sojourn remains clouded, I was hoping for some details. It's as if it never occurred.

Doc, have you requested that friends and family *not* mention the video? Because no one has, and I find it rather disconcerting, given it's now the second most popular of all time—approaching that mop-headed Canadian teenage wanker's music video with the one lyric song.

Mr. Wolff must have been there when it was recorded. He can clear up this whole misunderstanding. Please call him, I beg you: 503-070-0911 (cell).

Your refusal to do so hacks me off in Bukowski-esque fashion!

*　*　*

If I'm able to arrange it, would you be amenable to doing a joint session with Mr. Wolff?

As his letter stated, he's in Colorado and will be gone most of the summer. Have you already determined how long you're keeping me imprisoned? Also, it should be apparent by now that I have no intention of doing therapy with my parents, my teacher or my best friend. If you're bored with my company, there's a remedy for that you know.

June 25th

Today's Group was disturbing on several levels. Imagine a nest of hungry baby birds, necks craning in hopes of receiving a nice morsel of earthworm from mommy. Now, picture a pack of predatory velociraptors, each with 80 sharp teeth and 3-inch claws, ready to devour unsuspecting prey or, if necessary, each other. I'd say the atmosphere in Group fell somewhere between the two.

First, Ciera, who never volunteers anything, decided to share a poem. (Was this your doing? If so, bad call!) She should be applauded for her fortitude, but discouraged from any further attempts at dispensing her poetic wisdom. Second, it turns out "Crystal Strickland" is an alias. What's she doing here? Shoplifting an amino acid or a handbag isn't the reason. I'm certain there's a lot about her we don't know and never will.

Back to The Poem and the reaction of the voracious Group members.

VOICES

> Today familiar voices summoned me.
> Words of Judgment, words of blame
> Meant to damage self-esteem.
> Lies, hurled like Molotov cocktails,
> Devastate my fragile Heart.
> Oh, deadly Words, no Master of mine,
> I reclaim my Power,

> Unplug Soul's keyboard,
> Erase Memory's hard drive.
> Offering no Solace, I hit Delete!

There was momentary silence—like a breathless recoil from the shockwave following a rifle shot. Ciera scanned faces to gauge our various reactions. Joey grimaced and sorrowfully shook his head like he just been informed his dog died. Missy attempted to speak but instead elicited a moan, mournful and sympathetic. Richie belched (and may have farted). I faked a cough. Crystal nibbled at a cuticle The Jefferson twins burbled something incomprehensible. Then, once again, a disquieting silence reigned. When it became clear neither applause nor huzzahs were forthcoming, Ciera's head dropped at a severe angle, dramatically, like Sarah Bernhardt doing Camille.

Ever vigilant, you quickly covered. "Thanks for sharing, Ciera. It's really brave to address a personal issue in group. And, with poetry, too. Would you care to add anything?"

"No..." she mumbled, her eyes drooping as if Hypnos were forcing them closed.

"All right then. If you're sure there's nothing you—"

"Well...*maybe*..." she said, with the lethargy that often accompanies opiate hang-over. "I would like to know...how many of *you* hear voices." She slowly compassed the circle—managing to avoid eye contact with everyone.

Misty (zucchini-dildo) Smith, Joey (I beat off a dog) Gentry, Crystal (The Slunt) Strickland, (Ciera had recently combined "Slut" with her previous assessment—creating a humorous portmanteau), and the Jefferson (*idioglossia*) twins all raised hands. That left Richie (forever the asshole) Caytes and me in the "No-Voices" minority. (I do occasionally hear a voice, but it's my own. Does that make me a narcissist?)

Crystal spoke first. "I'm new here…so, just curious. What's with the shitty poetry?"

Misty audibly gasped. "You didn't just say that!"

Richie snorted. "Damn, girl! That was harsh."

Crystal was unapologetic. "Sorry…but I thought we were here to talk about issues, not discuss stupid poetry."

"I have an issue…with your criticism…of *my* poetry," said Ciera, whose neck, cheeks and ears were fiery red, first from embarrassment, now from anger. She suddenly seemed energized by a shot of adrenaline.

"Oh… Thought it was by someone much younger. Maybe you were younger when you wrote it."

"I wrote it…last night." Her eyes flooded with tears and she bit her lower lip.

"Just so you know, poetry or no poetry, you can eat crackers in my bed anytime." Crystal seductively closed her eyes and flicked her tongue like a sexy viper.

"Now you're talking!" said Richie.

As always, you proved the perfect, ineffective moderator. "No more of that, please."

Crystal *is* clearly a slunt. But, she's wicked hot.

As she often does, Misty came to Ciera's defense. "What makes you such an expert Chloé?"

"Huh…? Thought you said your name was Candy," said Joey.

"You told me it was Crystal," I said.

"Whatever you call yourself, you're definitely a *slunt*," added Ciera—anger now fueling her words.

"You know the rules. No name calling."

"But, you heard her! She insulted my poetry. I *hate* group!"

Being a pain magnet, she couldn't avoid the "Molotov cocktails" being tossed by the multi-named beauty. Though this would have been the perfect opportunity, Ciera was unable to hit "delete." Instead, she turned her chair away from the circle.

Antoine checked to see if he should assist Miss Self in reestablishing her seating arrangement. You waved him off.

"Chelsea…without criticizing her poetry, do you have anything further to add?"

"Wait a minute," I said. "What's with all the names?"

"Everyone…this is Chelsea Strickler," you calmly announced, apparently unfazed by her multiple aliases. "Why don't you tell the group a little about yourself?"

"Not much to tell."

"There's some reason you're in here," said Richie, "and it ain't just your bodacious ta-tas."

"Was that a compliment?"

"The only one yer gonna get from him," said Joey.

"*Quiet*, Hand Job, let her talk. Bet she's got quite the story."

"Not really. Just a little trouble downtown…at Louis Vuitton." She glanced at you to see if that absolved her. She then acknowledged the Jefferson twins, who'd perked up like Pavlovian pups.

"What kinda trouble?" Misty asked.

"You offer a blow-job in exchange for an employee discount?"

"That's enough, Richie."

"Cute. It was all just a little misunderstanding. My handbag got mixed up with one of theirs." The twinkle in her eyes said she wasn't the least bit sorry.

"LubbsmesumluviTAWN!" said Ophelia.

"Mmmrkjcbs!" exclaimed Celia.

Chelsea smiled. "Yeah, both very kewl."

"So, in other words, you got caught ripping off a handbag. Big fucking deal," said Richie.

"That's a felony," I added.

"Wrong again, dick wad. Has to be over $1000 to be a felony."

"Richie! Language…"

"Those *are* kinda expensive," Misty said.

The twins nodded agreement.

"Nineteen seventy-five," said Chelsea.

"Told ya," said Richie.

"Nineteen *hundred* and seventy-five."

"For a fucking purse?"

"Told ya."

"You'd know, faggot!"

"Richie, please go wait in my office."

"Aw, come on! Preston's a knob-gobbler."

"Antoine, please assist Richie."

"Probably gobbled your knob for all we know."

Moving in behind him, Antoine placed his hand on Richie's shoulder. "Let's go, sir."

"Get your paw off me, you big fat…loser!" He crossed his arms and refused to move.

"Office or Q.R.?" Antoine asked, calmly.

"You're not putting me in the fucking Q.R. No way!"

A simple lift of your eyebrow required no further discussion. In one beautifully choreographed motion, like Nureyev lifting a weightless Fonteyn, Antoine swept Richie up, chair and all—hauling him away. Being the vile little cretin he is, he managed to run through a complete list of expletives and kick over several chairs before he was de*posited* in the "Quiet

Room." I imagined Antoine finishing with an energetic *Brisé volé.*

Permit me to *posit* this. Shouldn't Richie be on the third floor with the other psychopaths? His anger issues are not going to be resolved in Group. It seems to exacerbate them. Forgive me if I exaggerate, but allow me to elaborate. I love any word that near-rhymes with masturbate.

More on Chelsea Chloe Candy Crystal's revelation later. Just seeing the word in print is like a Siren Song.

June 26th

Having lots of dreams. Dreams are a good thing, right? Ripe for analysis? Pretty sure Freud would approve. I wonder, though, do you think humping his wife's sister renders his opinions now and forever moot? Could explain him being hung up on repression and denial. Oh, well.

Still, I'd love to hear your interpretation, Herr Doktor.

A Vacation Memory

When I was seven, Suzanne persuaded Steven—using any number of beguiling methods that will not be elaborated on here—into taking a family vacation. He wanted to go to Vegas or Maui; I begged to go to Rocky Mountain National Park. I've always had an affinity for mountains, and the Rockies have beckoned me from afar. Once I'd tearfully explained to Mom how much it would mean to me, Steve didn't have an objection to stand on.

We drove across Idaho and through Yellowstone. The snow-capped Tetons were majestic, but there's something about the Colorado Rockies that create an intense harmonic vibration within me, as if my very DNA were linked to those red granite giants. Cognizant of the fact that matter cannot be destroyed, it's possible the mountains, the oceans, the Redwoods, even a mud hut in Gambia contain (or may contain) some of our atoms. Any physicist worth his protons will admit to that possibility.

However, what I'm referring to is: *consciousness*. It feels like part of my very essence is embedded in the glorious Rockies, and on that particular trip, I was drawn to them, magnetically, and galvanized by their power and immensity.

On the third day of our trip, we stopped alongside the Colorado River in a little roadside park, where we could have lunch, some KFC Steve purchased in Steamboat Springs. The thought of noshing on brea(dead) poultry nauseated me, so I pretended I wasn't hungry, even though I was famished. When he wasn't looking, I grabbed a dinner roll and stuffed it in my mouth like a squirrel with survival issues.

Suzanne announced how "refreshing" she thought it would be to kick off her shoes and wade at the water's edge. There was a large outcropping of slippery, moss-covered rocks, and she headed straight for it.

Stephen yelled, "If you fall in, the current will carry you away, and I'm not coming in after you." (So loving even then).

It didn't take her long to discover that the water, fed by melting snow, was, as he later so poetically described it, "dickshrinkingly frigid." In the meantime, he'd retrieved a tallboy from the cooler and parked himself at a picnic table in front of the 12-pc bucket.

After giving my dog, Scottie, a quick walk and a paper cup full of water, I attached his long leash to the bumper of the rented SUV so he could stretch his little legs while I explored the area.

I heard the mountains "calling." It never occurred to me to ask permission, so I took off across the road and started climbing. I mounted each new ledge with more confidence, a greater feeling of invincibility. As I continued my ascent, the thin crystalline air filled my lungs, which began to heave. Though the sun beat down, there was a noticeable drop in temperature, and a light breeze swirled around me—chilling the beads of sweat on my forehead. Within minutes, I'd scaled so high up that when I looked down, my parents appeared to be tiny insects—scurrying around, searching for something. Whatever could it be?

They began shouting, "Preston!" which sounded like Preston! 'reston! 'reston!

Each time I answered back, "Up here!" which sounded like Up here! 'pere! 'pere!

Steve finally located my voice. They were pointing and furiously waving to, 'Get down! down! down!'

I started down and quickly realized going up was an easier slog. After nearly fifteen minutes, I'd managed to descend only halfway when a rock about the size of a large cantaloupe slid out from under me. I fell backward, but the stone melon went crashing off the cliff—dislodging others with it and creating a mini-rockslide.

Suzanne and Steve raced back across the road to avoid being maimed or worse. They survived unscathed, but the roadway ended up peppered with small to medium-sized boulders—impeding both lanes.

When I finally reached the bottom, it was a joyless reunion. Mom was angrier than I'd ever seen her, though I knew it was the result of her fearing I might have been harmed. Steven's ire bordered on homicidal, fueled by the discovery that his cellphone registered no bars, which prevented him from dialing 911. It's now known as "Nomophobia," no-mobile-phone phobia, anxiety from having no network coverage. (Think *I'm* loony…?)

"What do we do now?" she asked.

"Do I look like a fucking Forest Ranger? I never wanted to come to the fucking woods in the first place! *Fuck! 'uck! 'uck!*"

"We have to do *something*," she insisted. "Those rocks could cause a wreck."

"Maybe we should put up a roadblock," I offered.

"Get in the fucking car and don't dare say another fucking word." He was steamed and adjectively challenged.

Though he'd never admit I gave him the idea, like a madman he began rolling the first of two large trash barrels onto the roadway, one on each side of the landslide. The heavy barrels, filled with rotting detritus and foul rainwater, were cumbersome, and he fell twice trying to get them in place—ripping his $1,000 custom-fit jeans and scraping his knee.

I will avoid the swearing sailor cliché, but I will say he easily outdid the "Cursin' Swear Bear" we'd seen for sale in a truck stop outside of Twin Falls, Idaho. His face was crimson, he was gasping for air and he looked like his head would explode. I now confess I rather enjoyed watching him flailing about.

When he finally joined us in the car, he slammed the door so hard I thought the glass would shatter. Jamming the key in the ignition, he violently turned it—holding it in so long the starter or the flywheel or both were in full metallic protest. Infuriated by the engine's inability to respond to his distemper, when it finally started, he peeled out of the parking lot—spraying a colossal rooster-tail of gravel and dust.

We'd driven about five minutes in strained silence, when I innocently inquired, "Where's Scottie?"

He hit the brakes—slowing to a crawl.

"*You* were walking him. What did you do with him?" Mother asked—alarm punctuating every word.

"Didn't I tell you not to let him bring that *damn dog*," said Steven.

The "damn dog," I'd insisted be named Scottie, was a Toy Pomeranian. Incongruous, I know; a little fiery-red fur ball, Scottie was a German and Polish breed. When I breathlessly explained how I'd attached

135

his leash to the rear bumper, Mother was aghast.

"Oh, my God, Steven. Pull over!"

He then demonstrated the truth behind the cliché "easier said than done." There was only the narrowest shoulder on these twisty mountain roads. Mother hopped out and, with some hesitation, ventured back, fully expecting to find the bloody remnant of crimson fur we'd dragged for miles. I could hear her unfastening the leash. She hurried back, leash and harness in hand, and jumped in.

"We've *got* to go back. He's pulled out of the harness."

"Goddammit!"

"I hope he's all right," I said, in my most melodramatic voice. "Hurry, Dad, hurry!"

"I told you...not another word." He reached behind the seat and, as if trying to put out a fire with his hand, frantically tried to swat me, just missing me by inches.

"But, I only—"

"Not now, Pres!" It was rare mother sided with him, and I was offended.

Through a head-jerking series of pulling forward and backing up, he managed to turn the SUV around, all the while mumbling unspeakable epithets. Luckily, we'd met only two cars since we left; due to Dad's maniacal driving, we'd caught and passed one and were fast-approaching the other.

"I think I see him," Mother shouted. "Yes, that's *him!* There, near the shoulder. He's running this way."

At that very moment, the car in front of us veered to the right, as if it were bearing down on what appeared to be a miniature fox. Tragically, we'd arrived just in time to see Scottie become roadkill. Steven began honking, incessantly. Mother—hanging halfway out of the window—

waved madly. As the car reached Scottie, it swerved to the left, barely missing him. Dad slowed and pulled to the edge of the road, but before he could bring it to a complete stop, Mother flung the door open and hurled herself out.

When she returned with Scottie in arms, he was shivering like the nearby aspens and soaked to the skin, a near-drowned rat-dog. Somehow he'd managed to ford a little stream in his attempt to follow after us. Before she could hand him back to me, the miniature whirling dervish went into eggbeater-mode—spraying water all over her, Steven and the dashboard.

"Put that little bastard on the floorboard before I toss him out the window!"

I had a proper retort, but I chose to suppress it. Mom handed me Scottie, and, though he drenched me, I embraced him, as Timmy would Lassie after he'd come home (for the umpteenth time).

We had to drive thirty miles before Steve's cellphone had bars and he could report the rockslide; what a memorable jaunt it was. For the uninitiated among you, straight roads in the mountains are non-existent; taking sharp S-shaped curves, or ones ironically called Nesbitts (bends shaped like a nose) at fifty to sixty miles an hour was harrowing. The car's engine, unless the temperature gauge lied, appeared to be on the verge of a meltdown. The more Steven seethed, the greater the speed. Neither Mother nor I dared say a word, though I could tell she wanted to scream, 'Slow down!'

As we whipped around a horseshoe curve, in hopes of breaking the tension, I pointed to a yellow caution sign, "Look!" 'Watch for Falling Rock,' it read. "I think Falling Rock's that missing Indian chief they're still looking for."

Dad glared at me in the rearview mirror. His eyes narrowed as he shook his head. "Son, what the hell's wrong with you?"

Mother tried to temper his distemper by pretending to side with him. "Not funny Pres." It didn't work.

"Your little rock-climbing antic was a selfish, thoughtless thing to do. What were you thinking?"

To have my "thinking" questioned by a man, who, I was certain, rarely thought about anything before acting, left me tongue-tied. For the first time I could remember, I was speechless.

"*Answer me.* What were you thinking?"

Finally, I mumbled, "The mountains were calling me."

"Goddammit, Preston Nesbitt. No more of your supernatural bullshit!"

"But—"

"I mean it!"

"Please, just answer your father."

I could've manufactured something less metaphysical and more acceptable, but I was rattled. When I repeated 'The mountains *were* calling me,' he threatened to pull the car over and "Tan your hide!" That was the archaic expression he used, and coming from him, it sounded even more ludicrous. I bit the inside of my cheek to keep from smiling.

"Well…?"

"I'm very sorry," I said, with all the pseudo-sincerity I could manufacture.

Mother and I exchanged wide-eyed looks. That did it. I snorted, then pretended to be choking on saliva. Mom pressed her fist to her lips and turned towards her window. Unable to stifle laughter, I ducked down behind the driver's seat, both hands tightly clasped over my mouth. Though unable to see him, I could feel his rage.

Later, when we'd made it to Estes Park and were settled in our cabin, or, as he christened it, "knotty pine hell," I heard her whisper, "I had no idea you knew how to tan hide…you old buckskinner you." She said it kinda sexy-like, and I knew where that could lead. It didn't take much to arouse Steven, a sultry whisper or corduroy slacks.

But instead of getting all riled up, he got all chocked up. I'd never before seen him shed a single tear. He answered in a pain-muffled voice, "I think we've both had enough death, don't you?"

Darned if I don't think he was trying to say he was concerned for my well-being. It only took an avalanche to pry it out of him.

P.S. Reread today's entry multiple times, and though I added a smidgen of whimsy, I noted the tone is noticeably different from most of my other entries. Perhaps it was the subject matter, but it made me aware of how much Nature has always meant to me and how I discovered a connection to the Infinite from the forests, streams and mountains.

That got me thinking about how much I'd benefit from an hour or two in Cathedral Park. Or, better yet, an excursion out to Kelley Point. Just you and me. Whaddya say…?

While you're mulling it over, I'll leave you with this little burlesque…a Steve Nesbitt special:

"Doctor, the second I'm left alone…I play with myself. Then, I feel guilty and depressed."

"Ah hah!" said the doctor. "And you want I should help you break this perverse habit?"

"No, Doc. I want you should cure my feelings of guilt and depression." (Drum roll…cymbal crash).

If I ever get out of here, the Catskills await.

June 27th

In *The Tin Drum*, Oskar's wrongfully accused of murder and forced to live in a mental hospital, where he loses his power to shatter glass with his voice. Because the doctors fail to understand him, they also confiscate his drum: his self-expression, his ability to summon the past and his power. It's really cruel to take away a person's freedom (unjustly) and, rather than helping, enable his unique abilities to slowly disappear.

I'm not comparing you to Dr. Hornstetter; she believed Oskar suffered from childhood isolation. Her diagnosis was wrong. He refused to "grow up" in an insane world. I'm simply trying to emphasize the "gravity" of my situation, with no "rainbow" in sight. Doc, I could use a reassuring *pynch on* the cheek. (Oh, for heaven's sake…Google it!)

Are you waiting for me to admit the video's a fake, so I can appear normal? Mr. Wolff said to tell you what you want to hear. The truth is…I'm as confounded by it as you are, though I've spent weeks trying to unravel the mystery.

I'm willing to do whatever it takes, but I'd appreciate a little feedback on what you need from me in order to be released from your ministrative machinations. I use that particular word, because your failure to explain my continued incarceration seems like a calculated ploy. That, and the fact that the U.S. accounts for twenty-five percent of the world's prisoners, has me more than a little stressed.

Without some indication as to why you're keeping me here, I remain adrift. I would have said discombobulated or flummoxed, but Chelsea's made me self-conscious about my archaic word choices. Confinement is beginning to have a deleterious effect on my psyche, not to mention my dream state. I find myself questioning my memory of certain events, just as Oskar began losing his imagination.

Believing me culpable in the creation of that video is comparable to finding Günter Grass guilty of conspiring with the Nazis, instead of transmuting his guilt into the creation of a masterpiece. His Art surpassed whatever weakness he possessed as a human being.

Can I be forgiven my peccadilloes, since I'm trying to do my part to make the world a better place? I'm only getting started in that creative pursuit, but my efforts are sincere, even though I often describe them facetiously. You've known me a long time. If you care for me at all, please tell me what I need to do to "get better." My anxiety level's accelerated, and lately I find myself analyzing myself analyzing myself.

Do you believe in Fate? Apparently, Preston Nesbitt's Fate is to be the featured player in the world's most controversial video, "Kid vs. Buick—and the winner is…?" The ever-present irony: the YouTube video you refuse to believe is real, because of it's fantastic nature, has unwittingly become his *raison d'être*. (I'm aware I'm speaking in the 3rd person. Give me some credit, won't you?)

A few weeks of summer vacay would be greatly appreciated before I begin university this Fall. For whatever psychological idiosyncrasies I may possess, I've proven I'm capable of functioning in an academic atmosphere. New York University will be no different.

If I can make it there, I can make it anywhere.

* * *

I wanted you to know I purchased "The Tin Drum." Please do not be offended when I say I put it down after Book One. Oskar is clinically insane. I see no correlation between the two of you.

Excellent! So, when am I getting out?

July 28th

Recently, you asked why I think I don't have more friends. Is there a magic number that would be sufficient, that would make me normal *enough?*

I have many acquaintances, but few friends. Finding someone who has your back, without stabbing it, is a rarity...a true, lasting friendship, rarer still. I think a person's lucky if he ends up with one or two really good friends in a lifetime. I thought Chris was one; I'm still holding out hope. Perhaps Ciera, if she stops emulating celebrity suicides, will become another.

Though I'd love to be liked, I'd prefer the majority respect me for my wit and intelligence. The turtle has its shell; the snake its venom; and I...a tongue of razor-sharp titanium. It doesn't keep me from being wounded, but it serves as a deterrent for those who know me and a scathing introduction for those who don't. Not proud of it Doc, but we all do what we believe is necessary to survive.

I came into this world wide open and willing to accept others and share my talents and enthusiasms—hoping for a little reciprocity. So far, that hasn't been my experience. As to why I don't have *more* friends, maybe this sorrowful little anecdote will serve to enlighten.

My Distrust of the Herd

In 5th grade, we studied "Native American" culture. It was yet another lesson in revisionist history, the "winners" concocting their version of what happened and passing it off as *Truth*. The truth is, and this is speaking truth to power, it was mass murder on a grand scale, and the resulting Diaspora set the tone for America's Imperialistic genocide, a "we're superior to you" British import.

In addition, we also inherited some pretty fuckupta ideas about sex. The Canadians got the French, the Australians got the criminals and we got the Puritans. (O frabjous day! Callooh! Callay!)

Anyway, once our class finished the unit of study, our teacher proposed to have a Culminating Activity, in this instance a party. Hopefully, it would be more authentic than our recent Thanksgiving Celebration: a fabled love-fest between the Pilgrims and the Injuns. I needed to remind everyone that a realistic Thanksgiving would be inviting our neighbors to a meal, killing them and taking their land. As per usual, no one found this either humorous or instructive.

As to the Culminating Activity: Our teacher, Mrs. Eunice Evans, whose knowledge of anything prior to WWII was limited to an obsession with Prohibition and its need to be reinstated, encouraged us to come dressed in "Native attire." Venison jerky, along with a drink of vinegar and cornmeal, would be provided as refreshment. (Yuck. No wonder my classmates seemed dispassionate and indifferent.) I, on the other hand, was crazy happy to be making my own Indian garb.

Though no prize was announced for "Best Costume," my competitive nature surfaced like sludge from a malfunctioning septic tank: odiferous, yet capable of producing something lavish and lush. Not a pleasant analogy, I admit, but the end product of competition often outweighs its inherent ugliness, or something like that.

After much pleading and begging, Suzanne drove me out to Savage's Poultry Farm, where I gathered a big cardboard box full of turkey and Guinea hen feathers. She then chauffeured me to the local Fred Meyer—"What's on your list today?"

Thanks for asking, Freddie boy. I'll need a big bag of tube pasta, like rigatoni without the ridges; two yards of red felt; a couple skeins of matching red yarn; a roll of ultra-thin wire; two small mirrored discs; a bottle of all-purpose glue and a large plastic bag of tin jingle bells.

With the turkey tail feathers, the hollow-shafted calamus covered in a strip of felt and secured with yarn and wire, I constructed a magnificent bustle, a sunburst within a larger sunburst. With the smaller Guinea feathers, I fashioned two fabulous arm rosettes with mirrored centers. The tube pasta was strung together with the yarn and became a beauteous hairpipe "bone" breastplate.

With the remaining yarn and bells, I whipped up some fancy anklets, reminiscent of a Clydesdale's fetlocks. I wanted Mom to purchase the angora variety, but she insisted it was too expensive. I could tell she thought it a little too "fairy fey"—wishing to spare me the inevitable taunting.

For several years, I'd beaded strips of varying widths on the antique Walco Indian Bead Loom I'd unearthed at a yard sale. Selecting one of my finest creations—featuring my spirit animal, the red-tailed hawk—I hot-glued it to a strip of elastic-backed felt for my headband.

Finding the remaining felt too cheesy for a breechcloth, while visiting Steve's recently renovated bachelor pad, I borrowed a brand new chamois, the deerskin he used to remove the water droplets after running his new BMW Z4 through the carwash. As partial payback for destroying our family unit, I fringed both ends and attached small shells across the bottom.

On the day of the party, Steve was "out of town" and couldn't drive me to school. Part of the joint custody agreement stated he would provide rides to my elementary school every other week. True to character, he usually managed to be on a business trip when that duty befell him. Though Suzanne insisted on taking me, I finally assured her I could make it on my own—explaining that I needed the extra time to get dressed in my fab Indian costume..........*

*To be continued. You insist we participate in Crafts. Just how you think making a wicker basket, a Popsicle stick house, a macaroni-covered purse (spray-painted blue) or a coiled clay ashtray is going to "heal" anyone, bespeaks way more about your befuddlement that it does mine.

June 29th

My Distrust of the Herd (Cont'd)

I fantasized that the many hours I'd spent making my authentic costume would impress Mrs. Evans, and that the result of my efforts would be wildly applauded, even by my recalcitrant classmates, most of whom would probably forego the opportunity to come dressed as Crazy Horse, Sacagawea or Hinmuuttu-yalatlat (more familiarly known as Chief Joseph). Chief Joseph was an Oregonian legend, and our study had focused on his "failed attempts" to keep the Nez Perce homeland from being purloined by the lying cheating government, who removed the tribe to Oklahoma, where they faced sickness, starvation and death. Anyway, that's what I gleaned from the lesson.

As testament to my ability to be invisible, I'd re-named myself, "He Who's Not There." If I didn't hurry, that would be prophetic.

Visibly vibrating with anticipation of my triumphant appearance, I stood in front of Suzanne's bedroom mirror—draping my deerskin breechcloth over my belt, between my legs, and smoothing it evenly over my junk and my trunk. I then tied on the giant sunburst bustle, arm rosettes and anklets, attached the splendid macaroni breastplate and slipped into my moccasins (purchased on our aforementioned Rocky Mountain trip) and beaded headband, adorned with the three hand-painted, red-tailed hawk feathers Mother purchased on E-bay.

Though the individual pieces of my costume were totally "sick" (get with it Doc), for some odd reason the parts did not make for a "wicked" (ditto) whole. I stared, blankly, into the mirror. Aha! The problem: Indians do not wear clothing over their clothes!

Failing to anticipate the reaction to my attempt at authenticity, I shed my costume—stripping down to my "Fruit of the Loom" undies. I would have gone totally *au natural*, but I was a little self-conscious about the size of my watering can (an allusion to Oskar Mazerath's tinkler, remember?). I'll let you determine whether I was embarrassed about its unfortunate dearth or its prodigious girth. And, in answer to the inevitable trivia question: boxer briefs.

Again, I assembled the ensemble. Though much improved over the previous layered-look, something was still awry. Of course, 'twas my complexion; devoid of pigmentation, I appeared to be just another pale-faced interloper. For the record, my etiolated skin tone in no way matched the deep tinge of my native heart.

Time was disappearing faster than the publishing industry and the music industry before it. What to do? I ran to the kitchen, grabbed a mixing bowl, some Hershey's Cocoa and the bottle of hand lotion Suzanne kept near the sink. Adding water and a few squirts of lotion to a heaping mound of powdery chocolate, I mixed a big batch of base "makeup." Once again, I slipped out of the outfit.

Twenty minutes 'til the tardy bell.

I hurriedly slathered on the chocolaty foundation—struggling to reach areas beyond the fingertips of even the most limber contortionist. I worried certain areas resembled bad finger-painting, with digit trails streaking down my thighs and across my shoulder blades like the rippling sand patterns in a Japanese serenity garden. At the very least, I prayed I wouldn't resemble just another *"White Eyes" in Indian drag.

THE QUEERLING

*Like blue-eyed, Jeff Chandler (ne' Ira Grossel), the blue-eyed Jewish actor who played Apache Chief Cochise in three different westerns. Oy vey!

As I frantically dressed again, another problem arose: my terra cotta skin was drying and flaking off faster than a speeding neutrino; on elbows and knees, it was exfoliating in chunks. Afraid my appearance more closely resembled an Indian leper, I decided to forego a final inspection in the mirror.

Portland was experiencing a cold snap, and this particular February morning, it was a bone-chilling 25 degrees. With blustery winds whipping in from the Columbia Gorge, it was downright frigid. I took several preparatory deep breaths—summoning my warrior spirit to help me *brave* the elements. Then, I rocketed out the door, coatless.

Noting how quickly my warrior spirit went limp, I darted back inside to grab my hooded winter jacket. Discovering it was too small to fit over my voluminous feather bustle, I sidled up to my bed, carefully draped the bedspread over the assemblage, and trudged out into the wintery blast.

A rare snow still covered the ground. Due to my makeup-stiffened joints, I had to swivel from one leg to the next—leaving behind a mysterious trail. It was the longest seven-block-walk of my life. By now I was late and frozen stiffer than the Daiquiris and Bushwackers Steven swilled down at every client lunch.

When I entered the building, I managed to avoid the attendance secretary, as I went temporarily stealth. Stealth I should have remained, because when I passed Boone Bivins—meandering out of the boy's restroom on his way back to his sixth-grade class—he did a double-take worthy of W. C. Fields in *You Can't Cheat An Honest Man*.

"Whoa, dude. That's fucking awesome. What're you…some kind of Indian or somethin'?" Boone's glassy eyes and dilated pupils revealed he'd just enjoyed his usual early-morning toke. Looking closer, he grimaced. "Holy shit! What's with your skin, dude? Looks like you stood a little too close to the campfire…like in the middle of it or something." Finding this hysterically funny, he continued to point and guffaw as I made my way to Mrs. Evans' room at the end of the hall.

As I approached the door, I could hear the party rockin' inside. Perhaps it was my need for attention (okay, okay…it *was* most definitely my need for attention) that made me decide to make a grand entrance. Letting my frozen bedspread slide to the floor, I flung open the door—leaping into the room with a vociferous "Waw! Waw! Waw!" war-hoop, my hand patting my mouth in that stereotypical war-hoop way.

In a split-second, the decibel-level in the room went from a 747 taking off at Portland International to zip, zero, zilch! There was a momentary pause in the action. Then, the explosive laughter that followed nearly blew the imitation hawk feathers out of my beaded headband.

As I surveyed the room, the twisted and contorted faces of my classmates suddenly blurred into a hideous Expressionistic painting by Otto Dix. I was horrified to discover none of them—*not a single one*—had bothered to don Indian regalia. No, wait! In the far corner of the room sat Tenilla Jean Dickinson, who had fashioned a headband and feathers out of multi-colored construction paper. She appeared to be wearing a dress pieced together from gunnysacks and fringed at the bottom like my chamois breechcloth. Her dark sympathetic eyes locked on mine; one kindred spirit out of the whole boisterous bunch, only one who took this opportunity to *be* an Indian.

Before I could blink, Mrs. Evans swept me from the room and into the hallway. "I love your costume, dear," she said, her pity not completely diminishing her sincerity. "It's the best one ever. But, honey, you need to go home and put on some clothes."

To ensure I did the right thing, she mashed the melting bedspread around my shoulders and ushered me all the way to the front door. As we passed the Principal's Office, Dr. Werner emerged. With a look of horror, she shrieked, "What in God's name has he done *now?*" Had I been armed with a tomahawk, the temptation would have been irresistible.

I did not return to school until the following Monday. By then, only a few, the imbeciles and halfwits, felt it necessary to say how 'stupid' I looked.

"Geez, I could practically see your weenie," said Buddy Funkhouser.

"That's what happens to big show-offs!" said Mindy Louise Meisner, who ate her own buggers and eye candy when she thought no one was watching. "My dad's a lawyer and he says it's illegal to own hawk feathers. I should report you."

"FYI, genius…Indians ain't cocoa brown. They're *red*," added Billy Birkhead III.

I wanted to smash him right in his Invisaligns. Instead, I said, "Shut your plastic pie-hole, Third the Turd!" That cost me a day in Detention, but it was worth it. By the time I returned to class, most of the taunting had stopped.

So, that's it. Bet you can glean a ton of psychological fodder from that pathetic pastiche.

If that weren't enough, permit me to describe the Paranoid Dream I experienced for months afterwards: I'm sitting at my classroom desk, fixated on memorizing the flags and capitals of Central and South American countries or some other innocuous assignment, when I hear snickering. It starts small but builds into full-blown mocking laughter. I look up to discover the entire class staring at me, as if I were an alien. Only then do I realize I am completely bare-ass naked. I could have said "wearing only a smile," but that would not only have been a cliché but also a hideous lie. I was mortified. Please note the root word does not mean embarrassed, it means death. I was humiliated to *fucking death!*

Re-reading this, I'm struck by how many unnecessary adjectives, adverbs, italics and exclamation points it took to recall this sorrowful scene of childhood devastation. Just reliving it, I'm totally spent! No…it's not neurasthenia. After a bloodletting, I require a nap.

P.S. Shared this story with Ciera. At the end, she sat there—weeping. Granted she's a push-over, but is it possible my life's more tragic than I ever imagined?

* * *

A story that revealing deserves a comment don't you think…? Oh, I get it. You expect me provide the analysis. Okay, fine. Here's what I think: (Placing lips on bare arm)…Zerbert! (You'll find it on YouTube).

July 1st

What invaluable lesson did I glean from the "imaginative" tale retold last week? Isn't that the point of all this? To learn by reflecting on the circumstances that brought me here, and comprehend how a different course of action might result in my eventual return to society?

If anything, "The Humiliation," as I like to call it, helped solidify my belief that the great majority of people are content to live safe, risk-free lives—allowing opportunities to zip by, like the contrails of a Boeing 767 jetting to new adventures in exotic places. How's that for a simile straining for significance? Here's an accompanying analogy: if not fed a proper diet, pigs will continue to eat their own feces until they die from malnutrition.

Still wonder why I'm not courting more "friends?" Why I'm occasionally misanthropic? Detecting a little anger? Well, sometimes sarcasm isn't enough to quell a slow-building rage.

In spite of how it sounds, my ire isn't a reaction to other's ignorance or apathy; it's directed at myself for wasting so much time in hopeful anticipation of a better outcome, cynicism resulting from failed optimism. Great expectation almost always leads to great disappointment. The biggest cynics were once the greatest optimists. Think Diogenes was cynical about finding an honest man? He's a mere carper compared to Juvenal, Rabelais, Swift and Voltaire. Count me among them. In fact, move me to the head of the class.

July 2nd

Some pre-4th of July Fireworks. The Solar Flare today was amazing. Reminds me of last year's spectacular Lunar Eclipse. Between the early moonset and the pollutants, it was blocked from view here in Portland. Fortunately, I was able to check out a live-stream on cable. Did you happen to catch it Doc? The panorama of the crimson orb from Tanzania was "awesome." (I use that word to mean awe-inspiring, unlike my peers, who think practically everything is awesome sauce.)

"Primitives" believed eclipses were a portent of doom. They envisioned the Sun and Moon being devoured by various creatures, from voracious frogs to demonic dragons. Today, untold numbers of folk believe 12-21-12 is the End Time. Hope they're right. When one thing ends, something new begins. Sounds like the perfect scenario for "a child of the Eighth Day." Gotta be an improvement, or at least a

Revelation...right?

Speaking of the Maya of the Mayans, you'd think they could have envisioned their own extinction and somehow avoided it.

* * *

I repeat. KEEP OUT of the Staff Lounge. It's important you remember we have rules. Those rules are to be respected by <u>everyone.</u>

Ah...there's the real Thomas, the one I suspected was hiding under that stoic façade all along. Way to go. Tommy Boy...let your Freak Flag Fly!

July 3rd

It was your turn to man the battle-station this past Sunday 'ol boy, but you were AWOL! Thought you might be "under the weather" (try explaining that one to Missy). Found out you're taking a three-day vacation? Just you and the Missus? Visiting relatives? Grandkids? A quick trip to the beach?

Must admit...missed ya.

July 4th

Independence Day. Not something teenagers cooped up in a mental ward would normally celebrate, but this year some of us are making an exception. Security's so lax I could flee anytime I choose. Just to prove it, I went to Powell's Books yesterday. Not the nearest, the main location downtown.

I was only gone a couple of hours; however, just knowing I could roam through those marvelous stacks of new and used books, each section color-coded (a good thing, too, 'cause one can easily get lost in the disorienting maze of that multi-floored warehouse), I felt totally liberated. Seriously, if you want my mental outlook to improve, permitting a weekly visit to Powell's would be an uplifting antidote to this soul-numbing environment. Besides, books are good *juju!*

Still, I returned. Don't ask why. And, don't punish the staff. I convinced everyone I needed the solace of the serenity garden. Thankfully, they honored my request…and then forgot all about me, or were happy to let me vegetate…rather than irritate.

Guess this confession will result in another visit to the Quiet Room, or an effort to improve security, but it's no use. Anything short of ankle-bracelets and GPS transponders will prove ineffective.

Still don't believe me? Try this: one of our finest went to the *7-Eleven* on S.W. Broadway last week for cigarettes. Not only did they sell them, they never bothered to ask for I.D. You might want to go over your credit card bill carefully next month. He bought a carton.

So, Happy 4th Dr. van I.

As for your "rules," remember this: Freedom's just another word for nothing left to lose. I shall now celebrate the only freedom I have left: masturbatory independence. You know, feelin' good is good enough for me…good enough for me and my Bobby McGee.

July 5th

Every major civilization eventually hits the shitter: the Babylonians, the Etruscans, the Mayans…and the Greenwich Villagers. Although we're the youngest country in the world, we're beginning to circle the drain. That would not apply to the size of our War Machine; inflated like a porn star's pud, it'll plug up the plumbing before it plummets into the cesspool where it belongs!

Nope, I'm referring to societal collapse, and I don't just mean the usual contributing factors: economic, environmental and social. I'm talking about a lack of...get ready for it: gross incompetence.

I'd like to blame "Comedy Central" for its irreverence toward everything and everyone, but I must, once again, point the finger at poor parenting.

A couple of us watched a program last night in the Staff Lounge—featuring imbecilic parents who attached baby seats to the back of Harleys; an unruly 9-month-old being duct-taped to a wall; a toddler sucking on a bong, while a stoned parent snoozed on the sofa; a 5-year-old girl practicing with a handgun at a shooting range, and a hyper-active kid confined to a pet carrier.

That's one form of incompetence. The flip side is parents who's "Love Language" is CA$H. Spring Break at WPI consists of trips to Gstaad, Bali and the Maldives. If your parents don't have a time-share in the Bahamas, you're broke-ass poor.

Half the kids at my school drive BMWs or Mercedes: "Beemers and Sadies." You're thinking the American Dream; I'm thinking Entitlement. Doc, most of these kids wouldn't be caught dead in Hondas, Toyotas or Volkswagens, which they refer to as "Rice Rockets or Sausage Wagons."

Where do these attitudes originate? Good guess. As it's unlikely we'll ever curtail defense spending, I'm on the verge of advocating the use of military drones to take out incompetent parents as they wander through the parking lots at Wal-Mart and Nordstrom. J/K (only a little).

Instead of college courses like "The Unbearable Whiteness of Barbie" and "Zombies! The Living Dead in Literature," a course on "How To Be A

Good Parent" should be mandatory. Perhaps if parents knew better, they'd do better. (One can only hope).

Seriously, what's happened to our culture? We've been dumbed down to the point where "reality" TV is about as intellectually stimulating as it gets. On "Court TV," I heard an attorney ask, 'Doctor, how many autopsies have you performed on *dead* people?' When "W" inquired, 'Is our children learning?'...the answer was painfully obvious: 'No! They is not!' The futile No Child Left Behind should have been called, No Teacher Left Standing. As a society, we're becoming more moronic by the minute.

P.S. Don't bother to change the door lock on the Staff Lounge. Some of the criminal element here could crack an impregnable safe.

July 7th

Feels like I've been "away" for the past two days. Drugs affect my memory. I'm unable to function on *Lithium*. Dr. Bollixed gave me a shot to "help calm" me. Guess my ranting extended beyond the page and into the lounge. Miss Vine alerted him. So helpful, that woman. Had you been here, I think it could have been avoided. My private sessions do seem to relieve my need to pontificate.

Please, no more vacations.

July 9th

Sunday...more interesting than most, with the arrival of Jamarcus Fremont.

According to an article in last week's *Oregonian*, Mrs. Olivia Jackson,

Jamarcus's mother, said she was "shocked" to discover her fourteen-year-old son was the arsonist who set fire to not one but two of her residences.

'Always told Jamarcus he could do anything, be anything he wanted to be. Done nothing but praise that child since he was a baby, and what good did it do?' (Obviously, Mrs. J., he took your advice to heart. Unfortunately, his passion is burning buildings).

In addition to incinerating her home three years ago and, more recently, setting her apartment ablaze, he's also responsible for a series of arson fires in north Portland. Part of the transcript from the court hearing was reprinted in the newspaper, along with testimony from some of his former teachers as to how "special" he is.

Love this: 'When Jamarcus got cut from the basketball squad last year, he was extremely disappointed,' said Ms. Carmelita Spikes, a student counselor. 'I spoke to the coach about reinstating Jamarcus, but he refused—saying, *The boy has no athletic ability. Can't play a lick.* What kind of coach discourages a young man who wants to play ball? This kind of rejection, along with being told he lacked the talent to be in a local hip hop group, damaged his self-esteem.' Mrs. Jackson added that her son was '…as good as any of them rappers on *BET* and a lot better looking. Why, that boy could make it in the movies if he wanted to. Be the next Denzel.'

When asked by the judge why he set so many buildings on fire, Jamarcus's response "rocked the courtroom," 'Eat sh*t, motherf*cker.'

In short, there's nothing like growing up on a steady diet of empty praise. Here's to all the soccer moms and bonehead dads who tell their kids how "special" they are when they're barely average. Be prepared for some pushback. If you're lucky, it won't involve matches and gasoline.

I'm disappointed you assigned him to another group. Could've been such fun!

THE QUEERLING

* * *

You are not permitted to read the newspapers in the Staff Lounge. Please understand that your refusal to follow the rules is an indication that you are not ready to be released.

OMG, you're beginning to sound just like Nurse Ratched. Is there a lobotomy in my future?

July 10th

Attempted a friendly salutation with Jamarcus this morning. BIG mistake!

"Yo."

"Don't *yo me*, bitch."

"Hey, man…didn't mean anything by it."

"Just got booked. I'm beefin' k?"

Nervous, I felt compelled to answer. "I heard."

"Heard wut, nigga?"

"About the…pyromania." When rattled, I have no filter when I need it most.

"Gettin' all up in my bidneh?"

"Huh? No… *No*. Just sayin' hey."

"I'm fuckin' dope, man. Tell me otherwise."

At this point, I'm not sure how to end the conversation, so I just smile.

"Don't smile, bitch. I ain't no liar…just don't reveal much."

"That's coo, man." For the love of God! I've never said "coo" in my whole life!

"You some kinda fag or wut?"

"No, I'm phat...er, coo." I am *so* white.

"Suck a bag of dicks!"

Time to remove Jamarcus from the list of "Potential Friends." Good call on assigning him to another Group. And, please remind me never to begin another conversation with "Yo." (I'd make his Psych Eval priority one.)

July 11th

I want my copy of *The Tin Drum* returned immediately! I didn't take it from Powell's; I bought it used. (Which I wouldn't have had to do if you'd let me have my copy from home.)

It's a travesty of great art to think I could purchase a hardback copy for only $7.75. Used paperbacks of that vapid vampire trilogy cost more.

In *The Tin Drum*, Oskar finally gives up his drum and allows himself to grow. When it comes to adulthood in this day and age, I'm still on the fence. Should I tumble and fall, who will put me back together again?

You?

July 12th

All that talk about "The Humiliation" recently has unearthed another dream, one that's haunted me off and on for years.

I subscribe to Einstein's theory that the physical world isn't "reality." According to AE, who was the closest thing we've had to AI 'til IBM's Watson, reality begins when we leave the physical world and reach the speed of light. Since I assume we're *"light beings" trapped in physical form, I guess Alfie was referring to death, or a release back to the non-physical. Still with me?

*Lends some credence to "You are the Light of the world, eh?"

The little man with the radioactive hair said that at the speed of light, there's no time, no space and everything that appears to be the past, present and future exists, simultaneously. Therefore, all we've *ever been* in this illusion we call the physical, all we *are now* and all we'll *ever be* is happening at the same time but at different frequencies.

So, frequency bleed-throughs from the "future" explain *déjà vu*. And, frequency bleed-throughs from the distant "past" come in dreams or unexplainable feelings. Residual memories fade away in childhood. (Well, not mine).

Now, to the dream...

I'm walking down a path when I decide to fly. But, not by transforming into a bird or any winged creature. It's as if I somehow understand that flying is possible, because I never doubt I possess that ability. Aware I can fly anytime I choose, I'm careful not to do so where I can be seen, for fear of frightening others or creating jealousy. However, on this particular moonless night, I feel safe enough, so I take off—flying low, nearly skimming the ground. Suddenly, I whizz past a shrouded figure who spots me and sounds the alarm. Within seconds, a teeming crowd forms.

Fearing for my safety, I fly higher—circling up and around what I eventually realize is a church steeple and a cross. Looking down, I notice some of the gathering throng carrying torches; the rabble appears to be either outraged or terrified by my flying ability.

Before I can escape, an arrow pierces the dark—felling me. I can only assume I'm dead the minute I hit the ground; however, since I always manage to awaken just prior to touchdown, who knows?

Doc, since it's your job to put a psychological spin on everything, dreams included, you're probably thinking "extreme paranoia." Then, too, the symbolism of the church steeple seems blatantly obvious for one who proclaims to be anti-organized religion.

But, how to explain a parallel past-life "memory" in which I, a Jewish convert, am being martyred, burned as a heretic, in what appears to be medieval Portugal, for my belief we are *all* Divine Sons and Daughters of God? That belief would not have made me a *heresiarch* per se, but to the Inquisition, any excuse to exterminate someone who did not adhere to strict Catholic orthodoxy was justifiable.

This "bleed-through" is an anamnesis, a remembrance of ideas I possessed as that poor soul, for I can describe in *full detail the tribunal or inquisition, headed by the Archbishop of Cranganor, who sentenced me to death by *auto-da-fé*…my baptism by fire.

*I recall this as clearly as last week's Group therapy, where Richie called you a "cocklapper," and you visibly shuddered. As drawing and quartering is no longer a permissible therapeutic practice, I could see you mentally tying the little bastard to a spit, over a raging fire, and delighting as flames "lapped" his Ritalin-stunted body. Made me wonder if you'd spent some time in ages past—punishing heretics like me?

To conclude…

The Book of Isaiah is used to condemn me: *"Ipse autem populus direptus et vastatus: laqueus juvenum omnes, et in domibus carcerum absconditi sunt: facti sunt in rapinam, nec est qui eruat; in direptionem, nec est qui dicat: Redde."*

My academic transcript contains no *Latin*, yet I can recite this incantation like a nursery rhyme. Translation: it basically says because we Jews did not recognize the true Messiah, we'll be forever a wandering, cursed and scattered people. I've never studied Latin and I don't profess to be an Inquisition scholar, but I can tell you what it feels like to be burned alive, the memory so visceral and real, that as a five-year-old, I'd wake up with flop sweats.

I'd stored this disturbing remembrance away 'til I read of the torture at Guantánamo. When Bush and Cheney spoke of "moral certainty" in detaining suspects and using the means necessary "to protect America," the nightmares resurfaced. In nearly 800 years, not much has changed, for it was with moral certainty that I was not only tortured but also barbequed.

Please ruminate on your moral certainty—examining the ethics of making this my permanent residence.

July 13th

I truly wanted and needed to go to Powell's City of Books on Burnside tonight. One of my favorite authors is in town. Naturally, Suzanne's going. I could have accompanied her, but 'No!' This was your chance to agree to something that would have not only improved my attitude but also my overall mental health; however, you nixed it without the slightest consideration.

This approach feels more like fascism than therapy. How about a little common decency? You know I'm not dangerous. No suicidal tendencies. So, what's the justification...?

I love books. Mom made me understand that literature's the Breath of Life! You've taken away my cherished reading materials: *The Tin Drum*, *The Idiot* and my 3-volume set of *The Complete Letters of Vincent Van Gogh*. Deprived of Culture, how do you expect me to thrive, to heal? I feel my soul beginning to wither and die. Truly!

Other than Ciera, most of the patients here are dolts. Only a couple read, and none have read anything without a Boy Wizard, a Vampire or Zombie...*ever!*

Don't call on me in Group. I'm announcing a moratorium on cooperation and declaring a work stoppage. If this is your idea of therapy, if this is your attempt to provide healing, succor...I have only two words: Epic Fail!

Don't let it upset your weekend, but I may not be here when you return on Monday.

Sincerely,

P. W. Nesbitt (former patient)

July 14th

Nice. Alerting Reggie to keep me under close surveillance all weekend. What's next, electric shock? A lobotomy? I've had it with this place.

July 15th -19th

Nothing! *Nada!* Nil! *Rien! Ei mitään! Niente! Niets!* Zilch! Zip! Diddlyshit!

July 20th

Your threats, I mean encouragement, worked. However, I'm not going to tell you who used your credit card to buy the carton of cigs. Go ahead, put me in the rubber room, attach electrodes to my skull, stick wooden slivers under my fingernails and light them. I won't give up the name.

Oh, all right. His initials are…Richie Caytes.

July 21st

Suzanne visited today. Her last few visits ended poorly, so I decided to be especially nice. She looked great. Since she adopted a Pixie Cut, her short blonde hair makes her look ten years younger. Mom has kind eyes (azure blue) and perfect teeth. Unfortunately, I got Steve's not-so-perfect ones, and my gray eyes are a genetic anomaly.

Wish I could say her appearance helped buoy my sagging spirits, but alas… Though she did her best to put a big, cheerful pink bow on her visit, I could tell she was distraught. I finally cut through the charade and asked what was troubling her.

"I don't mean to upset you, but I keep having this disturbing dream."

Suzanne's usually a seismic wave of positive energy, but she appeared depleted of her usual vitality. "It's really vague. All I know for certain is…I'm at a funeral." She sat for a moment—reliving the picture in her mind.

"That's it…?"

She looked up and took my hand in hers. "I'm sitting next to your father."

"Wow! Hard to imagine that ever happening, even for Nana Nesbitt."

"It was so *real*."

"Interesting."

"It gets even stranger. Turns out it's my funeral."

"Not that strange. Death in dreams usually means an end to something. Maybe it's symbolic of you finally letting go…of the marriage, I mean."

"But we were *both* heartbroken."

"I think Dad knows he screwed up. Why wouldn't he be sad? That's not so weird."

"Pres, I don't remember you being at my funeral."

"Well, that settles it. You know I wouldn't miss your funeral, unless Chuck Palahniuk or Gus Van Sant invited me to dinner."

"Don't joke."

"It was a *dream*, Mom."

"It didn't feel like one."

"That's the thing about dreams. On some level, they may be as real as this illusion we think of as reality."

"Oh, honey, I miss you."

"Miss you, too, Mom."

I then opted for the subtle approach; however, subtlety quickly morphed into the usual.

"How are things at home…? Who's cutting the grass…? That sure is a big 'ol house for just one person, isn't it…? Don't forget to set the alarm. Heard on the news the number of residential break-ins is on the increase."

"Really?"

"Yes… Just wondering if they've mentioned when I might get out of here? There are some really fucked up kids in here, Mom. Suicides, druggies, arsonists, animal abusers, psychos, felons, sociopaths, perverts and gangstas. Name it, we've got it! You or Dad could have me discharged. It needs to happen *soon*. The summer's almost over. It's only fair I have a little break before college starts. Please. Ask Doc when he plans to release me."

She stood and moved towards the window.

"I've asked him, repeatedly. He always says the same thing. When I know Preston's—"

"Delusions are gone."

"Yes," she said, sitting down beside me—draping her arm around my shoulder.

"How am I ever going to convince him that what happened to me wasn't faked?"

"What?"

"The video!"

I studied her expression. She made every effort to look supportive.

"You know me, Pres. I trust you completely. But sweetie, no one will *ever* be convinced you had nothing to do with that video anymore than they believe stories about your past lives or that implausible heron story."

I vaulted to my feet. "Ask Kirk! He was there, Mom! He had to have seen everything. I've tried to get Doc to call him, but so far he's refused. I don't understand why you won't ask him. Is it because you two…you know…?"

That's when Antoine burst in the door (again). "Sorry, folks. Time's up."

"But it hasn't been thirty minutes," I said.

"It's all right, hon. I need to run. I'm on my way to Eugene for an OSLA meeting…"

I'm positive the staff monitors visits. If a patient seems to be getting agitated, they end it. Is that how it works? Note to self: During visitations, *do not* become agitated!

P.S. You might recommend Mom get some therapy. This whole ordeal seems to be taking a toll.

July 22nd

Do you think it ironic that *patient* refers not only to someone under medical care but also to the ability to bear provocation, annoyance, misfortune, etc. with fortitude and without complaint or anger? Think about it...

Speaking of patients as opposed to patience: The newest member of Cellblock #9, Fletcher Mortenson, is a piece of work. In case you haven't noticed, he never stops pacing. It's like watching a neurotic rat contemplating whether he should risk death—trying to steal a hunk of cheese from a 30-lb. Maine Coon cat. If he keeps it up, the floor tiles will be grooved like sections of I-5. Plus, he pretends to be constantly "smoking." I've never observed anyone with this level of oral fixation: pencils, rolled up paper tubes, anything cylindrical. (You can imagine what Richie has to say about that!)

Fletcher wears a red and black plaid hunting jacket night and day. The rest of us aren't allowed to have coats, but this is permitted? Is it some kind of security blanket? How much more neurotic could he possibly be without it?

Normally, I'd just ignore him, but, like a demented owl, he watches me, constantly. He looks like he hasn't slept for days, his eyes encircled with dark purplish shadows. I'm not positive, but I think I read somewhere those can be an indication of neurological damage.

Yesterday, he finally spoke. "I know *whooo* you are."

"Who would that be?" I asked—acting nonchalant, but thinking 'this guy is a hoot!'

"You're that actor."

"Oh...*him*. Care to be more specific?"

He eyed me suspiciously. "That guy from *Social Network*."

"You mean Jessie Eisenberg?"

"The one in *Superbad* and the one about the pregnant girl who keeps the baby."

"Oh, that's Michael Cera."

"You *are* him. People are out to get me and they're using you."

"What…? No… My name's Preston Nesbitt."

"I recognize you Michael Eisenberg."

"Cera. Really, I look nothing like him. He's skinny, has brown eyes, no chin and a goofy grin. I'm a summer blond mesomorph with gray eyes, a prominent cleft chin and a winsome smile."

"You use weird words like him. You're *him*. Why can't you leave me alone…? Why does everyone wanna put me in a box?"

"Believe me, I don't want to put you anywhere."

"Yes you d-o-o-o-! You're afraid of my power. Afraid of what I'm capable of. They sent you here to make sure I don't transport myself to *Ouami*."

"Sorry…? I'm not familiar with—"

"My secret place. Where I have supreme powers. Where I can resist evil forces. You're here to spy on me."

"Actually, I'm in here because of a viral video."

"More spy talk. You're recording me now, aren't y-o-o-u?"

Like Owly (or Linda Blair), his head swiveled—searching frantically for hidden cameras.

"You've never heard of a viral video?"

"Stay away from me, Jessie Cera. I'm warning y-o-o-o-o-u! Keep out of my mind."

Clearly, Fletcher's out of his mind, so there would be plenty of room for me. Isn't there a separate ward for the real kooks? Don't say this is it.

* * *

Obviously, Fletcher has some serious mental issues. It would be wise if you would avoid him, at least until he has time to acclimate. He's convinced you're a spy, and your recent conversation really upset him.

Paranoid schizophrenia, right? I think treating him like he's nuts is part of the problem. Isn't it possible that some people actually can pick up on the thoughts of others? Thus, some paranoia may be the result of extra sensory perception. Before you dismiss that idea, remember: society once believed the Earth is flat (and some creationists still do). Fletch needs hugs not *hydroxyzine*.

July 24th

Waited a whole day to record this. I was too rattled to do it yesterday. Why the new method of interrogation? Afraid your usual procrustean *modus operandi* has failed to produce the conformity you desire? Think I'll suddenly admit to my participation in the video if you resort to Gestapo tactics? I would if I could, but what I've told you is the truth.

Recapping yesterday's unsettling Session:

I knew something was up the way you scarcely looked at me, while fiddling with your gold Cross pen—twisting it on and off like a tube of lipstick. Speaking of which, with your medium skin tone, I'd recommend something darker: mauves and berries. Whatever you do, stay away from the bright reds. A burgundy, perhaps? (Sorry, you know how jejune I get when I'm nervous.)

"Let's play a little game, shall we...?"

Those were the last words I was expecting to hear from you.

"I have a feeling I'm not going to like this *divertissement*."

You maintained your blank expression and continued to fondle your...pen.

"Okay, I'm in," I said, with faux enthusiasm.

You stared at me a few moments (to unnerve me?).

"What's the deepest, darkest secret you've never told anyone, Preston? And, if you don't mind, no need to perseverate your numerous masturbation marathons, I believe we've explored that area sufficiently."

"Good word, *perseverate*. I've noticed all you shrinks use it. Are you suggesting I'm too insistent in discussing my copius orgasms? Redundantly recounting my joyous ejaculations! Recalling, with glee, the frequency of sexual release? Sorry, but it appears the practice is inveterate. You know what they say, 'an orgasm a day keeps the doctor away.' Try it daily...multiple times. Hasn't worked so far."

"Let's just focus on something other than you stimulating your genitals for once."

Stimulating my genitals! HA! HA! You were *so* serious I had to laugh. "But, I'm the *champ*. It's a wonder the thing hasn't fallen off, or at least gone on hiatus. What's the record, eight or nine times in a day? I've managed seven and wasn't even fazed. Check that out for me, will ya? Might as well be in the *Guinness Book of Records* for choking the chicken as for the most controversial video. Though I haven't yet reached Gladwell's 10,000 hours, I've easily surpassed 10,000 orgasmos. Guess that makes me a true outlier, as opposed to an *out* liar, wouldn't you say?"

"Preston! I need you to be serious...*please*." (In eight years, you've never before raised your voice. You startled me!)

"*Geesh*, okay. Hmmm...deep dark secrets. How deep...I mean, how serious?"

"Very."

"*Très sérieux*. How 'bout this? When I was eight, while lying on my back between two rows of multi-colored zinnias in the searing July sun, I projected my consciousness into a black Tiger Swallowtail butterfly—viewing the blur of red-orange blossoms through multi-faceted eyes, tasting the petal's fruity aroma with my feet and antennae, and swilling the sweet "drink of the gods" with my probing proboscis. Even after an ear-splitting blast of the fire station's noon whistle jarred me back into my mortal existence, a hint of the saccharine nectar remained on my tongue."

I waited for a response. Nothing. Only more twisting of the pen and a concerted effort to remain calm. I explained that this experience, like so many others, had been received by Suzanne with her customary skeptical response to the metaphysical, an admonition to 'not tell anyone!'

"Whaddya say, Doc? It's been nine years. Has the statute of limitations expired?"

Not sure what I expected, but your expression indicated you weren't impressed with what I consider a fairly remarkable experience. You're rather intractable, you know that? Hoping to change the subject, I chose a new tact: interrogation.

"I'm sensing some cognitive dissonance. You obviously didn't appreciate my *secret d'alcôve*. Is your silence meant to denote displeasure of my story or my rudimentary French? Are you equating the experience with "magical thinking"—assuming I felt out of control as a child…with the divorce and all? Convinced these "stories" are my way of coping with stress…? Well I say, try loosening your grip on your restricted world view. It makes life more enjoyable and may prevent hardening of the arteries."

"The question was…something you've *never* told anyone. And, try something a little less—"

"Shamanistic?"

"Think, reality."

"From the perspective of a true shaman, the physical world is just *one facet* of reality. Believe me, there are others. I'm living proof."

I could see you were purposely taking slow, deep breaths. So patient, so in control. "This time, try focusing on an event that's a little more believable."

"You mean prosaic?"

"*No*, I mean believable. For someone whose intention it is to attend NYU in a few months, your refusal to take these sessions seriously shows a lack of understanding. Remember, our goal here is to have you functioning again in society."

"Ah...so there *is* a goal!"

"That's been the only purpose from the beginning. Please cooperate."

"But, if society's fucked up, and you've got to admit, as the amazing Reggie Watts so poetically put it, it's one big heaping 'Fuck Shit Stack'— helping me function in it doesn't sound all that appealing. Besides, from a professional standpoint, it's hardly *primum non nocere*...do no harm. It's more like, if you can't fix it, drug the sh—"

"Preston!"

"In fact, I'd say it's ethically the opposite of do no harm, it's—"

"Please, Preston!"

"Tell me, what's ethical about medicating—"

"Let's *not* get into that again!"

"Afraid of discussing what is unquestionably the egregious use of drugs in your profession...the pogrom against—"

"Just *answer the fu*... Just...answer the question, please."

Score! Finally, a human being emerges from the primal ooze of professionalism. You dropped part of the "F-bomb!" Way to go Doc! I could feel the web of self-defense mechanisms—surrounding my trust issues—beginning to unravel.

"Sorry. I...I need you to focus."

"Absolutely. Focusing. Need a second. Serious... (Clearing of throat). Uh, how 'bout this... Last March, over Spring Break, while visiting Nana Nesbitt in Glendale, I took a taxi to the Eagle Rock Plaza in Los Angeles. I heard *Glee* was filming there and Ryan Murphy might be on set."

"What...? Who...?"

I so wish I could have taken your picture at that moment. I've never seen you so frustrated.

"Surely you've heard of *Glee*...that really gay show about high school glee clubs? Watching it's like getting an advanced degree in musical theatre and bad acting. Ryan Murphy's the creator."

"No, never heard of it...or him."

"Nip/Tuck...?"

"Possibly that one. Believe my wife watched it."

"Booyakasha! First the F-bomb, now revealing a personal tidbit. Promise you won't beat up on yourself. Self-flagellation's so *outré*."

You stared at me with a look bordering on extreme annoyance, and I could tell you were using every ounce of restraint you possess.

"Okay, settling down... Not sure what it is about Mr. Murphy, but if I close my eyes when I hear him in an interview, I think I'm listening to myself, only a little more mature."

"Go on."

"Along with hundreds of others, I watched while the *Glee* cast was filming a flash mob number."

"...?"

It must be maddening—realizing you know so little about the world you live in.

"A flash mob is a group of people who assemble, via social media, and perform an act, then disperse. It's like Arab Spring but much less geopolitical. Song and dance instead of demonstrations and firing squads. *And*, it usually disperses without teargas or machinegun fire. Kidding. Lighten up."

You furiously jotted something down in your notebook. I hope it said, 'Time to join the 21st century.'

"There were at least six cameras shooting from various angles. If you look closely, you can spot me near the bottom of the escalator, just as Kurt and Rachel step off. It's on YouTube, but in this one, I'm not a featured player. You should check it out. And, while you're there, take a look-see at my video if you haven't."

"Uh huh."

"After an hour of watching them repeat the same dance sequence (the usual Flash Mob spontaneity was lacking), I snuck outside where some of the equipment trailers were parked. You can't believe the number of vehicles required for a location shoot. There were three or four massive eighteen-wheelers filled with lighting rigs and sound gear, six white vans—with a big red *GLEE* painted on the sides—to transport the actors, and a half-dozen make-up and dressing room trailers.

I walked past a couple of security guards who were smoking and kibitzing. They didn't pay much attention, because I acted like I knew what I was doing, as if I were part of the cast. Spotting a trailer with the hand-lettered sign, 'Mr. Murphy/Mr. Falchuk,' I was overcome with curiosity. Without contemplating the potential negative consequence, I gave a quick knock, then a firm yank…and *voilà!* It opened."

At that moment, you looked as if you were about to discover some criminal aspect of my personality. You leaned forward in your executive swivel chair, which, BTW, looks like something out of the Concorde. I've always found the leather upholstery rather ostentatious. It certainly bespeaks the prices you charge. Thank heavens McNabb & Associates has good health insurance. At $15,000 a month, Mom's school insurance would go bust. Even so, I won't be able to stay here forever. NYU starts in September.

As I was saying...

"There wasn't much indication the trailer had been occupied, except for a yellow newsboy hat (one I'd seen Mr. Murphy wear in a recent interview) on the little table by the kitchenette, along with a legal pad and a nylon-tipped pen (fine point, my favorite). Also, I spied an empty Starbucks cup (Grande) on the counter by the sink. This is a little creepy, I admit, but a "thirst for knowledge" led me to pick the cup up and sniff. No Caramel Macchiato or Vanilla Bean concoction, just coffee. I snooped around a minute before deciding to leave a note:

Dear Mr. Murphy (Ryan),

I'm not sure why I find you so fascinating. Perhaps it's your slightly androgynous aura, though you're not really my type. I fantasize about a hirsute Rugby player with the heart of a poet (not you, though the heart of a poet may apply). Still, you have that certain something and a fearlessness I admire.

I'm here visiting my grandmother, but I live in Oregon. Boring! Don't believe me? There's even a town named Boring...Boring, Oregon. It's only about twenty miles away from where I live in Portland. Fishing, hunting, biking, camping...and lots of tartan flannel. Even the Lesbians eschew flannel it's so ubiquitous! To be fair, Oregon's really beautiful. It's just that I prefer more stimulation, creatively that is. That's the primary reason I'm headed for NYU in the fall.

Something really amazing happened to me, Mr. Murphy. You can see it on YouTube: 'Kid vs. Buick—and the winner is…?' It will change the way you view reality. Or, at the very least, give you an idea for a new show. Keep up the good work. Diversity is good, and your aesthetic is right on.

Sincerely,

~Achilles

I sat for a few seconds, satisfied I'd recalled the note word for word. You waited for me to get to the point, until you could wait no longer.

"How exactly does this qualify as a deep dark secret?"

"Promise you won't judge me too harshly?"

"I'm not into judgment. You should know that by now."

"You're not really into trust, either…if you don't mind me saying."

You had that look you get when you're trying to decide if it's worth contradicting me—knowing it can lead to endless digressions.

"The secret…?"

"Oh, all right! I don't know why this is so embarrassing, but I feel a little like Joey sharing his dog flog story. I took Mr. Murphy's cap back into the tiny bathroom and *jizzed* in it. It took like twenty seconds. It was electric thinking the Ryan Murphy could walk in on me, knowing he'd be wearing my DNA to his next meeting with Network bigwigs."

You sighed and made a quick notation. After opening up to you, sighing felt like a psychological head-butt. The notation, as previously noted, was blatantly judg*mental,* syntactically speaking.

Is that sick? Are Joey and I more alike than I care to admit? When I think about it, wanting to help a pathetic animal motivated his act. Mine was about inflicting my sputum on an unsuspecting celebrity. *"Semen Stalking."* If this gets out, it could start a trend.

The scary part is it's someone I actually admire. Or, was that the motivation? Holy crap! Maybe I do need help.

July 25th

I was so disconcerted by yesterday's disclosure I couldn't get it off last night. That's never happened. I spent hours analyzing why I was motivated to spluge in an innocent man's hat. My confessed impropriety somehow short-circuited my joystick.

Though doubting the effectiveness of prayer, *I beseeched that the affliction be temporary. With no other creative outlet, with no other channel for my seeds of creativity, I feared I might dry up or detonate.

* Happy to report the beseeching worked…twice, before breakfast.

July 26th

NEWS ALERT: The alarm to the 2nd floor Emergency Exit is disarmed.

Word has it that Jamarcus and Chelsea have been having booty sex in the stairwell for the past week. Someone, I won't say who, looked through the glass and caught them in *flagrante delicto*.

Jamarcus, whose flagrante is reportedly *très delicto*, saw the spectator and made his own emergency exit. Later, I overheard him talking to Joey.

"We hizzit the skizzins. I be her nigga, she be my bitch. But, no emotions 'cause we focused on a grip."

I have no idea what any of that means. Though clearly misogynistic, it's very rhythmical and I dig the inner-rhyme. If only he'd been given a chance with that hip hop group, maybe a half-dozen buildings would have been spared.

Better reconnect the door alarm, unless hizziting the skizzins is part of their therapy.

*   *   *

This was helpful. Thank you.
No worries. Always got your back.

July 27th

You asked me to elaborate on what being a memory prodigy entails. I assume you mean other than being *sui generis?* First off, I want whoever reads this to know I'm not into memorizing a bunch of digits or the precise order of ten shuffled decks of cards. Becoming "Grand Master of Memory" holds no fascination for me whatsoever, though moonwalking with Einstein sounds like something I might enjoy. (I can only imagine the vacant look in your eyes. Are there any contemporary references that resonate? How Foer back must I go?). Sorry, for the snark, but I'm having a bad year.

Who's to say a GMM can even remember where he/she left the car keys? And, when it comes to relationships, the only mnemonic necessary for recalling the color of a lover's eyes is mindfulness. I'd venture to say people obsessed with repeating a series of numbers aren't particularly good at relating to others, and may not even comprehend the benefit.

Nor is my memory only associated with dates and times. There are those who possess that type of memory, which has more to do with lacking the ability to forget than it does to remember.

What makes Preston Nesbitt a memory prodigy is not only recalling experiences in detail but also reliving the accompanying emotions. It's as if I drank from the river *Mnemosyne, the mythological Greek river—insuring I'd remember *everything* when reincarnated, unlike most souls who choose to drink from the river Lethe, so they won't remember *anything* about their painful past lives. It's all described in the *Myth of Er* at the end of Plato's *Republic*. Blame Mr. Wolff. He assigned it to me as a special side-project sophomore year.

*For your edification: Mnemosyne was the Titaness who shacked up for nine nights with Zeus—creating the Nine Muses. It's believed that poets get their literary powers from their possession of Mnemosyne and with the help of the Muses. Before you shrug your dismissive shrug, know it inspired the likes of Virgil, Catullus, Dante Alighieri, Milton, Shakespeare and Chaucer. If they're crazy, I'm happy to be counted among them.

I swear I even have vivid memories associated with my birth. (I can see it now: head shaking, face in that scrunched up look—signifying 'hopeless.')

The birth memories are only snippets, flashes of sight, blips of sound and intense jabs of physical discomfort. But the infusion of fear imprinted it all in my hippocampus forever. From the agonizing rubber-ride to bright-white shock, filtered through bloody membrane smear, lung-ripping razorblade gulps of frigid air, explosive metallic crashes and jarring polyphonic exclamations—all elevating the level of adrenaline juice jangling my fragile nervous system—the fragmented memory remains.

Still, those fragments were nothing more than random bits of mental confetti 'til my Biology teacher made us watch a video of a woman giving birth. Bet M. Proust never explored memory at this (eye) level. Suddenly, it all came flooding back.

In addition to emotional memory, I have a type of photographic memory. On a test, I can sort through the picture galleries in my mind, until I find the page in the text where the answer resides. With a little effort, I can zoom in and read the **bold** or *italic* type. I'm not particularly proud of that gift, and it in no way indicates intelligence, but it keeps me from actually having to study for an exam.

Also, if I hear an answer, I can dial it back in almost on command, because I remember who said it, what they were wearing and the energetic atmosphere in the room. Still, that's not what I'm referring to Doc. I recall the words because they're associated with a *feeling*. That emotion locks in facts and makes them accessible.

Memory's what makes us human, but that's all changing.

For Nana Nesbitt's generation, who could identify their father's cigarette coughs, like birdcalls, in crowded theaters, churches and auditoriums, today's youth have little facility for remembering or recognizing anything so mundane. If you don't believe me, you should read some of the "What I did on my Summer Vacation" essays. Brain hemorrhage! Forget details. Forget mindfulness. No wonder kids my age think life is boring. To experience life's wonders necessitates being present…in the *now*.

When faced with multiple technologies, many engaging us at the same time, our brains are learning new ways to process information, usually in smaller quantities and in shorter time spans. Attention Deficit Disorder will eventually become the new norm. Admit it, it's already happening.

One's entire life can now fit on a hard-drive, a USB or a memory chip, which will eventually be implanted at birth, along with one of grandpa Ray's GPS transponders. Wanna recall your life? The info's right there at your fingertips, in your neural implant, or you can just Google it.

Having a digital database doesn't require a hippocampus or an amygdala, and it relieves one of having to pay attention. Besides, emotional experiences in "real" life pale compared to the heightened effect of virtual reality. Ever watch gamers in action? Adrenaline levels are off the charts, but most remain seemingly calm and detached so they can kill as many Templars, Orcs and Thugs as possible.

If this continues, eventually humans may cease to register any emotion. Orwell, Huxley and Phillip K. Dick had it nailed. Scanner, extremely dark.

My unique abilities are quickly becoming superfluous. When the mind becomes expendable, what's the point? As ol' Bucky Fuller once said, 'Humanity is acquiring all the right technology for all the wrong reasons.' Not sure I like the idea of being expendable…

July 28th

I'm so excited! Patient admissions are beginning to make things not only interesting but also bearable.

Enter Eloni "Sparkle" Matafeo…a 6'6" Samoan transgendered female! Born Mikaele Matafeo into a ginormous, both in size and quantity, Samoan family, Sparkle, now fifteen, says "Ain't *never* felt like a boy."

I can only imagine how painful this transformation has been, though in olden times, before Christian missionaries proclaimed the ancient healing powers of *Huna* to be "satanic," the tribe would've proclaimed her a "magical being" and regarded her with reverence.

Not the case here in the Pacific Northwest, where Eloni and her family have been at war with a group of Tongans for more than two generations. She says the beginning of the conflict dates back a wee bit further, about twenty-five generations, when the Tongans were finally "evicted" from Samoa. ("Kicked those loose ass pussies out!") Her speech is as colorful as her outfits.

"Me and my bros always gettin' in fights with them horsefuckers! Last week at Church's (Fried Chicken), I got jumped again, for like the fifth time. Ten or twelve of 'em. Good thing some of my outrigga niggas come along to get my back. I knock out three or four of their womens and put a hurt on a couple of big Ching Chong Boongs!"

Though Sparkle's been in trouble with the law for fighting and impersonating a female ("Not like solicitin,' just mindin' my own"), she's here because she tried to chop off her manhood and nearly bled to death. She didn't hesitate to go into the details, which I will spare you.

"Hate tuckin' my junk. But, surgery costs like hella much! Twenty large, maybe more. Second time I tried to get rid of that *thing*. First time, I was like twelve and my big bro stopped me. Bein' stuck in the wrong body's like bein' in jail. Sparkle needs to be free."

Though emphatic, her voice is soft and high-pitched. In spite of her bulk, she's extremely feminine. She looked me up and down, then planted her hand on her hip—elbow jutting out in 'I'm a little teapot' fashion. Cocking her head to one side, she announced, "Say, you kinda cute. Gotta girlfriend?" Sparkle has a honeyed complexion and a charming smile, with dimples like giant commas. And, though it's hard to be demur when you stand eye-to-eye with Kobe Bryant, she almost pulls it off. However, her Size-14 pink gators are rather inelegant.

Assign her to our Group. She can be "Chieftess" to my "McMurphy."

Can't wait to see what she does the first time little Richie Rich spouts off. Please, oh *please* let him bitch about her getting to stay on the girl's ward.

July 30th

Doc, you make everything sound so ominous. Actually, I welcome the opportunity to have an EEG. Perhaps once you get a good gander at my brain waves, you'll start believing some of my "outlandish" stories. You did use that very word to describe my heron tale, admit it.

I'm no expert when it comes to electroencephalograms, but I'm willing to bet you discover—unless I'm particularly teed off about something—my brain waves oscillate in the four to six hertz range.

You, on the other hand, only pretend to be calm, but you're a *Beta* man all the way. It's like a "tell" in poker; your jaw tightens ever so slightly when you're trying to concentrate and appear logical.

My calculation may be slightly off, but I'd say your Beta waves are cycling close to 30 times a second. *Quelle fatigue!* Bet you crash—dirty martini in hand—the minute you get home.

I've never spent any significant time meditating, but due to the paranormal phenomena and Out-Of-Body Experiences I've had—plus, what can only be described as shamanic episodes—I'd say my brain waves are transitioning around five or six times a second. That would indicate I'm living a significant portion of my waking hours in a *Theta* state. No need for mantras, candles and incense, it's like perpetual meditation without all the hoopla!

So, go ahead. Hook up those electrodes. However, don't be surprised if my prefrontal cortex lights up like the Perseids meteor shower on a moonless night in the Alvord Desert. Biofeedback...? Bring it on.

July 31st

Last night, I slipped into your office, via keys carelessly left lying around (where and by whom I ain't sayin'). Not looking to get anyone fired, but I didn't want you to think I jimmied the door. I prefer "having access" to "breaking and entering."

Why, you ask? My curiosity about Richie Caytes overwhelmed my sense of propriety or something like that. Blame it on an unfathomable need to understand my fellow inmates, an innate desire to assist in their recovery, or the resultant passive-aggressive feelings over your refusal to let me live my post-YouTube life away from the confines of The Healing Place.

Besides, the faster Richie's "cured," the sooner he's outta here. If I could, I'd employ the healing power of love. But, in this case, the one most in need is the most unlovable and the least deserving. (Ain't it always the way?)

Whatever the reason, I found myself rifling through your case files before I discovered his sitting atop your desk, in plain sight, as if you'd left it for me all along. *Dank, alter Sport.*

From the heft, it's apparent the lad's had a long history of battling authority. This kid's been a demon-child for more than a decade. Had I the time, I would've loved to have read through myriad police reports and innumerable court records, but instead I concentrated on notes from your private sessions.

It appears you're in the throes of trying to discover the cause of his animal abuse. I noted you underlined the word "power" numerous times. True, most animal abusers are seeking to feel powerful. As of yet, however, you've failed to unearth the root cause. May I suggest you spend more time on his relationship with Mommy Dearest?

Melissa Ann (Spencer) Arlington Benson Caytes is a very successful businesswoman, though apparently not as fortunate in the business of matrimony; it appears she's attempting to marry her way through the alphabet. (Okay. I rearranged the order a tad...for effect).

According to Richie, she's also sorely lacking in the Motherhood department. From what I gather, while Mrs. ABC was out transforming her modest little real estate company into a mega-firm (Caytes Realty, Inc.) by various and sundry tactics, she wasn't around much, and little Richie felt abandoned. Also, I suspect her addiction to Valium, probably added to some *in utero* problems that helped turn him into the terror he quickly became. (She carries a big prescription bottle in her purse, which Juma dutifully removes before allowing her to meet with Satan's Spawn.)

Sounds like a classic case of RAD, Reactive Attachment Disorder. Richie has the majority of characteristics: short temper, hostility, animal cruelty, manipulative, whining and scheming, impulsivity and pre-occupation with wickedness. If you want to know who defecated in Joey's bed, there's no need for DNA analysis. Yep, good guess.

Mrs. Caytes personifies every cliché of first generation money. She drives a $300,000 sports car, wears enough gold jewelry to sink a cruise ship, and if diamonds are a girl's best friend, she's got humongous BFFs on nearly every finger. I won't even get into what's she had suctioned, tucked, nipped, lifted, implanted, replaced, peeled, dermabrased, reduced, removed, resurfaced and lasered, but her forced smile is sardonic and horrifying. She comes strutting in here like she owns the place, but by the time Richie's reduced her to quivering mass of super-woman guilt, it's hard not to pity her just a wee bit.

You weren't around when she visited last Saturday, and I doubt Juma wrote up the incident; composition doesn't appear to be his strong suit. But, here's what I observed and overheard. This will go down better with background music. May I recommend Pink Floyd's "Dark Side of the Moon?"

"I know I'm a *terrible* mother, but everything I've accomplished I did so you and your sisters could have the things I didn't. I'm sorry I missed out on so much of your childhood. It was hard for me, too. Believe me, it wasn't easy trying to raise the three of you alone."

"*Alone*...bullshit! How 'bout the dozens of sitters and housekeepers you left me with?"

"I admit I've made mistakes."

"Like marrying my stepfather? Know how many times I caught that bastard beatin' off to porn in front of the Big Screen TV? He's porked half the receptionists, personal assistants and agents who ever worked for you...while you were out blowing potential clients to increase sales."

"*Please*, not that again... I'm not perfect. I promise to do better. I wish you'd had more parenting. But, all this acting out doesn't make it any easier. What do you want me to do, Richie? You're my son. I love you. Your family loves you. Grandma Spencer says, 'Tell that boy we love him...no matter what he's done.' Well, please say something."

I waited for him to declare what a miserable *biaatch* she is, an epithet he's anointed her with anytime she visits. Instead, there was silence. Then, about ten seconds later, I heard her scream, "No, Richie! What are you doing? For God's sake! Don't! Please stop!"

I peered around the corner to see what was happening. He'd dropped his trau and was bent over—mooning the hysterical woman, two inches from her face. Juma was trying to pull him away, but with little success.

I think you can add "improper sexual conduct" to that list. And, if it's not too RAD, might I suggest reassigning him to another Group or "elevating" him to the third floor psycho ward where he belongs.

* * *

Preston, there's no excuse for eavesdropping on the visitation of another patient. You know how upset you'd be if someone did that to you. As for breaking into my office and reading private files, this is a violation without justification. We will be addressing all of this in future sessions.

I'm a very naughty boy.

August 1st

Keeping me in the isolation room all morning was an over-reaction to my helping pinpoint Richie's psychological problems. If that's the way it's going to be, from now on, you're on your own.

P.S. Nearly 700,000,000 views on my video so far. Am I correct in assuming not one belongs to you?

* * *

Please do not use the computers. They're off base. And, do not encourage the staff to help you in this endeavor.

This is like denying an incubator to a preemie. I've had access to a computer since birth. Unlike Richie, I'm not trolling the Internet for porn. Be reasonable.

August 2nd

Steven, in spite of his 'crazy-ass schedule,' deigned to honor me with his presence this morning. I've been here for three months, and this is only his third visit. The others lasted a grand total of twenty minutes. This one was even shorter. The crux of the drop-by was to inform me he's up for full partner at McNabb & Associates. Oh, and he thought I might like to know I'm going to have a stepbrother. That's right. Ol' Steven's knocked up his girlfriend and she wants to keep it.

"You'd think by now I'd know how that works," he said (wink wink).

"Just remember, Pres, no glove, no love. A lifetime of regret comes along with a few minutes of pleasure."

Am I being too sensitive when I assume he's referring to Suzanne and me? And, have I mentioned how some homilies make me homicidal? J/K. No need to add that to my growing pathology.

They've already chosen a name: Ramayya Bekele Mengesha Nesbitt. Did I mention Makeda's Ethiopian? To ensure young Ramayya won't stick out during roll call, Steven says they're calling him Ray, a somewhat origamied version of his given name and his deceased grandfather's.

Makeda's only twenty-three, just seven years older than I am. She graduated from Portland State in Communication Studies. He showed me her picture. To my knowledge, he's never carried a picture of Mom or me in his billfold *ever*. I admit she's gorgeous. For some inexplicable reason, this majestic beauty wants to hook up with my Dad. Surely she knows he's rarely home and likely to cheat on her the first chance he gets. Probably already has. I asked if he intends to get married, and he said (get ready for it), "Got the milk for free. Kidding! Who knows? Gotta run. Big client lunch at Paley's Place. Makeda has me eating organic and sustainable. Not sure their wagyu beef tartare qualifies."

He stuck out his hand, as if he'd just closed a deal. I refused to shake it. "Take care, buddy. Wanted to keep you in the loop about your future sibling and my big corporate score. Please *don't* tell your mother. Just between us, okay?"

I'd like to request Steven be permanently removed from the approved Visitor's List.

August 3rd

AUSTIN GARY

Letter To Deadbeat Dad

Steve,

Wish I could say I enjoyed your last visit, where you stayed just long enough to drop the "bomb"...existing before it lay waste to everything. You're good at that by the way, not sticking around long enough to see the concussive effects of your casual pronouncements and cavalier infidelities.

Speaking of speedy exits, I'm still pissed you turned Scottie into a fur pancake-with-ears the day you left Mom and me. You'll never convince me you didn't do it on purpose.

As for your big news… Did you really expect me to be happy about your pregnant galfriend? If I thought you'd actually found "love," I might be; however, you've proven you're incapable of opening your heart wide enough to let anyone in for fear of being hurt…again.

Your sporadic attempts at Fatherhood suck. Maybe gramps didn't stick around long enough to show you how it's done, but chances are he didn't know either; probably couldn't bring himself to say, 'I love you, Stevie.' Guess that's why you're a walking wound.

Leaving Mom and me, you'll never know what you've missed, and how our love might have made a difference. You can keep searching, but you'll never find anyone better than Suzanne Allison Preston, who was a S.A.P. for thinking you were more of a person than you've turned out to be.

FYI, I'm sick of being triangularized every time you ask me not to say anything to her. <u>I'm telling her everything</u>! She deserves to know about Makeda and your off-spring (at least the ones you acknowledge). Also, stop asking me to spy on her. If she chooses to hump Mr. Wolff or the entire faculty, more power to her. Why shouldn't she have a life? You certainly never sacrificed any extra-curricular gratification when you were married, and you've been notching your belt in steady fashion ever since you abandoned us for Sheila, Cynthia, Mitzi, Desiree, Ben Harrison's mother and God only knows how many others.

Consider the trail of destruction you've left behind. Then, take a little responsibility for fixing your shit. Please!

Yes, I'm angry, but I'm even more disappointed by what a pathetic parent you were and continue to be. Do you think making 'full partner' squares anything? You've always used your job as an excuse for missing out on my life. "I'm doing this for you, Pres." No, Steven, you took advantage of your job to anesthetize your feelings and to avoid being a part of our lives. <u>You did it all for you</u>.

Ironically, even with your new position and increased salary, you'll still kvetch every time you send a support check. You may want to forego the tartare and opt for the soup du jour at Paley's Place, or better yet, start lunching at Fat City, because even with scholarships, NYU will cost you more than if I'd stayed with Nana and gone to Stanford.

Four and half more years and you'll have met your filial financial obligations. Maybe you can convince "Ray" to attend ITT or Glendale CC. BTW, hope you're planning to tell Nana about your newly acquired family; JSUK, when she calls next Sunday, I'm filling her in on the latest.

Don't know why I bothered to write. This is clearly a FWOT!

~P

P.S. Requested you be removed from my approved visitor's list. No need to make excuses for your "abbreviated" visits. We're done.

P.P.S. Never needed you to validate me, but that doesn't remove the albatross from around your neck for failing to try. Bad parenting's one thing, but being a hopeless cliché is another. S2BU!

August 6th

Terrible weekend—stewing over Steven's latest attempt to make life miserable. Woke up this morning with a fever. Reza took my temperature. 101.8. Burning up. Think my anger's trying to tell me something? No Group for me today. Miss me...?

August 7th

The Jefferson twins are gone. Apparently my discovery of *idioglossia* helped explain their incomprehensible speech. It's been a long time since I've felt useful to anyone. Thanks for the props Doc. Unfortunately, the positive vibe didn't last very long.

Normally, I wouldn't have accused Richie of being a "closet case" in front of the entire group, but his homophobic vitriol has gotten way out of control. He's accused every male here of being a "fag," even Antoine. (Just so you know, Caesar didn't seem all that offended.)

Yesterday, Richie caught Ciera and me lip-locked. It was a rather innocent moment. I'd been encouraging her to try and forget some of the horrible things her mother said to her in the past—hoping to eliminate some of her "not good enough" feelings. The next thing I knew, we were kissing. That girl has the softest lips! I told her that if kissing's ever added to the Olympics, she'll be a medal contender.

Interestingly, she admitted that she and her best friend, April, had put in some extensive practice-time all through junior high. Doc, I think it's likely that April's move with her family to Seattle last year helped flip the switch on Ciera's depression. You may want to explore that further.

Anyway, Richie happened by at that precise moment, and felt the need to open his toxic mouth.

"Swapping saliva with a faggot? Poor Ciera. Maybe you should slit your wrists now before you die of AIDs." Before either of us could respond, he disappeared around the corner.

Considering how many "queer" slurs he slung since he's been here, I don't think it's a stretch to imagine little Richie's homophobia is a result of his own repressed feelings. His speech is peppered with oral and anal sex references. 'You got a purty mouth.' 'Caught you lookin' at my ass again.' 'I'll make you my anal slave.' 'Your lips didn't get that way from suckin' doorknobs.' Every time he sees Joey, he grabs him and pretends to hunch his leg like a dog in heat. (Irony abounds). His obvious self-loathing is projected on every male here. So, I let him have it. My accusation seemed to register, wouldn't you agree? You'd have thought he'd been scalded the way he vaulted to his feet.

"Listen, fudge-packer. Better close your cum-guzzling mouth before I shut it for you!"

Ciera covered her ears and ran from the room. Misty LOL'd. By the look on Joey's face, I could tell he was relieved I was taking the verbal abuse instead of him. Chelsea just sat and stared, as if she weren't really present. You might want to check her stash of *Effexor*. She pops 'em like breath mints.

So, that's why I outed him in Group.

Getting right in your face, he demanded, "Gonna let the *queerling* get away with that?"

For once it would have been nice for you to take sides. Instead, predictably, you had him removed.

The *queerling!* HA! HA! I dig it! That deserves a title change for this, my modest memoir. Marjorie Kinnan Rawlings, *mea culpa, mea culpa, mea maxima culpa!*

August 8th

It's becoming increasingly clear you have no intention of releasing me. My own mother refuses to help. Are you hoping to wear me down, break me? No wonder long-term patients become lifers. Just like the "lonely madness" of solitary confinement, this system is designed to turn me into the very thing you've always believed me to be.

Shame on you!

August 9th

I'm a wee bit depressed. You'd be disheartened, too, if you were being held against your will and it spite of your earnest attempts to cooperate. You're convinced I'm not sane enough to function in this dysfunctional world. That's pretty depressing, wouldn't you say?

Even so, there's no need to prescribe a serotonin reuptake inhibitor.

Celexa, Paxil, Luvox, Lexapro, Cipralex or *Prozac* are overkill for a justifiable chemical reaction to…okay, I'll say it: imprisonment!

August 10th

Several years ago, Mr. Wolff took me to see *Richard II* at the Oregon Shakespeare Festival. Though the play's not a favorite, nor one of Shakespeare's greatest, I relate to the title character, portrayed as both mercurial and self-indulgent.

Tonight, I'm feeling a little like Richard, once a King with great freedom, now a Pale Ghost of my former self, imprisoned and facing my eminent demise. I can question why I'm here and argue why I shouldn't be, but now I see all such rationalizations as false flatterers—serving no purpose. *For what I speak, my body shall make good upon this earth.*

I've painted myself variously as a genius, an elitist, a judgmental schmuck and a solipsistic little jerk. To the two former descriptions, I've tried to add a *soupçon* of self-deprecation, an attempt to soften the "wise child" image. I can't deny my brilliance, but I can try to balance it by including my very human idiosyncrasies. If you really thought my abundant references to whacking off were done without complete awareness, you've been *P.W.N.'d!* Not everything's pathological, but often the thing that keeps us from losing our minds is scatological. (Not playing with my poo Doc. I'm referring to a type of humor. You remember humor, don't you…? Along with irony, it's all that gets some of us through.)

With the cult forming around my YouTube video, I'm trying to show I'm just one of the guys, down to earth, a regular chap. I'm not looking for followers or even admirers. The more I reveal my humanness, the less likely a queue will form. Would Christians still follow Christ if they could have smelled his feet? Would status-seekers, who spend multi-millions acquiring a Van Gogh, dare to invite that scruffy looking bastard into the mudroom of their McMansions—were he still kickin'? Doubtful!

Though I'm far from perfect, I do have some redeemable qualities. I'm hoping my attempt to help others will strike you as sincere, which it is for the most part. Is anything ever done without a small amount of self-seeking praise? The fireman, who acts on impulse to save someone, could be said to do so without forethought, but the forethought came with the choice of profession. The martyr for any cause chose to champion a cause—risking the dire consequence. That doesn't diminish the nobility of the choice, but it may reveal a premeditated wish to die a lauded death.

I suppose one could make the case for the ordinary man or woman who drowns while trying to save a loved one. But, who among us hasn't imagined what he'd do if ever confronted with the opportunity for self-sacrifice, particularly involving one's own DNA? (Steven would be wise to never test that theory.) Does anticipation trump the heroism of doing the right thing?

Therefore, be forewarned. This is my blatant attempt to curry favor. Though I cherish our togetherness, the grains of sand are rapidly forming the capstone on the pyramid of time. *How long shall I be (a) patient? Ah. How long?*

The trouble with using examples of kindness as a character reference is that it reduces my genuine desire of being helpful to mere solipsism. Caring becomes another self-serving act, generosity of spirit vanishes. Compassion and kindheartedness is cheapened when dissected. In spite of my criticism of the mass of humanity, I do care about individuals. However, my altruism is about genuine concern not eleemosynary. (I just love that word, which means: given as an act of charity.)

I could go into great detail about my attempts to raise Ciera's self-esteem, and I did so without thinking about racking up Brownie points. When I see how she's carved misery into her flesh, I want to go all Leviticus 19:28 on her ass. It truly pains me, in a non-co-dependent way, as one who knows how to transmute pain into humor, albeit black humor. Ciera, bless her, cannot find a scintilla of humor or irony in any aspect of her life. Therefore, I don't hold out a lot of hope for her survival. Still, I try. It is my impious attempt to provide balm in Gilead. Do not interpret that to mean I'm giving myself the power of salvation, since I'm apparently unable to save even myself.

I've already mentioned assisting Misty, but I haven't told you about the effect my talks with Fletcher have had on his paranoia. Have you noticed how he's stopped pacing? He no longer believes me to be a Hollywood actor, and he rarely wears that tacky hunting jacket. I enlisted Ciera, and between the two of us, I think we've helped raise his level of trust. Considering how nearly everyone in his life has abandoned him, he hasn't had much reason to trust anyone. I wouldn't say he's cured, but now, at least, he could hang out at the mall without mothers of small children reporting him to Security.

I'm aware I come off as an egotistic little twerp, but I'm not a bad person. In all the years we known each other, I've never mentioned that Mom and I deliver boxes of groceries to inner-city poor families every Christmas, even though we both think the Holiday is a hoo-dious blot on the memory of Christ, a disgusting celebration of Mammon, consumerism run amok...? (I could go on...for days.) Likewise, I gave every penny I earned last summer—as a reading tutor at Multnomah County Library—to *Save Darfur*. Normally, I don't believe in mentioning acts of charity, but I need you to better understand me.

I feel a great deal of compassion for Joey. Do you know his back story? What a survivor. Make sure he tells you about being left alone for nearly two weeks when he was only six. Little food and a trailer full of rodents. When he tried to go outside, he barely escaped an attack by a neighbor's pitbull. (You'd think he wouldn't be as fond of canines. But, he came to realize it had been abused by its owner and, as a result, it may have been the recipient of that controversial hand-job.)

I've come to his defense in Group on many occasions. I don't do it to impress you, but because I see a simple soul, who believes he's doing the right thing. Please tell me how beating off a dog makes him a threat to society? His heart's in the right place even if his hand wasn't.

My point is...though the residents of The Healing Place are not people with whom I would normally associate, I'm making the effort. I'm trying to see the good in everyone...even Richie, although the futility of that search rivals those for the Holy Grail.

It's said others hold up a mirror to us—revealing judgments against ourselves. What disgusts me in you is what I find distasteful in myself. What terrifies me about someone's violent behavior is what I fear lies hidden in my own potential for violence. If we're evolving towards something more akin to our true nature, which I believe is Love, then all such judgments must cease, especially those against the self. I'm not there yet. Not even close. Getting caught up in the illusion that I'm separate from God keeps me stuck. This being human business is hard. But, *look, what I speak, my life shall prove it true.*

Blessed are the peacemakers, for they will be called sons and daughters of God. Rather small compensation for ending up nailed to a cross or with an assassin's bullet. Oh, what tragic fate doth my future hold?

Methinks I am a prophet new inspired!

August 13th

Reread what I wrote Friday. It's mindboggling—realizing I have almost no control over didacticism. I start out trying to show I'm an okay person and end up lecturing. The thing is…I don't realize I'm doing it while I'm doing it. That "professorial" B.S. is undoubtedly an aspect of my Asperger's, my *Achilles heel*. Can't tell you how many friends it's cost me.

I'm as bad as the new kid, Adam, the one with Tourette's. His nervous tics are nothing compared to his verbal outbursts. The juxtaposition of his angelic face and his X-rated ejaculations is as freaky as the T.V. commercials that feature babies with adult voices.

This morning, I heard Miss Vines ask Adam to accompany her to Dr. Boullac's office. He's very compliant. Ever so polite, he said, "Yes ma'am." Then, something like, *"ratshittyassfuckpisscuntscrew"* came spewing out of his mouth. Miss Vines was horrified. Now she refuses to have anything to do with him. I heard her tell Reza he's "possessed."

As for my own form of Tourette's, any non-pharmaceutical remedies…? Got it! Whenever I start ranting, especially in Group, tug on your earlobe, and I'll try to apply the brakes.

I'm so glad we had this time together.

August 14th

When you dropped your notepad today, I couldn't help noticing that you'd traced and retraced the phrase, "active but odd"—indicating extreme boredom, mindless doodling, or your genuine assessment of me. Is this how the game's played? You require me to write about my thoughts and experiences merely so you can assign judgment, which you deny doing? And, after all this time, the best you can do is: "Active but Odd?"

Do you honestly believe I can't pick up clues on another's emotions? It's one of my special skills. You find my stories hyperbolic and incredible, yet dull and tiring? Funny, but you seem riveted to my every word. Obviously, I can blather on endlessly about any number of subjects, but I'm sensitive enough that when I see someone's eyes glaze over, I can bring it to a halt, though apparently not fast enough for you. You've had your fun, now it's my turn, Old Socks.

Mini-Analysis: Dr. Thomas van Ittersum

I find you "rigid and unimaginative" (try visualizing those adjectives circled again and again). You made up your obdurate mind about me months, perhaps even years ago: 'Preston's delusional, as demonstrated by the weird, shape-shifting stories of his youth. And, after eight years of therapy, he's gotten worse. He actually believes that freaky YouTube video to be reality.'

Yes, I do! Because I was apparently there and, though I may have forgotten what happened, as Mr. Wolff seems to have done, the video captured the fantastical event and nearly a billion have viewed it: roughly the population of North, Central and South America combined.

Have you even bothered to read some of the <u>one million comments</u>? I'm not talking about the haters, the impotent wannabes and the self-congratulatory snarks who derive power from trolling the internet in anonymity. I'm referring to the thousands of people who say something similar happened to them, and it took seeing the video to *re-member*…to reassemble the "forgotten" dream-like fragments and bring them into consciousness.

Why do you think it is that people don't consciously remember something so amazing? It's because none of us is supposed to remember. Once the accident occurs, the veil of forgetting descends *post haste*. Destiny connotes a plan. Free Will says, 'Really? Time for a detour.' Perhaps it's a necessity, like the illusion of time, to keep us from going insane.

Dr. Thomas van Ittersum, PhD. You hide behind the gold foil-embossed certificates you so proudly display, impressive documents—indicating time and money spent—yet proving nothing about your ability to heal, empathize, or even comprehend.

Granted, if someone comes to you, totally out of control, threatening to kill him/herself or someone else, medication can quell such destructive behavior. Yet, what satisfaction can be derived from drugging someone so heavily he can barely move, let alone jump out the window? You and I both know that without healing the wounded child within, it's all rather futile, unless you're one of the pharma-glomerates—pocketing billions—with no regard for the psychic damage inflicted upon the vulnerable.

Doc, is that why you're so walled off, to protect yourself from the knowledge you're part of an industry that yearly anaesthetizes millions? Or, do the few—who appear to improve under your care—justify the dozens who leave here no better, sometimes worse, and occasionally bereft…of life! Want to do something beneficial? Stop aiding parents in committing filicide. Please help:

END THE DRUG WAR ON CHILDREN!

August 15th

You're angry. Got to ya, didn't I…? Tough Noogies. May I give you some of your own advice for how to relieve anger? Try the punching bag, the foam-rubber baseball bat or the padded walls in the Q. R.

Knock yourself out!

August 16th

Suzanne called to say Steve's been arrested for failing to stop at a DUI Check Point. When finally apprehended by the Oregon State police—following a high-speed pursuit down I-5—his blood alcohol registered .18, more than double the legal limit.

This is his second offense and his license has been automatically revoked for a year. In addition, attempting to elude the police is a 3rd degree felony. Now he's facing possible jail time and a $5,000 fine, plus suspension of his license for another 1-5 years. His partnership with McNabb & Associates is "on hold."

He called Mom to bail him out...of course! At first, he wasn't going to tell her what was wrong, but then he opened up and a torrent of pent-up effluvia came pouring out. Seems Makeda decided to abort Ray, and she's returned to Addis Ababa to work for ETV2, the capital's main television station. He also discovered that in the past month alone, she helped him keep his Centurion Card by racking up nearly $75,000—shipping "gifts" to relatives back in Ethiopia.

Mom says she's never seen him so depressed, and worries he might do something rash. I neglected to tell her about my hateful letter and how it probably added to his mental anguish. After everything he's done, I still feel sorry for him. And, yes, in case you're wondering, I feel some guilt.

Be glad I don't suffer from the same disorder as Ciera, or I'd carve myself up like a Thanksgiving turkey.

August 19th

Mom left a message. Dad's court date is October 17th. He's hired Logan & Logan, Attorneys-at-Law, to defend him. One of the partners was a former state prosecuting attorney—specializing in DUI misdemeanor and felony cases. Hoping to influence the sentencing, he's agreed to enter a treatment program. Con man to the end.

Next to my dysfunctional Dad, I'm looking better, right?

August 20th

Couldn't sleep. Worried about Dad—fearing he might do something stupid like his father did. Admittedly, I've portrayed him in the worst possible light, not that he's undeserving. Still, he is my Father, and right about now he needs someone to cut him a little slack. Who'd a thought it would be me? Here's the letter I now wish I'd written, but one that, unsent, comes a little too late.

> Dear Dad,
>
> I have many memories of you from a very early age. When I was eleven months old, I was in my temporary crib in the living room of our condo on 11th Avenue, the one we lived in for two years before moving into our house. I know it was Christmas because I was able to reach out and touch the tree. I remember crawling around on the floor earlier that morning—boxes and wrapping paper strewn everywhere.
>
> You were sitting in your favorite chair watching T.V. Mom and Nana were in the dining room—setting the table. This would not normally be a memory of much significance, except I was able to grab

hold of a pine branch and pull it hard enough that the enormous tree toppled over onto my crib. Suzanne, who insisted upon authenticity, had covered it with ornamental vintage spun glass Angel Hair. When she heard the tree fall, she looked up and screamed, "Steven, the baby! He'll be cut to shreds!"

You rushed over and carefully lifted the tree off me. Mom did a quick physical exam and pronounced me unharmed. Nana said something to Mom that upset her, and it was a long time before she was invited to spend the Christmas holidays with us again.

The rest of the afternoon you held me, gently patting my back and softly kissing me on the forehead. The memory's not a long sustained "movie," but isolated moments reflecting genuine emotion. It's one of my favorites.

Another revolves around you trying to teach me to ride my bicycle without training wheels. "I learned when I was five," you said, "And, I didn't have *anyone* to help me."

Not to be outdone, I took off down the driveway—pedaling like a madman—heading toward the street. I was so focused on not tipping over that I failed to check for on-coming cars. Suddenly, you spotted the Anderson's van speeding our way.

"Stop, Preston! Hit the brakes!"

Confused, I lost control and crashed into the curbside mailbox—cutting a deep gash in my forearm. When you saw blood gushing, you panicked and rushed me to the Emergency Room at Providence St. Vincent Medical Center, even though we weren't Catholic or religious.

While the doctor closed the laceration with twelve stitches, you held my hand and stroked my head and kept repeating how "sorry" you were. Later, you admitted that since you'd had some time to think about it, you might have been six before you learned to ride your bike.

That was also the last time you ever kissed me.

Your father killed himself. It became the toxic secret no one wanted to discuss. As hard as that was to process, you must have realized <u>he didn't do it because of you</u>. His loss left you feeling empty and abandoned. Mom and I tried hard, but we couldn't fill that hole. Neither could sex or booze.

Dad, I know what abandonment feels like. You somehow slipped away, too...right when I needed you most. A year or two before you and Mom divorced, you were already gone. "Business," you called it. It felt like abandonment to me. Even when you were home, you weren't really there. And, though I'm pretty good at processing the "why and wherefore" of things, it sort of felt like I wasn't important enough for your time. I've been pretty angry about it ever since.

Some of my earlier acting out (like torching Miss Dawson's effigy), had a lot to do with how pissed I was at you and your inability to stay connected. That episode got your attention, temporarily.

Then again, you seemed genuinely concerned when I was court-ordered into treatment; however, your level of involvement soon waned, and compared to the effort you put into your job and your pursuit of immediate gratification, it was minimal at best.

I remember the last time I said 'I love you.' It was right before my 9th birthday. You'd packed up your things and were walking out the door.

"Dad wait! Why are you going? Do you have to?"

"Fraid so, buddy," you said—giving my shoulder a quick squeeze. You started away.

"Please don't go. I promise I'll be more like other kids! I will, you'll see. Come back... *I love you!*"

I waited for you to say it back, but instead you turned and

mumbled, "You bet. Take good care of your Mom. I'm counting on you."

For a long time, I thought all those stupid things like: *If* I hadn't insisted we take that vacation in the Rockies...or, *if* I hadn't blown up the antique stove...or, *if* it hadn't cost you $28,500 to replace Miss Dawson's garage and her stupid car, you wouldn't have left, or you might have returned. Even then, I knew those weren't the reasons, but that didn't stop me from trying to accept the blame.

I obsessed over the entire list of things that might have made you go: having to cope with my Asperger's; my smart aleck mouth; using my memory of who did what to whom and what was said as a weapon; enduring my referential tendencies; being assaulted by my "war of words" and my need to constantly "teach and preach," (your term); calling you Steve instead of Dad; loving Mom more than you...and being inundated with all my queer ideas and odd behavior. I know you don't understand me. Although you never say it or act like it, I do know you love me. And, you're proud I'm intelligent and have a bright future.

You're smart in your own way, too. You could probably have had a great career as an engineer like your father, had you not switched to a business major. I imagine you sub-consciously chose advertising as a profession because of that story about your dad meeting Terry Gilliam, who was in advertising at the time, your way of connecting with the father you barely knew...?

I appreciate how successful you've been in business, even though I think advertising is kind of evil and responsible for our consumer culture and people's need to constantly buy more worthless ~~shit~~ stuff. Sorry. You're good at it, and that's something. I'll never forget the time you wrote an ad for that discount furniture store and there were over twelve hundred people lined up before the doors even opened. Some of the slogans you came up with were kind of clever. Who else but you could sell a jingle to a funeral home?

I'm sorry about Makeda and Ray, too. I know you're up to your eyebrows in excrement right now, but remember, "This too shall pass."

There's more, but it's late and I need to get some rest. I just want to say I LOVE YOU, Dad. Mom still loves you, too. Please get better. Please!

Your son,

~Preston W. Nesbitt

* * *

Great letter, Preston. Let me encourage you to share it with your father.

August 22nd

Fine. You have my permission to scan the letter and send it to Steven. See, I'm cooperating every way I know how. I think it's only fair you tell me when I'm getting out. I should visit Dad, and I have a lot of things to get ready before I take off for the Big Apple.

I've been thinking about it; I'm willing to continue therapy through NYU's mental health clinic…whatever you want. If you don't believe me, I'll put it in writing. Just did.

September 16th

Almost a month since my last entry.

Cooperating didn't help, so why expect me to write in this <u>fucking journal</u>?

I can't believe you refused to release me in time to start college! Do you have any idea how many people applied to NYU? Over 41,000 freshmen! Only 2000 of us got accepted. That's 4.878%. How do you feel about my chance for future enrollment once they discover where I've been hanging out the past five months?

Some of my tuition, the part not covered by scholarship, and all the fees for the fall semester will *not* be refunded. I'll let you take that up with Steven, once he gets out of rehab.

If I thought self-immolation would help you understand how desperately I need freedom, I'd set myself on fire or have Jamarcus do it. But, of course, that would indicate suicidal inclinations and prolong my stay.

I feel like an pawn in a chess game, but to what purpose? Sacrificing my sanity for your personal enjoyment? You hold a position of power by virtue of what exactly…your unique insight; your ability to sit for hours like a stoic Buddha—listening but not hearing; your unassailable position on the psychological chessboard? You know what they say: at the end of the game, the King and the Pawn both go into the same box.

Apparently, I'm expendable. Why is that, exactly? Because I'm at your mercy and easily replaced by the next patient/victim; because, unlike most of the medicated, I will not supplicate His Majesty to gain favor; or, the real reason: because I'm the unwitting star of a video that defies comprehension?

Your refusal to say what I need to do to regain my freedom is cruel and bordering on sadistic. It's difficult to believe you have any intention of releasing me, though you continue to dangle that carrot. As a result, I'd resolved never to write another word, but you convinced me it's "nonnegotiable." So, I'm back at it, and anxious to oblige.

(Sarcasm acknowledged).

In return, perhaps you'd be so kind as to finally state what it is you need from me before you're satisfied I won't harm others or myself. Isn't that the *only legitimate excuse* for not letting me out of here?

The YouTube car thing wasn't a staged suicide attempt, and other than wanting to smack Richie around and tazer Steven's badoobies, I'm not a violent person. So, I'm guessing it all boils down to your diagnosis of:

Delusional Disorder

Here are the five independent subtypes, accompanied by my honest assessment: *erotomanic* (don't believe someone famous is in love with me); *jealous* (don't believe anyone is cheating on me); *persecutory* (don't believe anyone is following me to do harm); *somatic* (don't believe I have a disease or medical condition); and *grandiose* (don't believe I am the greatest, strongest, fastest or most intelligent person ever). *Really* I don't.

Okay, I admit I'm a clever little SOB, and it's true my memory sets me apart. However, scoring in the 99th percentile is indisputable proof there are people smarter than *me*. See there? Smarter people know *than* is a subordinating conjunction requiring the subject pronoun "I." So let's take delusional off the table, shall we? If you hospitalized everyone in the state who appeared to be delusional, Jeld-Wen Field would be overflowing like the Roman Coliseum on "See Lions Chow Down On Christians Day."

Doc, I'm willing to continue treatment, but I honestly believe I'd do better as an Outpatient. Confinement is incompatible with my temperament, and Suzanne grows more melancholy with each passing week. I *need* to get out of here.

P.S. Upon re-reading, my use of "so" is beginning to rival George Elliot's.

P.P.S. Must I resort to fictionalizing my life to make it more valuable? Please, somebody rescue me before I start running with scissors and cut myself into a million little pieces!

September 17th

Richie's gone! Hallelujah! Thank Yeshua! Praise Allah! Bless Buddha! Kudos to Multnomah County Court! Of course, "In doing what we ought, we deserve no praise."

As it turns out, not only did he torch a few unfortunate felines, he's also been implicated in a series of home break-ins—occurring within a few miles of his mother's multi-million dollar manse on Greenwood Rd. Not sure how many separate felonies he's been charged with, but it's safe to say he'll never cast a vote or run for State Auditor unless they amend the law. His mother's not beyond trying to finagle it.

It seems a video camera caught the little bastard trashing some trophy cases at Oswego Lake Country Club, before he and a buddy drove his Jeep Wrangler over the practice putting greens—engraving their disdain for the gentleman's game with a series of wheelies that did more than $40,000 in damages. (When it comes to felonies, seems he was the expert after all.) Can't believe you knew all about it and still made us suffer his presence.

Although Mrs. Cayte's high-priced attorneys provided the court with quite the canine and equine show—including a video of you commenting on Richie's progress while here (really?)—they were unable to convince the judge that The Healing Place was more beneficial than the Multnomah County Juvenile Detention Center, where he will reside until his nineteenth birthday.

Suzanne attended the hearing. I'd told her enough about young Mr. Caytes that her interest was piqued. I think she's starting to have doubts about the effectiveness of the treatment I'm receiving. Don't take it personally. She's just missing her fabulous son. That's fabulous...not fabulist!

Since Richie won't be seventeen until October, he was fortunate. His buddy got two years at Columbia River Correctional Institution. Just as well, though. A minimum-security prison would never be able to confine him. And, if they think M.C.J.D. can hold him, they're nuts. The only reason he stayed here was because he knew his days were numbered, and his mother thought the judge would be more lenient if they could show he was attempting to address his "mental issues." Like, for instance, being a psychopath?

BTW, Richie thought you were a real 'Fuck-tard.' You were probably aware of that when you decided to testify on his behalf.

Veritas vos liberabit. I hope, I hope.

September 18th

Overheard two staff members discussing how a certain wealthy parent of one of your former patients had promised a huge wad of CA$H to enlarge the facilities here, only to withdraw the offer. Apparently, her "love language" didn't extend to you after-all. You got played, playa!

September 19th

At your request, a discussion of what it means to be *queer*. "Without humor," I believe was the direction. Discussing queerness straight gives oxy*moronic* new meaning. Forgive me if I wander far afield. It's difficult for me to stay on the straight and narrow.

I don't pretend to be the voice of authority, but here goes...

For my generation, "queer" is often preferred because it rejects or encompasses the "uals," (homosexual, bisexual, asexual, transsexual) though it may be just another convenient and confining label. I'm glad it was reclaimed from the haters, but its political implications often transform it into a semantic weapon: 'You can't comprehend us because you're not one of us. Because we're different from the norm, we're *special*. So, fuck you!'

Thus, in certain circles, queer is an example of floccinaucinihilipilification (my new favorite word): i.e. "valueless."

I've responded intimately and intellectually to both sexes for as long as I can remember. I was born that way...*not a choice*. I have little concern for the packaging, only whether or not the person's intelligent, kind, caring and how we connect, energetically.

Ironically, many gays flat out reject the idea of bi-sexuality—believing Bi's to be closeted gays-in-waiting. Pretty sure the goal of Gay Liberation was never to make *everyone* gay, but not everyone got the memo. Sexuality is a mixed bag. Chris's dad liked to wear women's undies, but he was "all man." I know lesbians who actually like penises but reject them, because most are attached to pricks.

Even in Queerville, you can't get everyone on the same page. While some clamor for gay marriage, others oppose it as an attempt to normalize homosexuality. Still others insist the emphasis should be on supporting queer prisoners, organizing against police profiling and brutality in queer communities and fighting for universal health care that includes transsexuals. So you see, we're as diverse as the colors in the rainbow flag.

Psychologically, I've been most attracted to males who tend to be masculine but remote (to varying degrees). Steven, anyone? I prefer women who are strong, independent, intelligent and adverse to male-dominance. Suzanne, right? That would indicate preference for "type" *might* be influenced by environment/nurture.

I've always liked the song, "Love the One You're With," and I'm amused how offensive many people find it to be—only because, in our culture, love and sex are interchangeable.

Though I'm convinced it's not a natural state, monogamy is still the preferred myth. The Chinese have *fifty* separate words to describe love's different aspects and subtleties; we're stuck with only one. "I *love* ice cream, fast cars, my dog…and you."

No wonder we're confused.

September 20th

Sat straight up in bed at 1 a.m. Not to sound too *West Side Story*, but *something's* coming. I don't know what it is, but it's *not* gonna be great. At first, I hesitated even mentioning it, since you always assign similar feelings to paranoia. Not sure what any of this means. Believe me, if I knew, I'd tell you. No doubt we'll be discussing "irrational fear" soon…

2:59 a.m.

Too exhausted to write about it now, but that "something" just happened!

September 21st

Ciera's "episode" was harrowing. I'm usually one to defend the staff, but this time I blame them for gross negligence. How hard is it to keep the scissors, razor blades, letter openers and box-cutters safely locked away? We all know what drawer they're in; there's little about this place we don't know. Comes with the territory.

Why did the Lord give us agility, if not to evade responsibility?

Being institutionalized for a misdiagnosis makes misdemeanor misbehavior a justifiable misdeed, even for Miss Self. (Ogden Nash, eat your heart out.)

As to the incident...

I heard a scream, (Misty). Then, a few second later, Juma was calling for "Help!" I knew something serious had occurred and my first thought was: Ciera! When I stuck my head out of the doorway, I saw Juma and the new aide, Miss Patrick, rushing towards her room. Everyone was instantly out of his room and standing in the hallway.

"She's done it," said Fletcher, who apparently wears that fucking hunting jacket to bed. "She's finally done it."

A hysterical Misty was being ushered out of Ciera's room by Miss Patrick, who's so butch Caesar finds her attractive. I hurried through the commons area, towards the double-doors of the female ward, but Reggie was already securing them.

"What is it? What's happened to Ciera? Is she...?"

"No. Now go back to your room."

"I want to see her!"

"You heard me...back to bed!"

"Okay to let come in...mister Preston only," said Juma, who had emerged from Ciera's room—clutching a pair of scissors. "She's for him asking."

"But—"

"It okay. Come now, Preston…a minute only."

Reggie let me through, but when Joey and Fletcher tried to follow, he stopped them. "Move back boys. Back to your rooms! You heard me."

The other new aide, Larry, who'd apparently been napping in the staff lounge, herded them towards the boy's wing.

"Told you he was a spy," Fletcher said to Joey. "He gets privileges."

Reggie closed and locked the doors behind us.

I was afraid what I'd find: rivulets of blood streaming from her wrists, a bathrobe belt dangling from the light fixture. Instead, there sat Ciera—looking like a new arrival at Buchenwald. She'd shredded her gorgeous hair, which lay in tortured arabesques at her feet. Her blonde roots were tipped with only a few remaining strands of black. And, she'd circled and encircled her eyes with liner until she resembled a crazed raccoon.

"That *slunt* stole my poetry," she said in a grating rasp, caused by excessive crying and decrying. "Stole it and destroyed it!"

"Who did dis…?" asked Juma. "Who dis slunt she say?"

"Chelsea," I said.

"I'll check on her," said Miss Patrick, who'd returned from confining Misty to her room, a room adjoining the bathroom she shared with Ciera.

"Oh…your hair… Why…?" I couldn't disguise my alarm.

"I had to do something *extreme*." She picked up a whorl of hair from the pile, then let it trail to the floor, as if it were festive confetti.

"I've always loved *Rosemary's Baby*. Mia Farrow made that hairdo famous in '68. Everyone loved it but Sinatra."

"Don't make fun of me. My poems, all my feelings in words…gone *forever*. I want to die," she pleaded. "I truly want to die. Why won't you people let me die…?"

"Maybe don't say that to Doc. He takes wanting to die very seriously, as if it's a testament to his inability to perform miracles."

"I *mean* it! If you cared for me at all, like you pretend to, you'd understand why it's the only answer. Virginia, Sylvia and Anne knew there was only one way out of this—"

"They knew *nothing*. They're dead! They quit…gave up. That's the easy way out."

"Listen to mister Preston, Ciera," said Juma, "he tellin' you da true."

"But it's *not* easy! There's nothing easy about it. Pres, you love life too much. It's blinded you. Someday, maybe you'll understand. But not me…I'm not waiting for someday."

The way her eyes flooded with tears and her chin quivered, I knew she meant it. I've always known.

Doc, you've got to transfer Chelsea. Ciera refuses to be in a group "with that murderess of words."

September 22nd

Of course, you're nowhere to be found on the weekends, so it wasn't your fault. Still, did anyone bother to see if Ciera had any other sharp instruments hidden in her room? If she could steal a pair of scissors out of the Nurse's Station, there was nothing preventing her from taking a letter opener.

It's lucky it was dull, or she would have severed every artery in her wrists. As it turned out, she didn't lose too much blood. It's fortunate she was still under observation and someone got to her in time.

When will she be back from the hospital?

What are you going to do about Chelsea?

What does it take?

September 23rd

If it's not asking too much, please copy and forward this letter to the "unnamed" hospital where they took Ciera. It's important she know how I feel.

> Dearest Ciera,
>
> Please don't think my offhand remarks about Virginia, Sylvia and Anne were meant to trivialize your situation. I believe you when you say you want to die. I do understand despair, in spite of my attempts to always play the buffoon.
>
> I don't know why some souls are so overwhelmed by life once they enter the physical world. My understanding is that we all choose to experience certain things that give us the opportunity to heal and balance the "past" and gain greater spiritual understanding. Choosing to exit the planet now doesn't make it any easier next go-around.
>
> It's obvious you came here to learn to be more sensitive. Well, no one can deny your sensitivity, but as a result, you're addicted to pain. Maybe you brought that addiction with you, but the combination of living in the past and your belief system continue to feed it. How? By buying into the old adage that "pain is a valuable teacher." That means you subconsciously seek painful situations because you think they make you stronger each time you overcome one. The more painful the experience…the more valuable. Total bullshit, IMHO.
>
> Pain has only one thing to teach…*it hurts*. This I know from experience. And, I think if you're honest, you'll admit you've had enough. You're choosing to escape it by ending your life. There are other ways.

Everything in the physical world is based on duality: good/bad, light/dark, feminine/masculine, yin/yang, judgment/love. These appear to be opposites, but they're just flip sides of the same coin. Turn the Pain coin over and what do you find? *Peace*. That's the real lesson you came to learn. Do you want pain, or do you want peace? Every time you dive back into the past, the pain pool, you remain stuck. The present contains no pain…only peace. Now is the only safe place to be.

Knowing you, the very thought of living a peaceful existence sounds *boring*. That's just your Ego trying to keep you trapped. If you ever experienced even a little peace, you'd want more. It's the Peace that passeth all understanding.

Looking at my life, you probably think I'm a big hypocrite, but there have been many times when I've tasted blessed peace: quiet moments when it's just been Nature and me. I can't wait to get out of here and get back to having those experiences again. Boy, what I wouldn't give for an hour on that sandbar in the creek near my house.

Forgive me for saying it, but it's obvious your thoughts control you. You must take control. Raising one's consciousness is about being conscious of your thoughts. Checking out, taking your own life means your Ego mind wins…again. Ego…that's the real Debbil Miss Vines should fear. Yours has beguiled you into believing you're a victim: powerless. But, it's a lie! You told me once you agree that we create our own reality from our thoughts and beliefs. That means you have the power to change things because you can create something better. You must. There's no reason to keep seeing yourself as a "victim."

I love you, Ciera. I'm not talking about lusting after you, though you're attractive, funny, desirable and a great kisser. I see the little wounded girl within you, and I want to take her in my arms and tell her she's okay and deserves to be happy. But, *you* have to do it. You have to embrace her and assure her you're going to stop terrorizing her with your thoughts and threats…and actions. Would you continue to do harmful things to your body if you knew how much they hurt that sweet innocent child within…?

It doesn't help for me to love her if you don't or won't. Please start loving her, Ciera. She's a wonderful little girl and deserves it.

I know creativity's important to you, that your poetry's an outlet for your thoughts and feelings. But, *living* is also a creative process. Though it's not easy, it has value beyond our understanding.

Write me back, okay? <u>Soon</u>. I miss you…a lot!

Hugs,

~Pres.

September 24th

When I say, "What a fabulous start to the week," even Misty, who's as dense as a flourless cake, would detect the sarcasm. And, it just keeps getting better…

Two officers from the Multnomah County Sheriff's department invaded our sanctuary at 6:20 a.m. The resulting ruckus created by a room-search had everyone awake and speculating on the whereabouts of Joey Gentry, who escaped sometime after final bed check at midnight and before the morning staff reported at 6 a.m.

Joey, of course, is not the first to walk out of The Healing Place, but since his presence was court-ordered, the police had to be notified. While one of the officers questioned Antoine, who discovered him missing, another was in the main lounge area interrogating us.

"Any idea where we might find this…" he paused to check his notes, "…Joey?"

As a joke, someone suggested he probably headed back to Pets on Broadway. Chelsea, who was angry because she'd been 'rudely awakened by fucking pigs staring at my tits' said, "The little creep used to hang out in Pioneer Square with all the other losers." Another overheard him talking about going to New Pathways for Youth to try and get his GED.

The officer asked which of us knew him best. Because I'd made an attempt to befriend him, I was taken into the break room for questioning. "So, did this kid…uh…"

"Joey."

"…say where he might go when he got out of here?"

"Not really."

"Know where he's from?"

"Just outside Beaverton. A place called Evergreen Park."

"What's that…like a park…or a housing area?"

"A trailer park."

"Think he might've gone back?"

"Doubtful."

"Why's that?"

"I don't think he has family there anymore."

"He say where they are?"

"His mother left him and his sister when they were little. The sister ran off with some older guy years ago."

"The father?"

"Killed when their trailer blew up."

"Meth?"

"Joey didn't say, but it's why he ended up on the streets. Indicated he had no other place to go."

The officer quickly jotted something down. I couldn't help noticing his fingernails appeared to be manicured, each half-moon rising evenly from perfect cuticles. I always find this interesting, particularly in alpha males, who strain to appear ultra-masculine.

"Anything else you can tell me about him? Something that would give us an idea where he could be headed?"

"You might want to send a patrol car out to Stanley Avenue."

"Why's that?"

"There's an Adopt a Pet just off Johnson Creek Boulevard. He talked about getting a dog when he got out. Said it's not so lonely on the streets when you have a pet."

The officer, who smelled like peppermint body gel, made another quick note, and then looked around to make sure no one was listening. Lowering his basso voice, he asked, "They can't tell us *why* the kid was in here, but maybe you can. Off the record…just between us."

"Just between us, he was trying to prevent a dog from chewing through his chain and destroying the world."

He stared at me a moment, his eyes narrowing into accusatory slits. Slowly, he closed up his notepad and, without another word, exited the break room.

There's a certain power that comes from people thinking you're nuts.

September 25th

Found out why Caesar wasn't here Friday. It was all over the *K2 News at Six*. He was seriously injured in what authorities are calling a "hate crime." Apparently, he learned nothing from the last skirmish. The reporter said Caesar and a "friend" were walking—this time towards the Silverado Bar on 3rd Avenue Thursday night—when two men, who stopped to ask directions, jumped them.

His companion managed to get away and ran for help. In the meantime, the men beat Caesar so severely he's in critical condition in the ICU at Good Samaritan Medical Center. He's sustained a number of serious injuries. The medical report stated he has a skull fracture; damage to his liver, spleen and kidneys; several broken ribs; a punctured lung and multiple contusions. At the time of the report, they had postponed surgery to repair a torn eyelid and a detached retina in his left eye, because they suspect he may have a brain hemorrhage.

The security guard from the bar captured one of the assailants. Because he's a minor, his name is being withheld. The other attacker escaped in a '95 Chevy Eldorado. He's been identified as Jorge Carlos Nuncio-Hernández, 20, of nearby Hillsboro. Police are seeking any information about his whereabouts.

The "Q Center," Portland's LGBTQ Community Center, is having a fundraiser and the Hispanic Metropolitan Chamber has established a Fund at Umpqua Bank to help pay for Caesar's medical bills. I've used my allotted phone calls for the week. Please call Suzanne and ask her to contribute something in my name.

I'm sure you knew all about it. Still, you managed to hold Group without a word. It would have been nice if you'd said something. Everyone here loves Caesar. Well, almost everyone.

I won't repeat what Miss Vines said when she turned off the television and ordered us to our rooms; inappropriate and unprofessional doesn't begin to describe it. I can understand how his flamboyance has been difficult for her to accept, but I'll never understand that level of fear-based hatred by someone who proclaims to be a follower of the man who accepted and loved everyone as a divine child of God.

Reza called the hospital to check on his condition. Because she's not family, they wouldn't release any more information. Maybe they would if you called. Please do.

Violent crimes against people in the LGBTQ community are on the rise again, particularly against minorities and transgendered women. I know Sparkle can probably take care of herself, but not against a nutcase with a gun or a baseball bat. And, poor Caesar's just a harmless little man.

I'm angry. But mostly, I'm heartsick!

P.S. Don't think I haven't noticed you've stopped leaving notes. And, as always…it's a calculated move. Frankly, I'm getting tired of all the game-playing.

September 26th

Can't believe you used "confidentiality" as an excuse to keep me from knowing about Ciera's condition. Her well-being is of genuine concern. Do you plan to screen her letters, too?

* * *

It's standard policy. We would do the same to protect your privacy.

Look who's back with the comments! Knowing how much I sometimes needed you to respond, I view your absence in the comment department as passive-aggressive…which makes us more alike than you'd care to admit.

September 27th

Chelsea's outta here! She stabbed Misty last night at supper. (Not a life-threatening wound). I'd already left the cafeteria, so I can't report the details. All I know is Misty 'got in her face' about stealing Ciera's poetry and Chelsea jabbed a fork into her thigh. She's now at the same juvey facility as Richie. Jamarcus had to be restrained when they hauled her away.

Precautionary Note:

The new guy, Larry, Reggie, Miss Patrick, a couple of the night staff from the third floor and some of the maintenance people all smoke. I've seen them huddled outside the backdoor that leads to the parking lot. (What is it about "care-takers" and nicotine?)   I recommend a memo stating that lighters and matches are to be left in vehicles. I don't think you can be too careful. If Jamarcus could, he'd burn this place to the ground. Compared to some of the lunatics you've had here, you have to admit I look like the poster boy for sanity.

P.S. Thanks for checking on Caesar. Next time you call, please ask them to tell him his "amigo," Preston, sends healing thoughts and best wishes for a speedy recovery. Also, let him know this place is deadly dull without his vivacious personality. (Reza says to tell him she's praying for him…five times a day.)

September 28th

Jamarcus overheard Sparkle say how happy she is Chelsea's gone, and he went all Christian Bale on her ass. Big mouth barked up the wrong transgirl this time. She flattened him. Everyone—including some of the staff—applauded. Dearly loved it.

September 29th

Had "one of those" dreams last night. By that, I mean <u>it was real</u>. Before you dismiss it or assign a psychological condition…don't.

Setting: New York University.
Time: The present. Class: Expository Writing.

The class itself is nothing noteworthy. Grad student, Marjorie Epstein, teaches the course, which is populated by a diverse group of CAS (College of Arts & Science) freshmen. I'm pursuing a double major in English and Philosophy. None of my teachers even comes close to being as good as Mr. Wolff. Most are grad students more interested in getting their doctorates than teaching freshman-level courses. Our dorm room sucks, but who cares? I love the city!

In the dream, I'm reading—out loud—my essay on the "Quantum Mechanics of Simultaneous Experiences." Truly fascinating.

Without getting into the specifics, it deals with *superposition*, a theory known as Schrödinger's cat. Maybe you've heard of it? In the simplest terms, it suggests there are many outcomes that exist simultaneously. It's the observation or measurement of these various states that affect the outcome. Or, to put it simply: there's no single outcome unless it's observed. There have been various experiments proving superposition occurs at the subatomic level—demonstrating an individual particle can be in multiple locations *at the same time.*

I don't shy away from knowing things, but until this dream, I'd never heard of Schrödinger's cat. Draw your own conclusion as to why I would suddenly have this knowledge. Beats me.

My roommate, Izzy Feldman, is also taking the course. Please check and verify that one Isidore Jacob Feldman, son of Ira and Enid Feldman of Schenectady, NY, is, in fact, a freshman at NYU. Think *I* have a need to over-explain? You should meet Izzy. Believe me, he's the perfect example of "Active but Odd." He spent over an hour elaborating on what being an "authentic Jew" means. I'm not exactly stupid, but his explanation was incomprehensible. Maybe it's the Yiddish.

Izzy says he's kosher, but as a vegetarian, I'm way more kosher than he, though he won't admit it. He says he's "a sinner," but because he keeps *Shabbos*, he's still attached to Jerusalem. I say my Nana had me baptized when I was four months old. (Mom doesn't know). When I tell him that means "Once saved, Always saved," he responds with, "*Feh!*" This is going to be quite the year.

Back to English class and the dream:

Izzy's essay centered on the persecution of Jews—in particular, Jews who opposed Prohibition because they were whiskey importers, and how the WCTU (Women's Christian Temperance Union) was an anti-Semitic organization that blamed Jews for the nation's moral decay. None of this is as important as the fact that I "remember" everything about: my class, the teacher, my essay, Shabbos, Izzy's paper, our dorm room, and going to Katz's Delicatessen. Normally, I wouldn't eat there, but Izzy says, "You can't be a true New Yorker and not eat at the best Deli in the city." He ordered the Pastrami, $15.75. I pointed out it was kosher-*style* (not kosher).

"Listen, *Faygala*," he said—poking me in the chest like a demented woodpecker, "Not even Yahweh and Rabbi Rabinowitz could pass up Katz's Pastrami. Impossible, *ummeglich!*"

When asked the meaning of *Faygala*, he thought a moment, and then said, "Little bird." Judging from his smile, I suspect it has other meanings.

I ordered a Tossed Green Salad and the Vegetarian Baked Beans and Knishes. Izzy insisted on treating me because I edited his essay. I was grateful, since I'm already running low on spending money.

Though (unexplainably) Steven's a full partner at McNabb Nesbitt and Associates, he has me on a pretty tight financial leash, and man, it requires some major mullah to live in downtown Manhattan. Even so, there are lots of free things to do and see.

I made the right choice. Stanford's for people who need campus life, sports and frat parties. NYU's for individualists, though there are also scads of snobby, rich ivy-wannabes here who exist mainly to show how much money their rich parents possess, and for the rockin' nightlife. Still, I love it. Imagine having the entire city of New York for a campus!

Doc, this "dream" has no symbolic message. It didn't unfold in fractured scenes, cloaked in fog. It was an observable outcome of my very existence. If nothing else, it's temporarily relieved my sense of being confined against my will.

I'd love to hear your psychological explanation. In fact, I'd love to have feedback on anything I've said since May 2nd. At this rate, you could sit and listen to me forever. Is that the plan?

That's *fercockt*. Izzy can translate.

October 1st

I brought my entry from last Saturday to our private session. You promised to check into it. Yeah, right!

October 2nd

Can't believe you actually investigated my claims: Isidore Jacob Feldman *is*, in fact, a freshman at NYU. (No shit, Sherlock). Katz's Pastrami costs $15.75. And, miracle of miracles, a grad student named Marjorie Epstein, does teach an Expository Writing class for freshmen. But, there's no record of one Preston Wilder Nesbitt being enrolled this semester. (Of course not. Still, I'm a little disappointed).

When I asked how you thought I knew about all those things, you looked (a little too) pleased. "The internet. You've acknowledged using it several times since you've been here."

Doc, I swear I dreamed it...every last detail.

P.S. Suzanne stopped by the "Q" center to make a contribution. She was told the Fundraiser's been postponed and the bank's handling everything. Why won't anyone tell us how Caesar's doing? I'm concerned.

October 3rd

A letter from Ciera. It was opened and the return address excised, further proof this is more of a prison than a place of healing.

> My Dearest Pres,
>
> I was so happy to receive your letter. Daddy brought it to the hospital when he and mom came to visit last night. It had been opened for "security reasons." Mom says to tell you thanks for being such a good friend to me. They are both relieved my attempt failed. So am I. Bet that surprises you, huh? I knew I wouldn't die by the way I pierced my wrists.
>
> Want to know another secret? Of course you do. Promise you

won't tell anyone, especially Dr. van Ittersum. Chelsea didn't steal my poetry. I threw it away because I knew it wasn't any good. You knew it, too. I hated the way every boy including you thought she was so hot, and I hoped she'd get in trouble.

You were right about pain and me. I don't know about being addicted, but I've always thought it would help make me be a better writer. It sure worked for Virginia, Sylvia and the others. Doc says what I'm actually addicted to is drama. He told me I'm an "adrenaline junkie," and he's probably right. Life can be pretty boring without some drama every now and then. I never seem to know when enough is too much.

You've definitely been a good friend, but I've got to say it's your arrogant attitude that kept me from getting closer to you. Yes, you're smart, but so what? You always have to be right about everything.

People don't want to be reminded about something they said a month ago, or what they did last Thursday, and always being "right" about things pisses people off. I'm not saying you're not right a lot of the time, but you come off as a snob and a know-it-all and it turns people off.

You're scared like the rest of us. Admit it! That big genius act is just a way to protect yourself. We're not all idiots you know. Maybe you'd already be out of there if you didn't pretend to know more than the doctors.

I'm not coming back Pres. Mom and daddy aren't going to make me. Sure, I've got problems. Who doesn't?

I made up that stuff about daddy. You probably guessed that, too. I thought having an interesting back-story would help me become an artist. Stupid. I made up lots of stuff. My real name's Cindy. Cynthia Louise Self. Cindy Lou. Can you blame me?

Take care of yourself. I mean it! I'll always be able to say I once kissed the most famous YouTube star on the planet.

XOX,

Ciera (Cindy)

P.S. I know the difference between you're and your, but sometimes I slip up because I write too fast and also I have trouble thinking when I'm taking all those drugs. Remember not to tell Doc about my poetry. Funny, I just told *you* to remember something! LOL as Misty would say. Chelsea's still a slunt and they should lock her up and throw away the key. Hope you're right about living being a form of creativity.

October 4th

I've reread Ciera's letter a dozen times. She's right about me being scared. She's right about a lot of other things, too.

RIGHT: 'In accordance with what is good, proper or just. Correct in judgment, opinion or action.'

I'm weary from having to be right about: relationships, parenting, the drugging of children, the obsession with technology and consumerism. I'm exhausted because I can't switch my mind to *off*. You want to know what it's like being me? It's difficult to explain, but here's a little example of what goes through:

The Mind of Preston Nesbitt

You can't know how debilitating it is to have a brain that's analyzing, categorizing and commenting on every little thing. In the past, the only thing that slowed it down was repeating part of the 46th Psalm: "Be

Still...and Know I AM God." Uh-oh...here goes...

Mentioning the 46th Psalm brings up the theory that Shakespeare might have influenced it. Were you aware that the King James Version of the Bible was written *after* most of Shakespeare's most important works? (You'll have to find a copy of Psalm 46. I'm too enervated to copy it all from memory.)

Count down "46" words from the beginning of the verse and you'll find the word, "shake" (...the mountains *shake*...). Now do the same thing at the end of the verse. "Spear" is "46" words from the end (...cutteth the *spear*...). When the King James Version was being readied for printing in 1610, Shakespeare was (you guessed it!) 46-years-old.

Think that's it? Just warming up. The number 46 is the most important number in numerology. It's the Ruler Number. It denotes "the crown above the head" in ancient Chaldean scriptures. The qualities associated with one who possesses this number are: intelligence and intellect. Mention of the Chaldeans brings up the history of Ur...about *forty-six* hundred B.C. In the Babylonian exile, it's estimated that 46-hundred Israelite expatriates were brought away by the Chaldeans. Skip ahead seven centuries: 46 is the atomic number of palladium; the number of human chromosomes; the code for international direct dial to Sweden. In *The Hitchhiker's Guide to the Galaxy*, Doug Adams says, 'The Ultimate Answer to Life, The Universe and Everything is...42!' He's wrong. It's 46! I could go on and on...

Get the picture? It doesn't matter if the information is esoteric, banal or utter B.S. Once my mind's engaged, it runs the gamut. Sometimes I think I can hear it shifting gears and speeding through millions of interfaces—checking for connections between facts and theories: specific, random, true, false, plausible, improbable, serious or flippant. As you know, these "facts" can erupt from my mouth, spontaneously.

I want my brain to stop and take a deep breath. I need to go sit on the sandbar in the middle of the little creek near my home and slowly merge with the ethers.

What brought on these new insights? *Dreams*…lots of dreams.

Last night, I dreamed I was driving around Portland *with you* in your Lexus—pontificating about what's wrong with the world and what needs to be done to fix it…ways to make it a better place. Guess you'd finally heard enough.

"Why don't I let you out here on the corner, Preston, and you can share your philosophy with the masses?"

Why not? You know how I love a challenge.

So, there I am…standing on a street corner in downtown Portland—raving about the herd mentality. Three or four people gather and I quickly convert them to my way of seeing, my way of thinking and understanding. In short, I persuaded sheep to be part of *my* flock. Kind of like what Shakespeare did in *Julius Caesar*—showing how easily Brutus, then Mark Antony, could alter public opinion through Rhetoric.

The next thing I know, the scene's switched location. I'm now standing on a soapbox in the middle of Times Square. It's sheer chaos. I give the same impassioned speech, but this time no one, I mean *no one* stops to listen. I can't compete with the din. The crowd rushes by as if I don't exist.

Instantly, I'm transported to the streets of Mumbai. There in a market teeming with thousands, I bark out my words of wisdom to the throng of people feverishly buying knock-offs of brand name products, fakes so obvious I can spot the runny dyes, cracks and poorly glued seams from twenty yards away. Yet, people fight over them—pushing and shoving. No one notices me. A young boy, who entertains with a monkey, attracts more attention.

That's when I realized all my bloviating, all my insight and knowledge mean *nothing* to anyone but me. Knowledge *without* Wisdom is Fool's Gold…counterfeit and pointless. In reality, I am less than a little flea in a vast flea market that tries to pump himself up by being clever, by appearing to know something.

Epistemology is B.S.! Ever study Gettier's Smith-Jones problem? Total mind-fuck! Call me a skeptic. (Can't believe I would waste my time majoring in Philosophy at NYU.)

My life's a *non sequitur*, an artifice. I'm not even sure what's real, what's a dream, or what I even "know." I'm tired of being an ontological enigma. Though Descartes believed his ability to think proved his existence, I'm no longer certain of anything. Am I real? Are you? Did that accident happen, or was it a dream? I don't know. What does it even mean—"knowing?" I'm convinced it means but one thing only: I am the center of my own universe and that center is nothing more than *Ego*. And, Ego is nothing more than fear. Fear of not being noticed. Fear of not being accepted. Fear of never being loved *enough*. Love *is* the only reality.

Doc, I just realized something, something depressing, but something that smacks of truth. I'm every bit as self-indulgent as Holden Caulfield, maybe more. The very thought sickens me.

I could embrace the "why me?" syndrome. *Why* my extraordinary memory? *Why* have I experienced so many psychic phenomena? *Why* did I have to be the one to star in the most controversial video ever? *Why me?* But to what purpose?

Seems to me a journal, like writing a novel, is solipsistic…egotistic self-absorption. If I truly believed only the self existed, that would mean I've been writing this just for me, that I fooled myself into believing I did it for you. Yet, I have no way of knowing if there really is a "you." Lately, I'm not even sure of my own existence. Guess this journal is proof…or is it?

I sincerely want to apologize for filling these pages with useless verbiage, for a massive Ego that separates me from the loving being I want to be. And, please accept my apology for having to listen to my never-ending line of crap. I know you get paid to because I'm your patient, but I'd like to believe you care about me as a person. I'm pretty sure you do.

I didn't mean most of the negative things I said about you. You know how I am. Some of it was just showing off. And, some was because I was really angry you refused to let me out, and I couldn't understand why. I get it now. Is that the perspective you mentioned months ago?

Rereading this, it sounds like I'm trying to manipulate you into believing I've changed in some significant way—hoping you'll be impressed enough to release me. But, that isn't it. R. D. Laing said insanity is a perfectly rational adjustment to an insane world. These pages confirm that belief.

Last July, you asked me to share my deepest, darkest secret, and I fed you a bullshit story and you knew it. Well, it's time I told you the truth. Maybe you've known all along, but my deepest, darkest secret is: <u>I'm afraid I belong here!</u> I'm no saner than anyone of the patients I've put down with snarky comments and pseudo psychoanalytical bull. I've stated we're all connected, but because I've believed myself to be superior, I've denied that very connectivity. Spiritually, I'm a bigger hypocrite than all those I've accused of hypocrisy.

I am the Zeitgeist of the 21st Century!

I pretend to see the world from a new perspective, but I'm as phony as those fake handbags on the streets of Mumbai. For the past six months,

I've pointed out what's wrong with society…and, though I may be right in some instances, what good are my insights? True, I've offered up some alternative ways to live more empathetically, but I haven't shown much empathy in the process.

Remember the quote that begins this ledger of my now documented sins?

> *There's something in the basic nature of human beings*
> *that revels in the Theory of the Ideal,*
> *but finds its realization repugnant.*

It doesn't matter how close to Divinity, to perfection one comes, it's always the discovery of smelly feet and of human foibles that turns the rest of us into gleeful executioners. It's part of our need for dichotomy. We acknowledge two sides of a coin, but we can only view one side at a time. Believing one superior to the other, we fail to understand that here in the physical world, a world of our own creation, one cannot exist without the other.

They are One…a God with smelly feet!

This is my attempt at asking you to forgive me for my impertinence and my willful bearing, for my "Comedy Central" sensibility and my smart-ass mouth. And, to thank you for helping me see my own flaws. Reading through nearly 160 days of journal entries has made me realize that "peace will not rule the planet, nor love steer the stars" if I can't find peace and love within myself. I want to Doc. Help me!

October 5th

I'm pretty shook up. I'll journal what went down, but we have to discuss this in my private session. For once, you need to stop being only a listener and join in the conversation. You told Ciera she was an adrenaline junkie. It's time you gave me some advice. As for time itself, I've spent more with you that I have my own father. Things have gotten crazy. I'm worried.

Okay, back to what happened after today's Group:

Akiko "Amy" Fujita, the girl who "has it all" from my old high school, joined the prison population last night. On track to be valedictorian, she was president of the Honor Society, Girl's Republic Representative her junior year, 35 ACT, 2350 SAT and still it wasn't enough to keep her from overdosing on…are you ready for it…? *Heroin.*

Less than two months into her senior year, the pressure apparently got too much. Truthfully, I feel sorry for her. Both of her parents, her father, a respected neurosurgeon, and her mother, a city councilwoman and doyenne of the arts, placed unbelievably high expectations on her.

I got to know Amy a little when we were in a production of *The Seagull* last winter. She told me then her mother was 'livid' because she got a supporting role, Polina Andryevna, instead of the lead, Irina Arkadina. I played Irina's son, Konstantin Treployov. Yes, Konstantin kills himself, but remember…it's a play. Blame Chekhov or the director, Mr. Wolff. He insisted I was perfect for the part.

Amy has a pretty face, but unlike either of her parents or any of the other Asian girls at WPI, she was a little on the pudgy side. Thus, she was cast as the wife of a retired lieutenant. She said her mother called Mr. Wolff and 'bitched a fit,' but he refused to budge, saying, "We need students who can play some of the older character parts. Amy's talented enough to be convincing as an older Russian woman."

Mrs. Fujita refused to accept his explanation and went so far as to complain at a school board meeting that Mr. Wolff was playing favorites based on ethnicity and due to inappropriate relationships with some of his students. Ridiculous!

Anyway, when Amy got out of the hospital Monday, her mother insisted she was fully recovered and should be permitted to return to WPI. But, the school counselor and the principal stood firm, insistent that the only way she would be permitted to reenroll was to get a "clean bill of *mental* health" from Serenity Ranch or The Healing Place. Serenity's is a six-week program, so her mother opted for here—believing she would be released quicker (yeah, right).

I hadn't seen her since last April, and I couldn't believe how haggard she looks. She had to know I was an inpatient here, but she acted all surprised when she ran into me after our separate Group sessions. That's when she told me about her overdose and what followed.

"Heroin, Amy...? What the hell!"

"You're so naïve, Achilles. Do you think I'm the only one using? There are lots of us. If you weren't so straight and such a little moralist, we'd have probably let you in the group last year."

"Group? Who's in the group?"

"Who *isn't*? Some still in school. Some recent grads."

"Kids I know?"

"Jimmy, Celeste, Meghan, Paul, Yukio, Jason, Sara, Raleigh, Lisa, Chris—

"Chris...Roberts?"

"Yes, *your* Chris."

"But, where would he ..."

"Get the money? Like the rest of us, you find ways. I told my parents someone stole my cello. Besides, heroin's cheaper than blow and it's no big deal."

"But, Jimmy McClelland made the All-State football team last year.

How's that even possible? Can you function on that stuff?"

"Have you seen my test scores? Really, it's no big deal. We don't do it at school. We have parties. Everyone snorts. I only did it to lose weight, but I liked the euphoria. I refused to shoot up, but then Jimmy assured me it was safe and a better high. First time and I fucking O'd. Can you believe it?"

"Does your mother know about Jimmy and the others?"

"She pressured me to give up names, but I refused. I told her, 'Ask me one more time and you can fucking forget Yale next year.' I meant it, too. Law School wasn't my idea in the first place. I'm so sick of being their perfect little girl and of her micro-managing my life. Did your mother ever ride you about grades?"

"No."

"You're lucky. I always liked your mom. Guess it sucked when everyone found out about her and Mr. Wolff though, huh?"

I didn't know what to say.

"You *do* know, right?"

"That happened a couple of years ago. How did you…?"

"It's not like it's a secret. Someone hired a private investigator to record the comings and goings at Wolff's. Apparently, Kirk baby slept with a couple of married faculty members and maybe a few students. Everyone knows about it. It's right there on YouTube. It's why they both resigned."

"They?"

"Mr. Wolff and your mother."

Tried reaching Mom at home and on her cell. Both numbers have been disconnected. Steven's cell goes directly to voicemail. Reza says you're trying to get new contact information. What's going on? Would someone please tell me what's happening?

October 6th

(3:30 a.m. Can't sleep).

Amy's revelation unearthed buried memories of my last visit with Mr. Wolff. To say they're disturbing trivializes the impact they've had on my psyche. I awakened myself around 2:15 this morning—having shouted, *'Why?'* so loud that Juma knocked on my door to make sure I was okay.

Just another dream? You decide.

First off, the decision to go to Mr. Wolff's house was spur-of-the-moment. Normally, I wouldn't have done a drop-by without calling or texting first, but I was so intent on finally letting him know how I was feeling, I decided to forego the heads-up. I could tell he was surprised. In fact, he used that very word.

"Pres! Wow, this is a surprise." He looked past me, as if to make sure I'd come alone. "What's up, man?"

"May I come in?"

"Sure, sure…but I don't have long. Need to be somewhere in a few."

He was acting really strange, and I thought it odd all the blinds were closed and a dozen candles blazed in the living room.

"I was meditating when you knocked."

"I should've called first, but I…I…"

"Is something wrong? Sit down a minute. Tell me what's going on?"

I sat on one end of his big sectional sofa and he sat close by—pulling his bare feet up under him. He was wearing acid-washed jeans and a faded denim shirt with pearl buttons; it was half unbuttoned—exposing his hirsute chest. Like a rugged model for The Fashionisto, his hair always has that wind-blown look; it's dark blond with natural highlights, but his beard and body hair are darker. He's almost too good-looking, until you realize his face is just slightly asymmetrical. I was suddenly aware I was staring.

"Cool belt," I blurted.

"What? Oh, this?" he said—pointing to his brightly colored sash. "It's hand-woven by the Huichol tribe of west central Mexico. The dyes are all natural, of course, but can you believe how neon bright they are? Ever hear of them?"

I shook my head, 'no.'

"They're a pre-Columbian tribe, at least 35,000 years old. But, here's something extraordinary. You'll like this. Their spiritual leader is a former hippie from the Bronx. The story goes that back in '66 or '67, he was roaming the desert in the Sierra Madres—looking for peyote—when he became dehydrated and passed out. Fortunately, for him, the Huichol shaman, who was like 95 at the time, had a vision his spiritual successor would be found in the desert. He sent out a group that discovered this young guy, unconscious, right where the shaman said he would be. Crazy, huh?"

"Yeah, that's—"

"They believe dreams are prophetic visions. You should see their string art, Pres...all based on dreams. I have a large one in my bedroom I'll show you sometime. Anyway, after a 12-year apprenticeship, this guy from the Bronx became the Huichol shaman and lineage holder. Amazing, right?"

"Totally." My response was rather subdued.

"You seem distracted. Did something happen?"

"No, nothing. I just..." I was already shaking and my voice sounded submerged. This was a conversation I'd wanted to have for months, one I'd had in my head many times. But, now that the opportunity was here, I

THE QUEERLING

clutched. "I wanted to tell you...to let you know..."

"What? It's okay. Just say it."

"It's embarrassing."

"Hey, you know you can tell me anything."

"I just wanted you to know...you're my favorite teacher...ever." I could barely form a sentence, and what an inane sentence. My pulse was pounding so hard in my carotid artery I could actually hear it. I was certain he could probably see it.

"Thanks, man. You're one of my all-time favorite students. You knew that, right? Saved all your essays. Brilliant. Use them as examples every semester." He checked his watch.

"Maybe this can wait...when you have more time," I said. I was feeling insecure, and I wasn't sure I had the courage to say why I'd really come.

"That's probably best. How 'bout Monday after school? Stop by my room. We can talk more then."

"I love you, Mr. Wolff...Kirk." It just popped out. I was as surprised as he was. His face did one of those quick shudders, where you can tell the person's shocked but tries to look normal. He took an extra beat before responding.

"I'm really fond of you, too."

"No, I mean it...I do...love you. That's why I'm here. I've wanted to tell you for a long time. I had to let you know." My eyes watered and the candles radiated fractured light like stars in Van Gogh's night sky.

Mr. Wolff's so smooth. He tried to act like I'd just commented on an unassigned novel, or deciphered a literary monogram in a crossword puzzle. His blue eyes sparkled. I couldn't stop looking at his full lips, which were perfectly outlined by his thick beard.

"That's a big compliment. It's okay, buddy...relax."

239

"Don't you see...I'm *in love* with you? I have been since freshman year."

He didn't say anything for a moment, and I wanted to get up and run out of there. Finally, he leaned forward and touched my shoulder, just for a second—like he was reassuring me this was no big deal. I guess the following confession was to make me feel better...

"When I was a freshman in high school, I had a big crush on this junior boy, Myles Harris. He was a jock, but he was also this really smart guy. Captain of the Forensic Team and president of the Key Club. Really popular. Everyone liked Myles. I followed him around like a pup. Never told him how I felt, but he had to know. Was that the deal with you and Chris Roberts?"

"I'm not here to talk about Chris."

"You're right...sorry. What I'm saying is...I think guys have crushes on other guys, but never talk about it. It's part of our macho culture not to show our true feelings."

"But, this isn't just a crush. It's practically an obsession. I think about you all the time. Believe me, all the time. I have a whole notebook filled with poems I've written about you. Letters I never had the nerve to send. Don't you see...I'm attracted to you sexually?"

There. I said it. Instantly, it felt like the atmosphere shifted in the room. I couldn't look at him. My head fell into my hands. He sat for a moment—studying me.

"I'm going to tell you something, something I've never told anyone. If I weren't so fond of you, I wouldn't. But, Pres, you *have* to promise—"

"You can trust me," I said—raising my head and peering directly into his eyes. "I won't tell a soul."

He let out a big sigh. "In college...at Colorado State, I was at a Delta Upsilon rush party sophomore year. Never thought I'd join a fraternity, but… You do understand that I'm *really* trusting you here."

"You can, I swear."

"Anyway…I got smashed and somehow ended up in bed with this guy from Sacramento or Mendocino…I forget now. He was someone I barely knew."

I wanted to say, 'If this is going to be one of those "Christ was I drunk stories," just forget it.'

"He was extremely good looking, and I found him quite attractive. We'd hung out a few times, but hell, I had no idea what was going to…even though it might have eventually." He paused as if that were the whole story.

"What?"

"The alcohol made it easier. We were willing to do *anything*, everything for each other. Does that surprise you? I've always believed sex is the simplest, most complicated thing ever. That's all I'm saying. It never happened again, but the point is—"

"The point is I think about you constantly. I wonder where you are, what you're doing, what you're thinking. If you ever think about me. If you feel anything for me like I do for you, because sometimes I get this vibe when we're together…and—"

"Hey, man…I get it. Really I do. Though I certainly feel pretty hetero most of the time, I have some very deep undercurrents and conflicts—"

He was interrupted by someone knocking on the door. He sprang to his feet like he'd been electrocuted.

"Wonder who that could be? Sit right there and let me get this, okay?" He hurried to the door. I tried to see who it was, but he blocked my view.

"Hi. I'm a little early. I—" The voice was familiar.

"Oh, *hey!* Listen, I forgot all about our getting together this afternoon…to work on your monologue. I was just about on my way out.

I'm really sorry, but we're gonna need to reschedule."

"What are you talking about? Is someone in there? Kirk…?" She tried to move past him. "Do you—"

That's when I saw Rachel Markham, a girl in my class. When she saw me, she literally gasped.

"Hey, Rache. I was just leaving." I stood up.

She looked at him, then back at me.

"Why don't we get together after school on Monday? There's plenty of time before Regionals. That'll work, right?"

She said nothing, just hurried away. He closed the door behind her.

"Sorry about that. I *totally* forgot I'd promised to get together to work on her monologue. She's been pretty worried about Regionals. But, you know…that's Rachel…easily upset."

"Yeah, I heard."

"We still have a whole week to work on it."

"Apparently, it requires mood-lighting."

"What? No, no, trust me. It's *not* what you think."

"What should I think?"

"*Nothing*…believe me. But, hey! The good news *is*…since I'll be working with her after school on Monday, we can finish our conversation now."

"I gotta go…*Kirk*." I got up to leave.

"Wait. What are you doing? Pres…" He reached out and grabbed my arm. "Come on, man. Let's talk about this a minute. It's not what it looks like. Don't even think that."

"I've heard kids talking, you know. About you and Rachel and some others. I thought it was bullshit. Jealous kids making stuff up. But, apparently, it's your idea of a real world learning experience. One student at a time."

I moved to the door and started to open it. He came up behind me and held it so I couldn't. He pressed against me, his arm pinning my shoulder. I struggled to turn towards him. His face was only inches from mine.

"You're too smart to listen to gossip," he said, a little too forcefully. "Believe me, there's nothing to it. Not any of it."

"Is that what you told my Mom?"

"No...I—"

I turned and yanked the door open—forcing him to let go. I hurried down the porch steps and the brick sidewalk leading to the street. I wanted to look back to see if he were still standing there or following me. Instead, I rushed towards my car.

When I'd made it halfway across, he yelled, "*Wait!* Come on back, Pres! Let's talk! *Please!*"

I turned back to tell him to go fuck himself, and that's when I saw an old dark blue Buick—paint thinning in gray, bleached patches on the hood—streaking toward me. To me the car appeared out of nowhere. To the driver I was only a faceless shadow—flashing across the blinding light of the afternoon sun. *Time slowed...*

I could see the woman's face registering a look of Munchean horror as she white-knuckled the steering wheel and appeared to scream. In the back, there was a toddler buckled into a car seat. Peering over the seat, a young boy of four or five. (All of this in a millisecond).

What happened next was dream-like, otherworldly and unexplainable. The car, the woman and the children blurred into pinpoints of light—blazing shards of pointillistic energy—penetrating my very being. It was like Christiaan Huygens meets Georges Seurat. Particle or wave, the car became a light-rocket that either distorted reality or illuminated it.

I remember *nothing* about the drive home, only walking into our house and heading straight to my room.

Mom yelled up the stairs after me, "Lunch?"

"I have to sleep now," took all the energy I possessed.

That was around 2:45 Saturday afternoon. I woke up at 10:30 Sunday morning. I'd been asleep for *20-hours*. Twenty hours! I haven't slept more than six hours since I was eight.

When I walked into the living room, Mom was reading the Sunday *Oregonian*.

"Hi, honey. You okay…? You've never slept that long in your whole life. Are you *sick?*"

It felt like I was still walking through a thick fog. I tried to remember something, but I could only summon up a feeling…of dread. It wasn't until I saw the YouTube video I even knew I'd been at Mr. Wolff's. I wasn't supposed to remember.

No one was supposed to remember.

I know you've seen it. Who hasn't? If you watch real close, the video flutters, momentarily; you can see my arms out-stretched towards the speeding car and, though it's blurred, the car appears to pass <u>right through me</u>. At the same time, there's another image of me continuing on towards my car. I get in and drive away.

It had to be faked, right?

The flutter looks like an edit, with superimposed images. But, it's *not* a fake. It really happened…just like I said.

Steve was the one who called and told us it was on YouTube. Mom was upset by my insistence I knew nothing about it. We argued for an hour, something we've never done. She was convinced I'd lost my mind. The next I knew, she'd scheduled a private session with you. Turns out you two decided I should be admitted because I wouldn't admit it was phony, or because I'd had a break with reality.

I couldn't explain it then, but now I understand. Two "realities" clashed. Two frequencies intersected—both momentarily observable.

If there are two, it's possible there may be two hundred, two hundred thousand. A different one for every choice, for every action that affects our destiny. When you think about it, "meeting myself coming and going" takes on a whole new meaning.

Reality's what we believe it to be. The biggest illusion of all is *death*. Go to YouTube. Read some of the comments. Thousands of people say they've had similar things happen…unexplainable things, *totally forgotten* until they saw my video. Some are just quirky comments like, 'It's obviously a tear in the Matrix.' But, many are serious accounts and stories very similar to mine.

There's one from a teacher in Iowa. She wrote that about twenty years ago, she and another teacher friend were coming back from a meeting—driving on twisty two-lane country roads near Winterset. They're talking, not paying any attention, when all of a sudden, they come around a curve and there's an old tractor pulling a hay wagon—creeping along at about five miles an hour. She says they were traveling too fast to stop, and the next thing: 'streaks of light.' She swears they drove through it…through a tractor and a hay wagon! She also said until she saw my video, she'd totally forgotten about it. Neither teacher had ever discussed it. Not even a glimmer of remembrance in two decades. How could you ever forget something like that?

There was this other one from some guy who lives in Tennessee. He said back in the mid-90', he was driving an 18-wheeler in East Tennessee—running late, making deliveries—driving 65-70 miles an hour on treacherous back roads. He came shooting up over a hill, and right in the middle of the road, a passenger car had broken down. His headlights illuminated a family of five or six people standing around it. A sudden flash and… He wakes up behind the wheel of his semi, parked on the side of the road. He checks his watch; it's now 2 a.m.—nearly eight hours have elapsed. No sign of the car, an accident or the family.

He swears he was going way too fast to stop, and even if he'd tried to avoid the car, his semi would have jack-knifed and wiped out everyone. Once again, he hadn't thought about it one time, not *once*, until he saw my video. Then it all came flooding back.

Wish I could be more poetic about it. There are thousands of similar stories from people all over the world. 'I remember falling out of the tree and waking up in my bed. Don't know how I got there.' 'I was drowning in the pond, but the next thing I knew…'

These "accidents" are a constant occurrence, just as alternate realities exist at different frequencies, simultaneously—determined by choices we make and the calamities that befall us. The physical world is one hell of an illusion, but it sure feels real…

Don't you get it Doc? Schrödinger's cat isn't just a theory anymore. If a sub-atomic particle can exist in two places at once…we can, too.

I told you the truth. The video's real.

One Preston walked away…another

Epilogue

The following is an addendum to a journal, purportedly written by Preston W. Nesbitt, a sixteen-year-old mental patient from Portland, Oregon (U.S.).

It formed the basis of a report by his psychologist, Dr. Thomas van Ittersum, who presented it to the Institute of Physical Science (IPS), formerly a branch of the Physical Society of London on April 29th, 2013, exactly one year from the date of a viral YouTube video known as: "Boy vs. Buick—and the winner is…?" The IPS, with a worldwide membership of over 60,000, is a scientific research organization devoted to increasing the knowledge and application of physics.

The Nesbitt Journal, as it's officially known, was originally submitted to the American Society of Physicists (ASP); however, following a peer-review, it was adjudged "inappropriate" for scientific investigation and forwarded to one of Dr. van Ittersum's colleagues in Dublin, where it eventually made its way to the head of the IPS, who then passed it along to Dr. Heinrich Grunwald, the author of *Multiple Universes and Cosmic Anomalies*.

Dr. Grunwald was unable to authenticate The Nesbitt Journal, but was curious enough to begin an investigation, which led to its eventual publication as a work of fiction entitled, *The Queerling*.

The investigation verified the following: on April 28th, 2012, at approximately 1:22 p.m., Preston Wilder Nesbitt, then a senior at the Willamette Preparatory Institute in Portland, Oregon, was video-taped being struck by a 1998 Oldsmobile LSS sedan, driven by Mrs. Gloria Maenad of Sandy, Oregon.

In the video, it appears the vehicle passes through the young man, who, after a brief pause, is shown continuing on to his vehicle and driving away. The video appeared on YouTube April 29th, 2012, and, as of this writing, has received over 1.2 billion views and nearly a million comments.

The investigation revealed the video was recorded, remotely, by a private investigator hired by a Mr. Howard Markham. Here's where this event qualifies as an anomaly: Preston Nesbitt was pronounced dead at the scene at 2:27 p.m. on April 28th, 2012. Dr. Grunwald believes the video confirms the theory known as Schrödinger's cat.

From the video, it was determined the vehicle was traveling 47 mph, seventeen miles over the speed limit, when it struck the victim. In July of that same year, Mrs. Maenad was charged with vehicular manslaughter, but given a suspended sentence at the request of the victim's parents, Suzanne and Steven Nesbitt.

What then is the origin of The Nesbitt Journal, and why would an eminent psychologist present it as factual? Dr. Thomas van Ittersum, at a special hearing of the Oregon State Psychiatric Review Board on December

11th, 2012, gave the following testimony, under oath:

Mr. Chairman and fellow colleagues, I appear before you today, not of my own volition but at your request, in an attempt to explain what appears to be the inexplicable case of Preston Wilder Nesbitt, a former outpatient of mine at The Healing Place in Portland, where I have been head psychologist since the institution first opened in 1999. As you know, we are funded by the State of Oregon and through private donations, and licensed by the Oregon Department of Human Services as a certified Inpatient Mental Health Facility with Outpatient services.

On March 7th, 2004, Preston, then aged eight, received a court-ordered psychiatric evaluation; he was diagnosed with Asperger's Syndrome and possible Dissociative Identity Disorder, formerly known as multiple personality disorder. Prescribed *Haldol* by our chief psychiatrist, after several weeks, he developed difficulty breathing, suffered a series of seizures and was subsequently taken off the drug and given a low dose of cyclobenzaprine, noticeably calming his manic behavior with minimum side effects.

After several months of outpatient treatment, I determined there was insufficient evidence to support the DID diagnosis. Intermittently, over the next eight years, Preston received counseling under my care as an outpatient until last April, when he was struck and killed by a speeding car.

On Friday, October 5th 2012, I arrived at my office at approximately 9:45 a.m., following a special session of our Board of Trustees held in the Jupiter Hotel in downtown Portland. The meeting was a result of a patient suicide that occurred at our facility on September 30th, when a sixteen-year-old female in our care since March, used a letter opener, taken from the nurses' station, to puncture the radial and ulnar arteries in her wrist. She was unconscious with a faint pulse when another patient discovered her body in the shower stall adjoining their suites.

Efforts were made to staunch the bleeding. She was rushed to the emergency room at St. Vincent Medical Center, where she was pronounced DOA.

As she does every Friday, my secretary delivered a stack of patient journals, leaving them on my credenza. While chatting via speakerphone with a colleague on the status of the trustee's meeting, I began leafing through the pile, searching for the journal of the aforementioned female patient, Cynthia Louise (Ciera) Self, thinking her final entry might contain information vital to her case.

That's when I discovered Preston's journal, The Nesbitt Journal. As you can see, it's a large faux-leather notebook entitled: ~~The Thoughts & Lamentations of Preston W. Nesbitt~~. Notice how that title is struck through, and written beneath it, a new one: *Quips & Quotes From "The Queerling."*

Of course, I was confused as to the journal's origin and how it found its way into the stack of inpatient journals. When I read the first section marked "Prologue," I was even more perplexed. Then, when I saw the date of the first entry, I assumed it was a tasteless prank.

I questioned my secretary as to its origin, and she said she had no idea how the journal came to be in the stack, which she keeps locked in a filing cabinet, once collected from patients, following the Thursday afternoon Group sessions.

I spent the rest of the morning pouring through the journal, astonished to find accounts of patients Preston had never met, patients admitted after his fatal accident. The references to Ciera Self were particularly confounding. The journal contained selections of her poetry and details of her pathology no one without access to her files could have known.

In an account dated September 21st of last year, it detailed a suicide attempt by Miss Self, which resulted in her hospitalization. It noted she had used a letter opener taken from the nurse's station. A week or so later, Preston journaled the contents of a letter he'd received from her, stating she was alive and recovering from superficial wounds.

Other entries were equally as chilling, including descriptions of the court hearing of one of my patients, Richard Caytes, in which the journal entry described, accurately, not only the misdemeanors and felonies perpetrated by him but also my participation in the proceedings and precise details of the actual sentencing.

There was also mention of African American twins who were brought in for observation, but were released shortly thereafter. Preston's analysis of their "malady" was *idioglossia*, a rare condition. Upon reexamination of their files, I was able to determine his prognosis was more nearly correct than that of our staff's, which concluded the twins suffered from *pedolalia* or infantile speech.

Then, there were multiple references to two teenagers who were never patients at The Healing Place. However, after further investigation, I was able to find police records for both. One, a fourteen-year-old African American male, was incarcerated in the Multnomah County Juvenile Detention Center for a series of arson fires. The other, Chelsea Strickler, with an extensive record of shoplifting in the Portland area, had been diagnosed with Dissociative Disorder at Pathways Mental Health Services when she was twelve. Her record indicated the use of numerous aliases and multiple arrests for prostitution and larceny. Confined under the name Crystal Strickland, she had escaped from the Jan Evans Juvenile Justice Center in Reno, Nevada, last March. Her mutilated body was discovered three weeks later along Interstate 80, in the desert between Reno and Salt Lake City.

The accounts in The Nesbitt Journal referenced the charges against the young arsonist, and a specific shoplifting incident by Miss Strickler, one I personally corroborated, that occurred the prior December at Louis Vitton in downtown Portland.

One of our former aides, Caesar Fuentes, is mentioned throughout, but an entry on September 25th details a "hate crime" beating, which did occur the previous Tuesday evening, involving him and an unnamed companion. Mr. Fuentes, 32, originally hired as an aide to the Adult Ward before being transferred to our Intermediate Adolescent Care Unit in 2010, died from a brain hemorrhage on October 3rd. As an outpatient, Preston would not have had the occasion to ever meet him, yet his description of the incident and Caesar's personality is indisputable.

The October 5th entry mentions an Amy Fujita, who was also never a patient at The Healing Place. Our investigation revealed Miss Fujita, 17, a student at Willamette Preparatory Institute, was pronounced dead of a heroin overdose, September 19th, 2012, at the Portland Medical Center, where her father is chief of neurosurgery. A classmate, James McClelland, was subsequently charged with possession, trafficking and the fatal injection of Miss Fujita. A probe by the Portland Police Bureau uncovered extensive use of the drug at the Institute, where Preston had been a student since junior high. Details of the girl's heroin usage and McClelland's involvement were chronicled in the journal.

Many conflicting details occur in the journal's entry of August 2nd that describe a relationship between Preston's father and a Ms. Makeda Abebe, a foreign exchange student from Ethiopia. Portland State University confirmed that Ms. Abebe, a 2009 graduate in Communication Studies, is currently an employee for a public relations firm in San Diego. Contacted by Dr. Grunwald's investigative team, Ms. Abebe, who is single, acknowledged that Preston's father, Steven Nesbitt, spoke to her college Mass Media class during the 2008 fall semester. She stated that she and a small group of students met with him briefly after the seminar, but she had seen him on only one other occasion, when she applied for an opening as a media buyer at his advertising firm, McNabb & Associates, following graduation. She said Mr. Nesbitt had supported her hiring, but the job was eventually given to a friend of the McNabb family. She thought it strange that he personally called to give her the news, instead of the personnel director, but that was the last time the two talked.

Mr. Kirk Wolff, 43, a highly respected English teacher at Willamette Preparatory Institute, was charged last summer with the statutory rape by an authority figure of a former female student. The student's father had hired a private investigator, who, in an attempt to record the comings and goings at the Wolff residence, inadvertently recorded Preston's fatal accident and placed the controversial video on YouTube.

Mr. Wolff was arrested in Boulder, Colorado, where he was attending a writing program at Naropa University (June 23rd entry). Released on a $25,000 bond, Wolff maintains his complete innocence. He was suspended by the Institute, and is awaiting trial, scheduled for next month. He faces multiple charges, which could result in a sentence of up to 20 years in federal prison.

Every teen mentioned in The Nesbitt Journal has been identified as legitimate. Some were actual patients at The Healing Place; others have records documenting activities detailed in the journal. As far as could be determined, none, except Miss Fujita, ever met Preston.

His parents, Steven and Suzanne Nesbitt, remarried last summer and relocated in Glendale, California, where he teaches advertising arts and she's head librarian at Glendale Community College. When contacted, they said they had no knowledge of a journal, no interest in seeing it, nor did they wish to comment further.

I have known Preston Nesbitt since he first appeared before me in 2004. I can state, categorically, that the voice of the journal entries is, indeed, his. These are the rhythms and the vocabulary with which he expressed himself. The sarcasm and black humor is representative of how Preston dealt with his painful past. For years, I have heard his rants and observations in various forms, though many were new, and, as previously stated, were accurate observations of people he never met. No one who knew him would doubt the journal's authenticity, which makes its existence even more confounding.

Preston was a sensitive. Emotion was the lodestar that guided him, and it was the fetter that kept him shackled to the past. I can attest to his prodigious memory, and in my thirty years of practice, I have never encountered anyone with his ability to recollect and link associative information, as if it were being fed by a vast database.

Beyond his obvious linguistic precocity and a high degree of consciousness, Preston's particular genius was based on full access to his unconscious. Unlike some narcissists, who refuse to see beyond their particular universe, Preston cared for others and his concern for the welfare of humanity was genuine. That is not to say he wasn't critical of people and society in general, as this journal illustrates. But since much of it was done with humor and wit, I attribute his sarcasm and ridicule as an attempt to expose the frailties and faults of mankind, exhibiting the characteristics and concerns commonly associated with a satirist. Oftentimes, when he became too self-absorbed, he instinctively sought to reconnect with Nature to bring himself back into balance.

Like other savants, Preston's abilities were advanced beyond his years, yet, like them, he remained somewhat infantile and naïve. Had he lived into adulthood, I believe he would have retained that childlike quality. He was a fascinating patient, and if I may admit to a bit of unprofessional conduct, there were times, I did "sit idly by" and enjoy the verbal "regurgitation," as he dubbed it. On a personal note, when I think of Preston, I recall the Portuguese word he discovered to describe the ambivalence one often feels towards an absent loved one: *Saudade*...the happiness in having known him and the sadness in losing him.

As for the source of The Nesbitt Journal, J. Jacobs & Associates, a board certified forensic handwriting and document service, authenticated the entries to be those of Preston W. Nesbitt. And, I can verify that the written responses and comments attributed to me are, inexplicably, in my own handwriting.

So ends Dr. van Ittersum's report to the O.S.P Review Board.

* * *

These are the facts, as we know them. Dr. Grunwald and his staff continue to study the case and are convinced similar cases exist. They are currently investigating more than a dozen in various locations, from Helsinki, Finland, to Pondicherry, India, to Kosciusko, Mississippi.

What we are witness to, ladies and gentlemen, is not a mere conundrum or mystery; we are in possession of a scientific anomaly for which no feasible explanation currently exists.

Is this proof of multiple/parallel universes? And, if so, are we witness to a "bleed through" from one frequency to another? As stated in the final entry (Oct. 6th), did one Preston die April 28th, 2012, and another...walk away? I would also propose the questions: Did a third attend his freshman year at NYU? And, was yet another an inpatient at The Healing Place and the author of The Nesbitt Journal?

Contacted before the publication of this material, Dr. van Ittersum commented: "It's been said that the mystic 'forgets his fellows on his flight to the divine.' That was never true of Preston. And, since his passing, I've come to regard his mystical qualities and his magical stories with less suspicion. As he challenges in his entry of June 7th, 'Why does everything that belies our understanding of reality come off as apocryphal?'"

Why, indeed!

* * *

The *Nesbitt Journal* and Dr. van Ittersum's report comprise the entirety of *The Queerling*. At first, the Nesbitts objected to the title, but when they read the journal, extant, they gave it their blessing, saying "Pres would have loved it."

Suzanne Nesbitt composed the novel's dedication. It reads:

To Queerlings Everywhere:
Celebrate Your Diversity! Embrace Your Godliness!

THE QUEERLING

ABOUT THE AUTHOR

Austin Gary currently lives in Calgary, Alberta, with his husband and best friend, Brad Wilkinson. He is the fiercely proud father of award-winning stage director, Rachel Rockwell, and songwriter, producer and drummer for heavy metal band, Five Finger Death Punch, Jeremy Spencer. He is also extremely proud of his son-in-law, Broadway sound designer, Garth Helm and his creative and loving grandson, Jake.

For more information, visit his author website: Austin-Gary.com. Or, http://en.wikipedia.org/wiki/Austin_Gary

Author photo by Jaik Kaymann

Made in the USA
Lexington, KY
04 November 2013